The Great An

Also by Paul Flower

*The Redeeming Power of Brain Surgery (a novel)*

To the teacher who taught me to love books
and also gave me life.

This edition published in 2019 by Farrago,
an imprint of Prelude Books Ltd,
13 Carrington Road, Richmond, TW10 5AA, United Kingdom

www.farragobooks.com

ISBN: 978-1-78842-157-7 (print)

# The Great American Cheese War

Paul Flower

Farrago

# PART ONE

# This Means War?

# Chapter One

Dying had its advantages. That's the way Hank Vanderway saw it.

Hank's oldest son, Jack, was a hippie. Jack was forty-eight and an architect in Boulder. He wore an earring like a woman and had that long hair of his pulled back in a ponytail. He was married to a woman, thank God. But he and his left-wing college-professor wife were too hippie-selfish to have kids. Jack had long irked Hank to no end. Soon, there would be no more Hank. No more irk. Death was good that way.

Hank's daughter, Mary, wasn't a hippie but was married to a jerkoff with no spine who did something with whatever annuities were. The two of them had made a couple of babies who were brat-holes. The kids would likely grow up to be Satan worshiping drug mules. Not Hank's problem. Not anymore. Advantage again: death.

Hank was dying because of a bioweapons attack—monkeypox borne by intentionally infected prairie dogs—launched by the government of Wisconsin against the sovereign state of Michigan. He repeated this fact to his longtime political adversary and friend, Frances Griffendorf. Frances, as usual, didn't seem to be listening. Didn't matter, Hank figured.

Nothing mattered. Well, except saving the people he loved and the state he'd served for so much of his eighty-three years. That mattered a lot.

He had to do something soon. He'd be dead before Christmas. If not before before Christmas.

"What's the date?" Hank said.

From her usual position, behind an open *Detroit Free Press* across from Hank in their usual booth at Bob Evans, Frances said, "August twenty-second, the year of Our Lord 2021—what it's been all morning, since midnight or thereabouts, sweetheart."

They were the oddest of aging couples: Frances, a big-hearted, tough-as-Mackinac-in-February liberal Catholic lesbian from Iron Mountain; Hank, a surly, long-married Vietnam vet with his roots deep in the conservative soil of West Michigan's Dutch Reformed community. A mutual love-hate for the Detroit Tigers and penchant for cross-party cooperation had brought them together during a rocky period in the 1986 baseball season. They'd been political buddies ever since.

Hank stared at the omelet on his plate, bloated yellow-orange cheese bleeding from it. He'd chopped the thing up, releasing some of his tension on the eggs and ham and cheese. The sight stirred his bowels. He breathed in the breakfasted air: coffee, bacon, and ham. The scents were also disappointingly nauseating. Hank sighed. He thought for a moment. "You know, it's been thirty-nine years since I told the missus I love her? That's what she tells me. Night of Henry Junior's funeral, so she says," he said. He looked around the crowded restaurant, watched a grade-school kid with longish hair wolfing pancakes, hair nearly in the syrup on his plate, and wondered why the kid wasn't in school. "She brings it up every year on our anniversary." He silently vowed to make amends with Helen before he died.

Hank looked to Frances for a reaction. None came. To the omelet, Hank said, "I've had a good run. I've had three good terms in the legislature. Almost. Once I'm gone, they'll have a special election and some homosexual Democrat will win." Before Frances could protest, Hank held up a hand to the newspaper. "It's a fact. And you know it. Half the candidates who run for the state house from my district are homo and Democrat."

"Not that there's anything wrong with that," Frances said. She turned the page and glanced at her old friend.

"Oh, don't get your oversized panties in a bunch," Hank said. "You know, I don't hold it against you."

"You don't."

"No. I don't. We've had that discussion a million times. You're totally fine doing whatever you want up there in the Upper Peninsula at night. Your life. Your soul."

"Well, thanks once again for that."

"It's just that I am going to do whatever I can in my final days so help me God to keep a queer from Saugatuck out of my seat in Lansing. Hank Vanderway is not going to roll over. And not only that, he's going to do whatever the Lord will let him do to save this state from a threat you should be taking a lot more seriously. Hank sees Wisconsin from here. You should too."

"Love it when you use the third person when talking about you, Hank Vanderway."

Hank picked up his fork. With a trembling hand he stabbed an ambitious bite of the omelet remains and jammed it into his mouth. His stomach somersaulted but Hank chewed with determination, his gaze shifting back to the pancake-loving kid with the hair. A young woman across the table from the kid was looking at her phone, thumbs tapping on its screen. Something sick slithered in Hank's big belly. He turned to stare out the window at the crowded parking lot. It was a gray

11

morning. Humid. Chance of thunderstorms later. A thirty-something guy with a beehive of a beard, wearing jeans, a tight-fitting black T-shirt, a fedora, and tattoos wrapping both arms, sauntered toward the restaurant door. "We had a chance to fix this state and this country," Hank said. "At the national level, we had the right people in place in DC—the right man. But no. That opportunity passed. We could have been great again. We blew it. Now, when things go bad here, we've got a do-nothing woman for president. We're on our own."

"Well, at least you've got one of your own here in the governor's house. He's a moron. But he's a Republican moron," Frances said, returning the political fire.

Hank growled. "You need to show that young man some respect." He leaned to his left, reached down and pulled the Glock 19 he kept in a holster inside the waistband on his right hip. He laid the gun on the table. A tiny elderly woman gazed over the partition that separated the booths. She froze and let out a tiny yelp.

Frances peeked over the top of the newspaper, her eyes wide behind thick-lensed glasses. "Really?" She looked around the restaurant. Several other patrons had heard the yelp and were looking their way. Frances smiled and raised her hand in a gesture of assurance. "Don't worry, folks," she said loudly. "He's harmless. Licensed to carry."

In the last legislative session, Hank had led a drive to eliminate most of the state's remaining gun-owning restrictions. He'd shown the Glock quite often in public ever since, relishing the reactions.

The elderly lady's oatmeal suddenly seemed fascinating to her. In the booth behind her, a couple of guys in suits raised handguns and nodded toward Hank. He nodded back. The guys stuck their guns back inside their suit coats and resumed their conversation.

Frances sighed heavily and returned to her newspaper. Hank took a slurp of coffee, put down the mug a little too firmly; coffee sloshed on the table. He pushed the pistol toward the saltshaker, away from the brown puddle. "You don't care? Fine. But me being poisoned like this, by the government of a neighboring state, no telling what happens from here forward."

Hank closed his eyes, tried counting to ten but only made it to three. He imagined Frances and some of their other friends joking around at his upcoming funeral. Bud Spavik, a fellow MSU Spartan who'd taught phys-ed in East Lansing for four decades, would be standing in the funeral home imitating how Frances used to push Hank's buttons. Dom Bowser, Sid Loften, and Walt Vandermeer would cackle, showing no respect even though Frances's wife, Barb, would be throwing them dagger stares. Sid, ex-infantry, who'd done the whole nine yards in the last year of 'Nam just like Hank before going to State for his bachelor's, would be the only one with the guts to look at the open casket with him, Hank, in it. These images also belly-slid through Hank's brain at night but in the light of a Michigan day he figured they didn't matter. Not anymore, they didn't. The state was going to Hades in a hand basket. Now, if the Wisconsin terrorists had their way, so was he. He opened his eyes. The bearded guy had taken a seat at the restaurant's lunch counter and seemed to be flirting with Hank's favorite waitress, Julie. Hank frowned.

Frances was repeating a question.

"Huh?" Hank said. He sniffed and dabbed at his nose with the wadded-up napkin. The napkin smelled like cheese.

"What makes you so sure of this being anything but a lousy case of the flu?" Frances said.

"I told you. We were over there on the fishing trip and the symptoms fit and the whole thing goes right along with what our guys have been saying about Wisconsin planning to, you know, attack," Hank said. He started to shove another hefty forkful of omelet into his mouth but his gut squirmed. He put down the fork and squeezed a thick finger through the handle of his coffee mug and steadied the mug with the other hand. Hank scowled as he slurped the coffee. "Damn new mugs they got; what was wrong with the old mugs?" he said.

Frances studied Hank over the back page of the sports section, which featured a Farmer Jack ad. Hank noted that pork chops were on sale at Farmer Jack. He'd always liked a good pork chop. This wouldn't matter anymore. God didn't serve pork chops in heaven, God being Jewish.

Hank wondered if he should have gone to church more.

"You know you're awfully pretty when you're dying?" Frances said.

Hank scowled and put down the mug, disentangled his finger, picked up the fork again and jammed its load into his mouth. He swallowed hard. "Muscle aches, hot and cold, dizzy, sick to my stomach." He clicked the symptoms off on his fingers. "Had them all, off and on, since last month. Since we all got back from the Wisconsin-Stupid-Dells. Bet they had those dogs running all over our stuff when we were out fishing. You're lucky you don't like to fish."

"You've been listening way too much to Ham DenBraber and that nutbag on the radio." Frances snapped the paper back full and slouched behind it.

Hank cleared his throat and tried to swallow the anger and omelet rising from his stomach. "Listen. Ham's just a kid but Grand Rapids re-elects the boy to state senate in a landslide, you know he's a straight shooter. His future is in DC, I tell you. He's a smart one, and he's been talking for months now about the threat."

"Parker confirm this big Wisconsin plan of attack, did he? Parker, your radio friend, the 'voice of true America'?"

"Graham Parker has got sources," Hank said. "He may have come here from Australia originally but he lost an eye in-country, in 'Nam, you know, fighting for us. I for one am proud to have served with the likes of him, and to have him based over at WOOD Radio. He's a local guy talking the truth out all over the country. All over the world, with the Internet. He's been talking to little Billy Hoeksma about this stuff too, I tell you that. Him and Ham both been talking it up."

"They've got the governor of Michigan worried about monkeypox."

"Worried about Wisconsin. Ham briefed Hoeksma a week or two back."

Frances turned a page. Said nothing.

Hank lowered his voice to a growl-whisper. "Listen. Everybody thinks Wisconsin's economy is all happy with cheese but it's not. Not anymore. Cheese is gone."

"Tigers beat the evil empire last night in the Bronx. Think we could pass a bill to find out where our bullpen has been lately?" Frances said, reading. "Won the game but gave up four in the seventh."

Hank's meaty fist slammed the table. Silverware and porcelain clanked. Frances lowered the paper. Hank's face was grayish and his upper lip was sweaty. The two of them stared at each other. Slowly, almost carefully, Frances folded the newspaper and put it aside. She took a sip from her coffee and eyed Hank through the steam from the mug. "Look, I've heard some of the stuff from Parker and the others. You know that. I just don't buy it. And I don't buy the paranoia." Frances put down her coffee mug. "I mean, you have to admit, you've always been a sucker for big, hairy conspiracies."

Hank glowered.

Frances sighed. "OK, OK. Look. You've been telling me this thing in bits and pieces." She gave Hank a come-here motion. "Give it to me straight. The whole story."

"Really?"

"Really."

"You gonna listen?"

"Cross my heart."

Hank frowned. His stomach rumbled. "OK. But first, I gotta go to the can." He slid to the edge of the bench seat and nodded toward the pistol. "Watch my gun."

# Chapter Two

Hank returned to the booth, gushed out a sigh, took another slurp of coffee, put down the mug, and picked up his pistol. He waggled it absentmindedly, collecting his thoughts, scanning the room. The elderly lady in the adjacent booth was gone; a wadded napkin splotched with lipstick was next to her half-eaten bowl of oatmeal. Hank turned toward Frances, who nodded at the gun.

"You want to stand down there, partner?" Frances said.

Hank thought about it and then holstered the weapon. Finally, forearms resting on the table, voice lowered, he said, "This is what our sources tell us."

"Do tell," Frances said in a sarcasm-hued whisper, leaning in. "You have sources."

Hank ignored the bait. "About thirty years back," he said, "some forward-thinkers in the Wisconsin state assembly saw the lay of the land in the dairy industry. Competition was killing them—other states, you know. So they started funneling grants into cheese research. Called it the Cheesus program." Hank paused to mop his forehead.

"Cheesus. See there? That alone… how can you… Cheesus." Frances shook her head.

Hank plowed ahead. "Thing was, only certain dairy operations with connections to Madison got the grant money from the program. And when the ones that got the money came up with special cheese recipes, only certain powerful dairy guys had access to them. There was no provision in the grants that said they had to share."

"And we know what happens when we don't share."

"A lot of what you call subversive activity is what happened. I mean, you heard of the Shawano Six, right?"

"Can't say I have."

"Of course not. Secret society. Very radical, disenfranchised, that sort of deal."

"Radical cheese guys."

"Darn straight. Somehow, these guys…"

"All six of them."

"Yes…"

"From Shawano?"

"Thought you'd never heard of them."

"Just guessed."

"They got hold of the recipes, and started shopping them around the whole country, trying to sell the technology to the highest bidder."

"Black market for cheese technology I'm guessing is pretty intense." Frances chased a laugh with coffee.

"Here's where it gets interesting." Hank paused to slurp his coffee. He leaned in closer. "One of the key players, some say the leader, was Devon McAllister—that actor."

Frances snorted and coughed. Coffee burned in her nose. "You mean Denton McAllister?"

"Dev-on, I heard."

"So, Devon—Denton McAllister, the movie star, stole cheese secrets in Wisconsin?"

"He's from Shawano."

"Well that explains it."

"Seriously. This was all back before he was, like, a star. Someone hooked McAllister into this—because of his family connections is most likely why."

"Family…?"

"Oh, everyone knows McAllister's related to El Chapo— the drug lord guy? The Mexican? McAllister's birth name was Rodriguez. Everybody knows that. He's, like, El Chapo's second cousin, I guess."

Frances tried to bury a snicker in her coffee cup.

"Thought you was gonna listen."

"Thought you weren't going to sound like Breitbart."

Hank gave his old friend a long stare, fighting the urge to get up and walk out. He took another slurp of his coffee, trying to control the tremor in his hand, and carefully set down the mug.

"OK. OK. I'll behave." Frances raised her hands in mock surrender.

Hank took another deep breath before continuing. "So somehow, McAllister gets involved. He's young. He's smart. And he's got these, like, third-world criminal tendencies— knows smuggling and how to sell illegal stuff on account of his not-all-that-distant cousin. So he finds out some local guys, some farmers over here in Michigan, were interested in starting a cutting-edge cheese operation. They set up this meeting with McAllister. It was going to be on a Saturday afternoon in Jenison, heart of, you know, Michigan dairy country. But it was county fair time and the dairy and cheese people here got busy and sent word through their back channel to push the meet back. The back channel didn't work, for some stupid reason— this is before the Internet and, like, cell phones. So McAllister waited a day or so and then just headed over here to Michigan, hoping to make contact and get the deal done. That's when things got all hinky."

"Hinky."

"Hinky as heck. McAllister got here on a Sunday night and all the farmers were at evening church. Of course. No one to meet with. So he's stuck playing with himself or whatever these Hollywood guys do, in some hotel in Grandville. He's calling these guys and they're not answering."

"They being at church and all."

"Right. And right then, he gets the call."

"From the farmers."

"From his agent in La-La Land," Hank said triumphantly. "He takes off to Holly-flipping-wood—ends up in California a movie star and what else ends up there with him?"

Frances thought, frowned, and then raised her hands. "I give up."

"The stolen recipes," Hank said triumphantly, smacking the table.

"Cheesus?"

"Cheese. Us."

Frances took a long drink of coffee, then wrapped her hands around the mug, closed one eye, and looked at Hank. She held Hank's gaze, studying his grayish, sweating face, trying to picture what was going on in his old brain.

"So they got the cheese," Frances said. "The best cheese."

Hank leaned even closer to Frances, his tone now conspiratorial. "You see it, don't you? California's been selling cheese hand over tit ever since. All because of one radical Hollywood type with a bad gene pool and a bunch of real powerful, you know, greedy cheese industry folks. And let me tell you, the governor has been ticked about it for a long time. Furious."

"Governor? Hoeksma?"

"No, not ours. Theirs. Wisconsin's."

"Oh, Oleson?"

"Yeah, the esteemed Governor Oleson of Wisconsin. He's not only a big liberal fat cat, he's from one of the powerful cheese families, of course. His granddaddy's the guy that came up with pre-shredded. Bet you didn't know that."

"Certainly didn't."

"Yes, sir. Oleson's family was supposedly going to get those recipes, too; the ones McAllister stole. Oleson's been vowing revenge ever since. He's been playing the long game. He knows touching Mr. El Chapo the second, McAllister, is going to be next to impossible. So he and his family have been working on a way to get back at Michigan for our part in the whole thing."

Frances stared at Hank. "How come I haven't heard any of these details till now?"

"'Cuz you're too busy listening to Dan Dickerson and stupid Tigers baseball on the radio."

Frances mentally conceded the point. "And this gets all sinister, with the monkeypox and prairie dogs and you and Ham DenBraber maybe dying—how?"

Hank managed a strained smile. He eased his weight back. Looked down at his plate. With his fork, he speared a piece of green pepper that had wandered away from the massacred meal. Head still down, he said, "Around 2001 or so, someone got the idea to start converting Wisconsin's empty cheese factories into something more ominous." Hank took a deep breath. He raised his gaze. Frances could hear Hank's chest rattling. "Old man Oleson's the one who most likely come up with that idea."

"Governor Oleson."

"No, his old man."

"So Wisconsin's governor's father…" Frances said.

"…is the one that started using old cheese factories for making weapons. Sick weapons."

"Like what?"

"Monkeypox."

"They, what, manufactured it?"

"Yep. Bi-o-logical warfare."

"Who? How?"

"Doesn't matter."

Frances couldn't contain herself. "Come on, Hank. They're making weapons of mass destruction to get back at Michigan for something Dev—Denton—McAllister tried to do on behalf of criminal elements in the cheese underworld. Really? Play that back for yourself."

"These are evil people, Frances. This is about pure…" Hank searched for the word. "…just badness. Wisconsin folks, they look lazy and fat, a lot of them. But they smell weakness and they exploit it. That's the way the Packers always play, and you know it."

"The Packers? The football…"

"They take advantage of the weak. And these Olesons may be the worst of the lot. The old man, they say on one side of the family he's descended from Vikings that came here in the Dark Ages." Hank frowned and leaned toward Frances. "And you know what they say about Vikings." He leaned back and shook his head.

"No, can't say that…?"

"Rapists."

"Vikings?"

"Darn straight. Just as soon take advantage of a woman as say hello."

"So all Vikings are evil?"

"Yes, ma'am. Proven fact. It's how God made them. Black guys shoot hoops better than anyone else. Your average Mexican is happy working outdoors or moving illegal stuff across borders. All the same thing."

Frances's coffee was cold. She took a swallow, grimaced, and then looked at Hank. Her buddy's eyes were glassy but there was no mistaking the fire in them. "So, Oleson knew you were coming and decided it was finally time to attack," Frances said. It was all she could come up with.

"Give the woman a prize." Hank smiled. "Way I figure it, they let some infected prairie dogs out of a lab just to let us know what they got and to see what the virus would do." Hank sniffed. "Shot across the bow."

"And you got caught in the crosshairs."

"Yep. A few Michigan public officials happen to be on vacation and at least one of us, maybe more, come back infected. Tie it back to the whole thing with McAllister and you got plenty of motive." Hank gestured to Julie the waitress. He lowered his voice and added, "Burned when I peed this morning and you know that isn't good."

"That's just your prostrate."

"Pros-tate," Hank said.

"What I said." Frances picked up the paper and opened it. She slumped in her seat, feeling comforted by the thin wall now between her and Hank.

"What do you need, Hank? A prostate exam?" Julie had glided over. There was a smirk on her tired-but-pretty face. She leaned across Hank's plate and poured warm-ups into their coffees. Hank breathed in her waitress perfume: baby powder and kitchen. Julie had always worn it well.

"Careful. He's cranky today," Frances's voice said from behind the paper. "Thinks he's dying."

Julie's baby-browns clouded. She cupped Hank's face with her free hand. "You OK, Hank? I don't want to lose a customer. I lose many more and I'll be back mowing yards full time. Last I did that was two marriages ago."

Hank's chest went tight. He swallowed again. "What I want to know is where you got these stupid mugs. Got no handle on them worth a spit."

Frances smiled, relieved to change the subject. "That's not what he really wants from you."

Hank felt his face go hot. Julie gave Frances's newspaper a backhanded slap. Frances jumped and a giggle escaped. She winked at Julie and snapped the paper back to its original shape. Julie straightened, hand on her hip. "You two. I swear, you'll be winning elections and a hundred years old, sitting here trying to solve the problems of the world and flirting with the help."

"Can't happen. Term limits. Besides, only one of us will make it," Hank said.

Frances heaved a sigh, folded the paper, and tossed it on the table next to her bowl of oatmeal. "Julie, my dear, this meal's on me today. He's got monkeypox. Caught it from prairie dog crap in our sister state across the big pond." She picked up a fork and began eating her eggs.

Julie's laugh cut through Hank's aching belly. Julie the waitress was a nice-looking lady and Hank liked thinking she was attracted to him even though he, Hank, was a public servant with a good reputation, a congressman married going on forty-one years, and Julie was younger than his living kids. The laugh confirmed that Julie was just a waitress to him. He thought about it for a second and decided it soon wouldn't matter who was what to him.

"You two kill me." She shook her head, turned, and walked toward the kitchen. "I'll find out where we got those mugs, Hank. Personally, I find them to die for."

Hank shoved his plate away and scowled at Frances. "You asked how I know. About the monkeypox. I know because I sent a blood sample to a guy. Up in Greenville."

Frances stopped chewing, her mouth open. Looked like a fish with a mouthful of paste. She swallowed, took a sip of orange juice. Put down the glass. Gave Hank a look. "You're serious," she said.

"Been serious as a stroke from the get-go."

"You sent a sample of your blood to some whack job conspiracy theorist."

"It's all legit," Hank said. "Listen. The guy in Greenville, name's Clayton Store, he's got this website. Just a prick of my blood on a clean, dry paper towel, seal it in a Ziploc. Twenty-nine ninety-five. Put it on the credit card. Result came back last night. Positive. Monkey. Pox."

Frances started to do the fish-mouth thing again then stopped. A smile sparked in her eyes. She groaned, shook her head, and wagged a finger at Hank. "You're good. You're real good. Had me going there," she said.

Hank's fist hit the table again. He shot a glance around the restaurant then swung back to Frances. "Shut your pie hole just once and think," Hank said.

Frances smiled. "Say, what kind of pie you suppose these guys here are making for lunch?"

"Peach," Julie the waitress said. She'd come back and was taking an order from an overweight guy in a Green Bay Packers sweatshirt in the booth behind Hank. "And no, you can't have a piece now."

"If I had some it would plug my pie hole," Frances said.

"It would. But it won't. Not yet anyway." Julie was breezing by, back to the kitchen, her scent trailing her. "The mugs are from Racine, Hank, a sales guy gave us a deal on them."

Hank's mouth was fish-open now. He watched Julie disappear through the swinging doors by the cash register. "Racine," he said, the word coming out broken. "Ra-ceen, Wisconsin."

"Seems to be a theme today," Frances said.

Hank's eyes had shifted. He was staring at something far off, something that wasn't where Frances could see it. Hank's eyes were bloodshot and there were lumpy bags under them. To Frances, Hank looked like crap.

"You look like crap," Frances said.

Hank wanted to agree. But, to him, it didn't matter anymore. For him, death would make everything mute.

# Chapter Three

Governor Bill Hoeksma was staring into the mirror above his office bathroom's sink, trying to recite the 23rd Psalm from memory, when his phone buzzed.

The call was trouble. He could feel it in his bones. All of his calls were trouble. Governor Bill hated trouble.

"Criminniny," the governor said. He'd been practicing the psalm recitation for an upcoming speech to an evangelical group. He sucked at memorization. He hated talking to groups. He hated the way trouble always seemed to find him.

Governor Bill exited the bathroom, pulled the phone from his pocket and looked at the screen. It was Ham DenBraber, majority leader in the Michigan State Senate and Governor Bill's closest friend and political ally.

"Yo," Governor Bill said as he sat in his desk chair. "Don't tell me. Let me guess. Something's wrong."

"Listen, we need to talk, like ASAP," Ham DenBraber said. There was a wiggle in Ham's voice.

"You're not losing your nerve on this minimum wage deal, are you Ham?" Governor Bill, at Ham's urging, had proposed a cut in the minimum wage. The vote was coming. He would get his way with the vote; the Republicans had the numbers. But the issue had caused considerable civil unrest in Detroit and protests in Grand Rapids and Ann Arbor. "You know the whole thing was your idea."

Ham found his voice. "Governor, Bill, listen, this Wisconsin thing has gone beyond politics," he said. "There's a life and death component."

"Really," Governor Bill said. Out of habit, he flipped open his laptop and waited for the screen to flicker to life. He opened and scanned an email from his wife. The cat had ear mites, the note said. Willie, their four-year-old, had ringworm.

"Governor, if you could give me five—"

Governor Bill slapped the laptop shut. "Haven't we pretty much talked the Wisconsin thing to death, Ham?" With a finger, he tapped the plastic baseball-cap brim on the Sparky Anderson bobblehead doll that squatted next to his stapler. Sparky bobbled, grinning. "I mean, you guys have told me about Cheesus and all that and so on and what have you." Governor Bill Hoeksma tapped the side of Sparky's face. Sparky wobbled crazily. Governor Bill imagined Sparky was telling him "no" about something; for a moment, this depressed him.

"Governor, this is important. Critically important."

Bill Hoeksma hated being governor, especially in moments like these. But he had himself to blame. Twenty years before, he had pissed away his high school and college years on girls, alcohol, drugs, and apathy. In his family, that had left him with few career options. Bill's father, William "Will" Hoeksma, had built the home appliance manufacturer Amerispin into a global colossus. The firm employed thousands across the globe, and spent millions on public works in its home city, Grand Rapids, as well as on political influence in Lansing and DC. Amerispin had rewarded Bill's hard-driving sister, Bev, and manic brother, Mel, with incredible wealth. Bill, forever the black sheep, had nearly flunked out of the University of Michigan. When he was in his third year at U of M, a come-to-Jesus confrontation with his father led to detox, celibacy (within reason), a public declaration of faith at the family's Christian Reformed Church, and the gently forced decision to forge a career representing the family interests in politics.

With the family money and power behind him, and a goofy likability putting lipstick on the pig of his inexperience and total lack of intellectual curiosity, Bill had won two unremarkable terms in the Michigan House of Representatives and one in the state senate. Then, two years ago, his father had hatched a law-and-order campaign for Bill to ride into the governor's mansion. Bill loved guns; he'd been a collector, shooter, and hunter since his teen years, and he had legally carried a 9mm Sig Sauer in a shoulder holster during the campaign. When a video and photos of the handsome, young, gun-toting politician, sans suit coat, hit social media, it went viral. #Gunvernor—a cute wordplay his father hated—had trended on Instagram and Twitter. Gun-rights groups were smitten. Members of the state's growing network of private militias began showing up at rallies. Bill connected with some of the militia leaders via Facebook. Their support, in particular, had helped greatly, particularly when they appeared at polling places in traditionally liberal neighborhoods of Detroit on Election Day. Bill Hoeksma had easily beaten a West Bloomfield Democrat whose name now escaped him.

Thus, Bill had regained his share of the Hoeksma golden egg. On days like this, he wasn't sure it was worth it. He was up to his eyeballs in shit he didn't understand. The deal with Wisconsin was the smelliest of it.

"Unless someone is, like, dying, Ham, you're going to have to give me a pretty good reason to spend any more time on this. Is somebody dying, Ham? We got cold bodies washing up on the lakeshore?"

From Ham, there was a heavy sigh. He coughed. "Well, governor…"

Governor Bill frowned, his finger an inch from the brim of Sparky's cap. Sparky Anderson bobbled uncertainly. "Well? 'Well' what?"

"I can explain. I'll be right there."

Ham ended the call.

Bill dropped his phone on his desk and sat back in his chair. That was so like Ham—to leave him hanging. Bill wasn't the sharpest knife in the drawer but neither was he the dimmest bulb in the lamp; so said *The Detroit News* in its editorial endorsing him for governor. Too often he thought Ham treated him like a child, the way Bill's dad did.

Ham and Bill had first met in the spring of 1990. The occasion was a meeting of the University of Michigan's Young Republicans. Ham was the guest speaker. Bill Hoeksma, future governor, had slouched in the shadows outside the meeting room door, head down, until the last of the others, a pretty redhead named Marci who would in two years marry Ham DenBraber, kissed Ham and skipped off down the hall.

"That was uncalled for," Bill Hoeksma said.

DenBraber, startled, turned from gawking at his future wife. "I… we're dating."

Bill Hoeksma's eyes lingered on the tight-jeaned Marci rounding a corner at the far end of the hall. "No. I didn't mean kissing her. I meant singling me out; telling the group I didn't care. During the meeting."

"You spend a week prepping a speech then have some apathetic hippie sleep through it."

"Hippie?"

"If the shoe fits."

Bill let loose a long, stuttering belch. "You don't even know me."

Ham DenBraber sighed and stared at a point over Bill Hoeksma's head. "Bill Hoeksma," he said, "son of conservative political powerbroker William H. Hoeksma, Sr., CEO of Amerispin, Grand Rapids-based home appliance powerhouse. Bill Junior is heir to a shared fortune estimated at one-point-five billion with a 'B;' has a nose for women, parties, alcohol, and, rumor has it, occasionally, cocaine."

"The cocaine thing is just like you said—rumor," Bill Hoeksma said with a snort.

Ham DenBraber shot Bill Hoeksma a disgusted look and bent over to pick up a briefcase.

"Hold on," Bill Hoeksma said.

Ham obeyed—a move he would in later interviews attribute to the intervening hand of God. He put down the briefcase, straightened, flicked nothing off the front of his tie, slowly folded his arms, and gave Bill an arched-eyebrow glare.

Bill avoided the gaze, instead studying his battered Converse basketball shoes, searching for one more belch or something more profound. Finally, he looked up at Ham, a sly grin slithering across his face. Something, something Ham would also recall years later as divinely inspired, sparked in his eyes. "Ham DenBraber," Bill Hoeksma said, "the son of the 'Dealing Dutchman,' Dirk DenBraber, General Motors' number one volume dealer in Michigan, Indiana, and Ohio. Earned your business degree from Calvin College last year. Now getting your Masters in poli-sci at Michigan."

"Nice," Ham DenBraber said. Despite himself, he smiled. "Shows you can read a bio. Impressive."

"More than just read. I'm into this crap," Bill said.

"What... crap?"

"Politics. The agenda. Your agenda. Ours. The Republicans."

"You have an excellent way of showing it."

"I know. I know." Bill Hoeksma ran his long, thin fingers through his shoulder-length hair and glanced around them in the empty hallway before leaning toward Ham DenBraber. "My dad, you know, is like the f-ing king of this state. And I'm the troubled youth. The heir with the hair. The family shame. I know what the press says. But it's not fair, really. I got this brother, he's running the company now with Dad and my sister; he had his share of problems when he was younger. Honest to God. But my dad won't cut me any slack."

Ham DenBraber clucked. "You poor, misunderstood billionaire-in-waiting."

"No. Wait. Hold on. No excuses. I'm aware of my, like, failures. I mean, I've been reading a lot lately. Reading the papers and getting in tune with stuff and reading, like, the Bible." Bill Hoeksma took a deep breath. "I'm going to start going to one of those Bible study deals."

Ham DenBraber let loose a pent-up sigh that sounded like an explosion.

"Honest to God," Bill said without a trace of a smile.

Ham DenBraber scowled. "I'm sorry. I shouldn't doubt you. I mean if you really are interested, there's one I go to."

"Cool. See, I'm moving now. In a certain direction. On a personal and, like, even spiritual level. A good direction. And, like, I'm seeing the political world more clearly too. I believe this... this... this George Bush is the real deal. I mean, he's former CIA and all. That's kind of freaky. But he's also a businessman. He gets it. He sees the 1990s, like, as a decade for the conservative, like, revolution, to really take hold. He's going to finish what Reagan started—get us back to the good American things like hard work and strong families, and marriage and faith, and he'll get rid of the welfare mothers and crack down on these union nuts and give states back the powers they should have to straighten up their backyards and let businesses compete again." Bill stopped and gave Ham a long look. Ham just frowned and gestured for him to continue.

"See, well, I've been thinking," Bill said. "My dad and I don't get along all that well but, you know, he's the real deal too. Like your dad is. Guys like them, they're the backbone of the state—the whole country, actually. But it's going to take people, young guys like, like you and me, to follow up. We're it. We're the next generation, right?"

Ham DenBraber opened his mouth. He didn't know how to respond. Bill Hoeksma didn't give him a chance. "Of course I'm right," Bill Hoeksma said. "And you know it. Just like you know you've been planning to run for office when we graduate next year. I read about that. And I was thinking maybe, you know, here I am, getting cleaned up, grounded, and becoming an important member of my community. And, hey, maybe we could work together."

Ham DenBraber studied his wingtips.

"I mean, to start maybe you could teach me the ropes on how to manage a campaign."

"You. Want to get into politics," Ham said slowly.

"Yeah, ahh, yes. Yes. I do."

Ham stared at the figure in front of him. "You're a wreck, you know."

Bill smiled. "Yeah. Pretty much."

"And you sound desperate."

"A little."

"A lot."

Again, the smile. It was disarming, Ham thought. Under the week's worth of beard and the shaggy hair, there was something weirdly likable about Bill Hoeksma. "So, why?"

Bill smiled and shrugged. "My old man, he's pretty… he says I need to do this."

Hank thought for a moment, his eyes on Bill's Conversed feet. He suddenly smiled. His gaze met Bill's. "He's cutting you off, that it? Unless you do this?"

"Well, not—"

"Come on."

"Maybe not completely," Bill said.

Now Ham DenBraber snorted.

"OK. Yes. Yes. He is," Bill Hoeksma said to his shoes. "He is cutting me off, you know, unless I get this political thing going and, you know, start hanging with the right people—flying right."

Ham DenBraber studied Bill Hoeksma. He was a wreck. And definitely not a poster child for intellectual achievement. But there was something about the guy. A sense of humor, maybe. Charisma, definitely. Ham's professors had always said you couldn't teach charisma. "What's in it for me?" Ham finally said.

Bill Hoeksma smiled and raised his gaze again. "One point five billion. With a B."

The door to the governor's assistant's office opened and Senator Ham DenBraber plodded in. Kelli Alexander, Governor Bill's assistant, looked up from her desk and smiled. "Good morning sen—" Before she could finish, the double-doors to Governor Bill's office swung open, and the governor stepped out. "Don't get up, Kelli," he said with a smile. "I was expecting my long-lost partner in crime. And here he is." Ham managed a strained smile, gave a half-hearted wave to Kelli. The two men went into the governor's office. The doors closed behind them.

Governor Bill sat in his chair, and then swiveled to face the senate majority leader. Ham lumbered to a stop in front of the desk and swayed there, mouth open. He looked at Governor Bill, gulped, coughed, wheezed, sneezed, wiped his nose, and sniffed, then stared, glassy-eyed, over Governor Bill's head. He leaned forward and put one meaty hand on the desk, for support.

"You don't look so good, Ham man," Governor Bill said.

Ham DenBraber studied the Lansing skyline through the window. His mouth opened and a word that sounded like "smog" or "grog" came out. Ham groaned something else— "smerth" or "smurf," Governor Bill Hoeksma never was sure— and crumpled to the floor.

Ham DenBraber said nothing more.

# Chapter Four

On the morning of September 12, 2001, Will Hoeksma, Sr. had stood, naked except for his boxers, at the steam-stained mirror in his immense silver and marble master bathroom. A TV recessed in the subway-tiled wall next to the bidet carried the images of the smoking rubble in New York, the announcer droning, barely audible.

Will regarded his image. *Not bad for a guy on the backside of fifty,* he thought. The wispy hair on his chest was gray but he was tanned and lean. When he worked out shirtless in the company health center, he drew stares. He knew this because he watched in the health center mirrors. He loved the stares. They were why he'd installed the mirrors.

Will was a busy man. Politically powerful. Top dog at Amerispin. Had a lot going on. He could handle it.

But now. This.

Terror in America.

He'd seen it coming. Yes, he had. It was biblical, the clash of civilizations. It was political—Clinton's passivity and tail chasing had led them down the bloodied garden path. It was predictable.

It was an opportunity. Heck, a responsibility.

As he dressed, Will thought it through. More attacks were coming. Governments would be overmatched. They would need private sector support from right-minded men. People who knew people. People-like-him people.

Good, godly men—men blessed with heart and spine and resources—would need to make the world safe from jihadist freaks.

The cause was righteous. If there was a profit to be made, so be it. To the victor.

For the hundredth time since the first reports from New York, Will murmured a prayer for the victims and first responders. He took a deep breath. He smelled aftershave and a hint of money.

Every big business deal he had ever made, every initiative he'd spawned—and there had been many—had a moment of pure inspiration such as this. His mentor, his late Uncle Jake, had talked about these moments a lot.

*When you see opportunity, don't be a pussy. And when you go for it, stay the hell calm*, Jake's long-dead voice said in Will's graying head.

Jake's older brother, Will's father, Bill, had been both a pussy and not calm. His temperament, bad inner ear, and nervous stomach kept him out of military service and on the outskirts of his driven, ambitious son's life. Jake, on the other hand, served in World War II, where he nearly earned a Purple Heart and other medals of valor, returning home with a lifetime's worth of almost-true stories and a Third-Reich-like silver eagle medallion he and a hooker had wrestled from the dead hand of a Nazi soldier. From Will's grade school years onward, Jake and his nephew had been peas in a non-pussified pod. Jake started Amerispin Appliances in his garage and built it with military-style discipline, precision, and ruthlessness. Unmarried and technically childless, he funded Will's college education, kept him out of the man grinder that was Vietnam, and hired him the day he graduated. From the marketing department, Will rose quickly on his own merit—Uncle Jake would have it no other way—and took over the top spot at Amerispin following Jake's death in 1985. A love of America, weapons, and winning had been at the heart of Will's inheritance. He had never served in the military. But he always felt as though he had.

Uncle Jake had prepared him for this day.

That fate-filled September 12, Will arrived at his office in the Amerispin tower in suburban Ada at precisely 6:30 a.m. The vast corporate headquarters building was mostly empty at that hour. Will appreciated the solitude. It gave him time to pray, read emails, and figure his first steps through the post-September-11 world. He stood for several minutes in the quiet half-darkness of the grand, vaulted lobby, studying the large painting of Uncle Jake that hung, dramatically lit, behind the reception desk. "Amerispin Jesus," employees called the portrait. Jake seemed especially messianic that morning. His right hand rested on two stacked books: one the Holy Bible, King James version; the other his bestselling memoir *Winning by Winning*. Jake's pale blue eyes seemed to be commanding Will to win.

By noon, Will had made some calls. By the end of the week, he'd circled back to accountants and market strategists and faced-to-faced with military experts.

By early 2002, he'd made his move. He launched Silver Eagle Security, a paramilitary company "committed to defending American interests, American values—true Americans."

Will's army quickly grew to include several dozen ex-soldiers, including former Rangers and former SEALs, a nobody-knows-who list of experienced spies, three of his preferred Washington lobbyists, and several offshore bankers and law firms. Contracts came. Business expanded. Silver Eagle's arsenal and reputation grew accordingly. When he encountered skeptics or naysayers,

Will brushed them off with the nuclear self-confidence and bluster that had kowtowed his father and mother during his teen years and brought business rivals to heel.

Will schmoozed and dined and whined. Spent millions. Bent rules and coerced the timid.

As with Amerispin, the Hoeksma touch proved golden. Silver Eagle became one of the leading private security firms in the world. The (invisible) Silver Eagle flag flew over counter-terrorism campaigns across the globe. The original business plan expanded to cover revenue opportunities in other key verticals, including assassination, mass-protest mitigation, enhanced interrogation, and Will's private portfolio of "Black-Silver Ops."

As he'd predicted, the paramilitary marketplace became as crowded as an Iraqi open-air market. The fact that Silver Eagle was rated by trade groups as the number two fully integrated private security provider was a source of endless pain for Will. That the top firm was owned by a fellow West Michigan guy—another Dutchman, Benjie Teegarten, who had drawn inspiration from Silver Eagle's success and earned a small edge in the global market thanks to a series of successful strikes against terror groups in Bangladesh—made the pain worse.

Now, nearly twenty years after that morning in September, Will felt the pain was about to end. He had a plan that would make Silver Eagle a household name. And the plan was in motion at last.

# Chapter Five

The first thing Governor Bill Hoeksma did after Ham DenBraber collapsed was nothing. He sat, still as death. A clock ticked in his head or maybe it was his heart in his chest or the sound a fat senator's body makes as it's cooling down from 98.6—he wasn't sure. Finally, slowly, he leaned forward, aimed his mouth toward the door and said, "Kelli." The word came out whole but croaky. He tried again. And again. The fourth time, he must have screamed it because an instant later the door swung open and in rushed Kelli, and whoa. She stopped. Her face dropped from his to the seemingly dead Ham.

Governor Bill forced himself to stand. Slowly, he walked around his desk and stood over his friend. Ham appeared to be breathing, maybe; Governor Bill wasn't sure and he didn't want to touch Ham if Ham was dead. He looked at Kelli. Her eyes were wide and her lips were pressed together like she was about to cry or scream or something. She looked cute, Governor Bill thought, and instantly felt guilty for thinking it.

"I'll call 911," Kelli managed to say. She turned and left his office, slamming the door behind her.

Kelli liked Ham DenBraber. She liked him a lot. OK, to be honest, she loved him. Did he know that? She wasn't sure. She wasn't feeling well today, as it was. Now she just wanted to cry. Instead, she punched 911, told the dispatcher in a frantic-but-she-thought-professional tone there was a possibly dead, at least very ill, governmental figure in the governor's office, and then she sat at her desk, eyes closed, thinking, praying. She counted to a hundred and seventeen, started over, got to thirty-six and opened her eyes. It dawned on her that she was going to be overrun with reporters and police and who-knew-what. Kelli slapped the desk and stood, stalked to the alcove behind her desk, and made three pots of coffee on the three-burner BUNN restaurant-style auto-drip coffeemaker; two pots were French roast, the other was nutmeg spice extra decaf. Kelli knew no one else would drink the nutmeg spice extra decaf; however, she had a fondness for it and sensed an expanding need to indulge herself. Two paramedics arrived with a gurney and gear; she opened the doors to the governor's office. The paramedics rolled in and shut the doors behind them. Two state cops arrived and introduced themselves (Baker and Nofsprig). Three Michigan State University campus police, flush-faced and winded, arrived; their overzealous dispatcher, a passionate Republican with a bit of a man crush on Governor Bill, would later be reprimanded for deploying officers outside of their jurisdiction. Two Lansing city police arrived. Kelli offered coffee. They all wanted nutmeg spice extra decaf, black. She made another pot of it, dumped the spare pot of French roast and started a second pot of nutmeg spice extra decaf. The state cops snaked police tape across the chairs in Kelli's office. A city cop, claiming jurisdiction, yanked it down. A campus cop called Nofsprig an idiot. Nofsprig took a swing at him. The doors to the governor's office swung open and the paramedics came out with Senator DenBraber on the gurney. His face was gray and sweaty. They had a transparent oxygen mask over his nose and mouth and one of the paramedics was holding a clear plastic IV bag filled with a clear liquid, a tube from it snaking to the senator's unconscious right arm. Everyone realized that this meant he was alive, which took both the tension and some of the excitement out of the room. One of the paramedics laughed at something the other paramedic had just said. Kelli scowled at the paramedics and quickly closed the doors to the governor's office. A city cop asked to speak with the governor. Kelli said, "Give him a minute." Trooper Baker asked to see the governor. Kelli said, "Not yet." Ninety-seven seconds later, Trooper Nofsprig asked to see the governor. Kelli let Nofsprig in to see the governor. Nofsprig took the governor's statement, and then returned to Kelli's office. The governor always called Ham when there was a crisis and now he couldn't call him (Ham) so he told Siri to "call Dad." Siri said, "Calling Dad." Kelli called her intern, Tammy, and asked Tammy to get donuts. Kelli refilled everyone's coffee. Governor Bill ended the call to his dad—no answer. Kelli made more nutmeg spice extra decaf and took a bathroom break. A campus cop called for backup. In the bathroom, Kelli wondered for the third time that morning why she hadn't gotten her period. She didn't feel well and worried she was pregnant. She vowed to name the child Ham, if it was a boy. She began to cry as she thought about how her husband, Stan, had always said he liked Senator DenBraber and how Stan liking Ham was such an important thing for Stan, since he had a hormonal imbalance from a bicycle injury suffered as a teen that made it hard for him, Stan, to emotionally connect with other people. Stan had joined a private militia with some guys he knew because when he talked about guns and liberty with like-minded people, it helped fill his rarely satisfied need for connectedness. In the bathroom, Kelli forced herself to stop crying by reminding herself that Ham's situation would have no noticeable effect on Stan. Governor Bill called his father's number again, this time without Siri's help. Kelli returned and offered coffee to everyone who didn't have coffee. The cops all said, "No thanks." Kelli began to cry again. Tammy arrived with donuts. Another campus cop arrived, wearing sunglasses and a knit cap. One of the city cops pulled his gun. The other cops pulled their guns. All the cops yelled, "Gun!" Tammy screamed. Kelli stopped crying and screamed instead, then had that uncomfortable moment when the screaming turned to laughing. Kelli wondered if she was losing her mind. One cop said, "Emote much?" Everyone, Kelli included, laughed. The cops holstered their guns. Tammy said, "No gun," in a squeaky voice. Everyone giggled. Governor Bill ended the call—no answer. A state police detective arrived. A reporter called Kelli. Kelli put the reporter on hold. Governor Bill pressed the call button and held it down, re-calling his dad. Another reporter called. Kelli hung up on the reporter. Governor Bill left a voicemail apologizing to his dad for not having talked to him in so long and asking him if he'd maybe call him back. Kelli poured the last of the nutmeg spice extra decaf. Tammy offered to get more donuts. Kelli told Tammy to "bite me." Tammy ran to the bathroom in tears. A reporter from TV 10 arrived. A reporter from the *Lansing State Journal* arrived. Kelli offered the new arrivals French roast but no one wanted it. Nofsprig and Baker left. The state police detective left. Governor Bill asked Kelli for a donut and coffee. Kelli offered to have Tammy "run to fucking Starbucks." A reporter for the Associated Press arrived. Governor Bill, sensing Kelli's mood, said never mind about Starbucks. A reporter called back. Kelli hung up on her. Governor Bill paced. Kelli ordered the reporters into the adjoining conference room. Kelli entered the conference room and told the reporters what she knew about Ham's condition—nothing—then told everyone there was no coffee. One of the reporters said softly, "That sucks." Kelli told the reporters to get out of the stupid building. The governor found the wireless headset for his cell phone, in a desk drawer. The reporters left. The remaining cops left. The governor put the headset on. The governor called his father. The phone vibrated. He grimaced, cut off the call to his dad, and pressed the answer button.

# Chapter Six

The Silver Eagle Security training complex had grown to cover several thousand acres of farmland and forest near the tiny hamlet of Borculo. The sales literature called the base "a muscular but discreet, government-grade military operation without the annoying political oversight." To Will, the massive private-military layout was a perfect blend of Michigan's natural beauty and the state's unshaven, bare-knuckled, outdoorsy personality. This was a place where a man could walk among the pines, wade through meadows hip high with Queen Anne's lace, and blow shit away till the cows came home. Then, if you felt inclined, you could blow away the goddamn cows.

The Borculo complex had a manmade lake for amphibious assault training, indoor and outdoor shooting ranges, and a heliport for the company's small fleet, which included a Hughes MH-6 Little Bird, two Bell AH-1 Cobras, and three Sikorsky UH-60 Black Hawks. Prospective clients—nerdy, sweaty government bureaucrats, bling-dripping hired "intermediaries," and shades-wearing advisors to the anonymous and probably criminal—usually jetted in. Silver Eagle's landing strip could accommodate small-ish corporate jets and the three General

Atomics MQ-1 Predator unmanned aerial vehicles Will had recently purchased through a murky Pentagon back channel. These drones had seen action in Serbia, Yemen, and Iraq. Each was equipped with two AGM-114 Hellfire missiles.

The drones were hangared at a second airstrip in a secluded area near Allendale, just a few miles from Lake Michigan.

Will's gut danced at the thought that he might launch the drones soon.

Sitting in his parked SUV, staring through mirrored sunglasses at a Silver Eagle trainee-associate (TA) in an asbestos suit, Will felt the burden of command. For the first time, the coming conflict weighed heavily on him. This concerned him. Jake Hoeksma's nephew had never shirked confrontation or fretted over conflict.

Will forced himself to focus on the TA in the fire suit. He'd been set on fire and was flailing at the flames that engulfed him, but in an oddly reserved way.

The setting was perfect. Nearby, a lawnmower roared to life. A dog barked. Will felt a welcome surge of confidence. Despite the gravity of the situation with Wisconsin, all was good.

In the vehicle's passenger seat, a young weasel of a copywriter from Silver Eagle's ad agency was watching the TA training exercise with a familiar expression of fascination and horror. Will smiled, thought for a moment, then sniffed and cleared his throat. "That's our brand, you know," he said, pride filling his chest. When the kid didn't respond, he continued, "That TA there? He's top-drawer people. The best. He's Silver Eagle people. He is meeting every one of the basic requirements for certification in Fear Management Training, what we call F-Mat. Not many young people on earth can do that."

The skinny twenty-something copywriter clawed at a lunarscape of acne on his weakly whiskered jaw. He didn't—couldn't—speak. Like most guests, he was transfixed by the training demonstration; the trainee was flapping his flaming arms like a wounded phoenix.

"It's the heat that makes him flap like that. If you notice, he's staying on his feet and he's not trying to extinguish the flames," Will said with a nod and another sniff. "That's in the manual. We only hire ballsy people. The ballsiest."

"It's really really, ummm, awesome." The weasel's voice squirmed out of him. "I mean, he's staying inside the Designated Flame Confinement Area; you know, the orange circle spray-painted there, on the ground." He shot a quick glance at Will, and then turned back to the spectacle. "I wrote the field manual, sir."

"Right. Yes. Of course," Will said, irritated at the kid's impudence and his own forgetfulness. The Wisconsin thing was throwing him off his game, which made him wonder about his age. He'd spent decades juggling irons and fires. Was he losing his edge, now when it counted most?

*Don't be a pussy*, Uncle Jake's long-dead voice murmured in his head.

Will flipped open the console that was between him and the weasel. He pulled out a Ruger Mark IV semi-automatic. His other favorite handgun, a Colt 10mm, was nestled in a specially designed pocket of the Silver Eagle windbreaker he was wearing. He released the safety on the Ruger, chambered a round, buzzed down his window, extended his left arm, feeling the reassuring bulk of the hidden Colt rocking in its hammock, and squeezed the trigger.

The eardrum-wilting boom of the gunshot and the crash of a lawn tractor slamming into a tree nearly drowned out the weasel's scream.

Will drew his arm back in, carefully placed the gun on the dashboard, and fumbled for the window power switch. The glass whirred closed. His ears were ringing but Will's gaze remained locked on the two Associate Technicians (Ass-Techs) overseeing the TA test. Dressed in Silver Eagle Security uniforms, one Ass-Tech was a football slab of a guy, the other a thin giant. The giant was wearing a Bluetooth headset and appeared to be talking into it. The football guy had dropped to the ground and was doing one-armed pushups. Both were keeping their eyes on the burning trainee.

"What the fu…?" The copywriter's voice clawed to be heard. Will, preternaturally calm, faced him. The kid's eyes, behind ridiculously large black-framed glasses, focused momentarily on the scene beyond Will's left shoulder. "You shot… the lawnmower? You could've killed the guy…" He turned back to the TA testers. "They didn't even…"

Will smiled. He waited, letting the kid sputter.

Finally, Will said, "Are you done?"

The kid was again looking past Will, a frown creasing his forehead, eyes blinking. "There's a guy… He was mowing. You shot… He crashed into the tree."

"He will be fine."

"But…"

Will held up an index finger.

"This is insane," the kid said. "You could've killed that guy on the mower."

"Correction. This is a lesson to you. This is my brand. Be ready for anything. I only hire good people. Tough people. The best people ever. No pussies."

The kid glanced beyond Will, then to the flaming TA, then back to Will. His face fell. He shrugged. "Whatever. I mean, I guess."

"You're damn right, you guess."

Will gestured toward several bunker-like structures beyond the burning trainee. "Now, look. Those buildings back there," Will said. "Those are where my spies work. My spooks. They manage all my intelligence tactics. Ex-CIA, most of them.

Couple are ex-Mossad. Do our cyber security and cyber espionage projects. Very cyber. Secretive. Spook stuff."

The kid, still obviously shaken, looked at him, thought for a moment, and wisely said, "R... really?"

"Really," Will said, swallowing a smile. "And here's something else you don't know." He shot the kid a glance to underline *don't*. "I make it policy to never enter those buildings." Another glance. A smile. The kid looked genuinely surprised at this information. Will felt a rush of warmth, his legendary confidence fully returning. "It's my don't ask, don't tell policy."

The kid didn't smile.

Will stared at him. "You a fruitcake, kid?"

"A fruit...?"

"A fudge packer? You on the other team?"

"You mean, uh, am I, what—gay?" The kid's thin, pale face turned pink. "No. No." He was suddenly defensive, recoiling. "Of course not."

Will smiled. "Of course you're not," he said. "Of course." He reached across the center console and patted the kid's blue-jeaned thigh. The kid, as expected, recoiled.

Outside, the TA suddenly began screaming. The copywriter's gaze snapped back to the scene. His face blanched. His glasses reflected fire.

"Oh, don't worry. They always eventually do that the first time." Will sniffed and picked up the handgun from the dashboard. "Gets worse when they release the Dobermans." The leather seat groaned. Will held the gun in his hand, stared at it. He looked the TA. "Got no idea where the damn dogs are. Should be on him by now. Gonna kick someone's ass over that. Details. Details. Details."

"This is crazy, man. Crazy," the copywriter said softly, eyes locked on the flailing fiery arms. Even his voice sounded like a weasel's voice.

"Danger's in your head," Will Hoeksma said, his gaze on the tableau, a muscle in his jaw pulsing. "Yeah, it's hot as hell but there's no way he's going to burn alive or anything like that. The new associates scream, until they get a handle on this fire suit thing. Until they realize we're not going to invest one-hundred-thousand-plus to train them and then turn around and kill them. Yeah, they blister up a bit. But they come out fine." Will turned to face the kid. The weasel scowled, his eyes still on the trainee.

"How old are you?" Will said.

"Twenty-two."

"Well, let me tell you, Mr. Twenty-two..." Will Hoeksma said, the gun jab, jab, jabbing toward the kid's face.

"Todd," the weasel said.

"What's that?" Will said.

"Lindquist," Todd Lindquist managed to say. "That's my name."

"That Jewish?" Will said.

"Who, me?" the weasel said.

"Lindquist. That Jewish?"

"No. No. No, Mr. Hoeksma."

"You got a problem if it was, Mr. Twenty-two?" Will suddenly flipped open the center console, threw the Ruger in, and slammed the console shut. He stared out at the trainee. "I said, you got a problem with Jewish people?"

"No. Not at all. I mean..."

"Well, I do. I don't like them one bit," Will said. He shot the weasel a mirrored frown. The weasel looked a little pale.

They sat for a moment. Finally, Will said, "Look. You're wondering why you're here. You're wondering why you of all people, some twenty-year-old..."

"Twenty-two, s... sir."

"Why I asked the agency to send you over."

"Well, yes. Yes, sir, I did."

"Well, for starters, I got fifty years on you and know what in the damn hell I'm doing. So I suggest you keep that in mind. And number two: I'd hoped you'd be up for the job. I've put some things in place that we're going to need some help with—some stuff that needs to be written and so on. And I don't need to babysit some bedwetter. You a bedwetter Lumnuts?"

"I've been working on your account for the past year, Mr. Hoeksma. I've done the backgrounding; I can handle this."

"You can handle this?" Will nodded toward the burning trainee. "Are you sure of that?"

The kid swallowed. "Yes. Yes, I can. Of course. I mean, yes. *Yes*. I do know your business. I just want you to know that. I worked on the online ad campaign too. Along with the employee manual and stuff."

"You did."

"With Rich's—my creative director's—help, of course. And Shanna, she was the art director."

"You come up with that condom ad?"

Todd blushed. "Yes, actually I did. But we, you, never actually ran it. It was just one of my—our—ideas."

"So you're apologizing for it."

"No, no. I mean, I thought it was a killer idea. Actually."

"Comparing the protection you need for sex with the protection my company provides; that was 'killer'?"

"Well, I mean, for the audience, for young guys like my age, it would really, you know, cut through the clutter."

"An ad tying intimate relations to my firm; that's a clutter cutter? That what my brand is about, Lundgren? Penis jokes?"

"It's Lindqui… no… I mean, yes, but… OK, maybe, maybe that idea's a little out there," Todd said. "Look, ummmm, sir, like, some ideas, like that ad, are just part of, you know, the process. We want to grab people."

"Really. That's how you work?" William Hoeksma said. "After fifty years in the business of selling shit, you think I'm without a clue, Mr. Lambjack?"

"Uh, sorry," the copywriter said, his eyes wide through his glasses. "Mr. Hoeksma, I didn't mean to…"

"You can drop the Mr. Hoeksma."

"Yes, ummm, Mr. Hoek… ah, um, Will, William."

"Call me 'sir.'"

"OK. Yes. Of course."

"Sir."

"Sir," the kid said. He gulped and turned to face Will. "I'm sorry. I'm very sorry."

Will let the apology fester for a moment. When he spoke, it was in a conciliatory tone. "Well, I can certainly understand how a twenty-two-year-old artsy fartsy ad guy like you would think I was just a dumb old client."

Todd laughed.

"You think that's funny?" Will said, suddenly stern.

"No, no, sir," Todd said, his face now pale.

"You don't think my humor is funny?"

"Well yes. I mean, if you do, sir."

Will looked at the kid and rolled his eyes. The weasel was green and easy to manipulate. This was good. He was also brilliant—Will had chosen him for a reason, although Will would never acknowledge it. He'd had his human resources people do a deep background check, which had told them Lindquist was a bit of a creative genius and an excellent writer who handled technology with the ease and cocky confidence of most twenty-something males raised on Xboxes, laptops, and social media. His parents were flaky, composting, off-the-energy-grid, Prius-driving, left-wing freaks who ran a health food store in Kalamazoo but who seemed politically impotent and, therefore, harmless. Lindquist had one sibling, a sister who had taken a vow of poverty and entered some kind of monastery in the farm town of Fennville. She would not be a problem. Lindquist had started out as a journalism student but had gotten his degree in creative writing at Western Michigan, where he'd smoked a considerable amount of pot, spent a lot of time playing video games in his off-campus apartment, and distinguished himself as an unfocused, talented, somewhat nervous smartass. Lindquist was "easily influenced by others," according to the background information. The current conversation confirmed this.

"You keep your head on straight, you're gonna do just fine, Lambchops," Will said. He picked up his cell phone, thumbed in the security code, and checked to see if he had any texts. There was one.

# Chapter Seven

"Hello," Governor Bill said into his headset. He slipped the phone into his pants pocket, sat in his chair, and turned to avoid looking at the spot where Ham DenBraber had fallen. The doors were now open to Kelli's office. Kelli was talking with a small group of staff members. Some were crying. Others were open-mouthed. One, a cute young woman who worked in media relations—Donna or Deena or Desiree—was crying and open-mouthed. She was also taking notes. Governor Bill remembered Donna-Deena-Desiree was the only remaining member of the communications team they'd budget-cut two years ago. He had authorized her to speak on his behalf, in any situation, especially those involving the mainstream media. Governor Bill refused to talk to the mainstream media; they always distorted what he said. He was happy to see Donna-Deena-Desiree taking notes.

Kelli stopped in mid speech and vomited into her wastebasket. She had said something earlier about not feeling well.

"It's Tuttle," Tuttle said in Governor Bill's ear.

Tuttle. State police commander. To Governor Bill, he was "the colonel." He'd been an enigmatic, long-haired scarecrow with a near-mythic backstory when Bill's father, Will Hoeksma, met him in his University of Michigan dorm back in the early 70s. A shaggy Vietnam vet majoring in criminal justice with a 4.0 grade point average, Tuttle served two tours as a military policeman, but his real deal during the war was smuggling black-market goods—mostly stuff stolen by other Americans—from Vietnam to the US. Will heard Tuttle "nearly tortured to death" three Vietnamese men who threatened to expose his illegal operation. Legend had it that Tuttle spent his first year after the war in Singapore as a night watchman at a tattoo parlor, where he'd fallen in love with a local girl whose radio show, "Singapore Sal," played American popular music. Turned out Sal was CIA, so the story went, and she recruited Tuttle, who'd gone on to handle several ops for the agency before getting homesick, quitting the spy business cold, and returning home to Michigan with a special place in his heart for Asian cuisine and pop hits from the 60s and early 70s. Fascinated by Tuttle's legend and seeming lack of moral compass—a quality Will valued in certain employees—Will Hoeksma cultivated a friendship. He'd made Tuttle head of security at Amerispin, and then had relied on Tuttle to help launch Silver Eagle. Shortly after Governor Bill took office, the state police commander had suddenly retired during a health crisis, and Governor Bill, on the advice of his father, had appointed Tuttle to replace him.

Governor Bill Hoeksma pushed away from his desk and leaned forward, elbows on knees, eyes clenched. "Colonel, we have a thing here."

From Tuttle the response was tinny music and Tuttle humming.

"Colonel?"

"I've been briefed," Tuttle said at last. Behind him, the music swelled; Toni Tennille warbled about Muskrat Susie and Muskrat Sam. "Governor, I have you on speaker phone, but the room is empty. You can speak freely."

"Ham DenBraber is seriously ill," Governor Bill said.

"Yes, governor. Affirm that. I affirm and confirm."

Governor Bill swallowed hard. "The medical—ambulance—people have been here. Police."

"I am aware, sir."

"I. Gosh. Shit." Governor Bill wiped tears away, tried to smooth the hitch in his voice. "Excuse my French."

"No problem, sir."

"I don't usually swear like that."

"I know, sir."

"He. Right here. In my office."

"Yes."

"Paramedics said he is one sick puppy. I had to wait for them. With him here. I didn't—what could I do? I just sat. I've called my father but he's not answering."

"I have text-messaged your father. Assumed you'd want him informed. Now, sir…"

"I can't believe he did this. Ham, I mean." Governor Bill closed his eyes for a moment then opened them. "How did you hear about it already?"

"Governor, my officers, several state troopers, responded to the scene."

"Oh. Oh, right. Yes. Certainly," Governor Bill said. "I suppose it's his heart. You know, Ham, he certainly never works out. I tried to get him to hit the gym, to run with me. Bike, maybe…"

"Governor, I believe you have to consider the other possibility here. As we've discussed…"

"Which makes me think I should have my cholesterol checked." Governor Bill reached for a Post-it note pad and stopped. "Tuttle, that music. The Captain and Tennille?"

"Yes, governor."

"Could you turn it down a notch? I can't hear myself think."

"Sorry, sir." The music faded slightly. Tuttle cleared his throat. "Governor, we've discussed the possibility of a viral attack from Wisconsin. Senator DenBraber and I briefed you on this. We brought Hank Vander… Representative Vanderway with us, as you recall."

Governor Bill thought about this. "Shit. Wait. Hold on. He wanted to talk to me about that."

"Who?"

"Ham. Wanted to talk about the Wisconsin deal."

"When?"

"Today. That's why he came. Why he was here." Governor Bill looked to the outer office. Kelli, pale, was returning from somewhere with a wastebasket. She was saying, "Maybe something I ate." The others were moving out of her way. Some young guy he didn't recognize—probably an intern—reached to help her with the wastebasket; Kelli slapped his hand.

"And did he?" Tuttle said.

"Now my secretary seems to be ill. And I'm not feeling all that great myself."

"Did Senator DenBraber talk to you about it?"

"No. No. He had no idea. I felt fine until he…"

"No, sir. Did he mention the Wisconsin situation?"

"Oh, right. Yes. No, no he didn't. He said he was going to but when he got here, he went… collapsed before we could really get into it."

"Sir, frankly, this is why I called. As you know, Senator DenBraber felt fairly sure that something had happened to him and the others while they were over there on their trip. So did Representative Vanderway. Given the senator's condition, it appears Wisconsin has attacked us."

"Whoa, Tuttle. Whoa." Governor Bill hated to be rushed. "Rushed" usually led to decisions he regretted because he didn't understand exactly why he'd decided what he'd decided. "Ham is certainly not the picture of health. He just seemed a little weak—like he had a cold or the flu or something," Governor Bill said. He thought for a moment and a possibility dawned on him. "Are you saying… could this virus… could I be in danger, Tuttle?"

"Not likely, sir. I do want to have someone look you over, health-wise. But you weren't in Wisconsin with our people. Our greater threat right now is what Oleson and his people will do next."

"Oleson?"

"The governor, governor."

"Oh, right. Sure. Of Wisconsin." Governor Bill touched the back of his hand to his forehead and then found his pulse in his neck. He counted beats for 15 seconds, reached for the Post-it pad, snared it, picked up a pen and wrote

17
x4

on a note. He did the math. Sixty-eight beats per minute. Even better than he'd thought. He felt for the lymph nodes in his neck. No tenderness. At least they didn't seem tender. Not sick-tender, anyway. If you pressed hard enough, well, anything felt tender when you pressed hard. Didn't it? He forced himself to stop thinking about it.

"Governor?"

"I'm here, Tuttle."

"Sir, as we've laid out for you these past several weeks, these are evil people. That's why we need to move forward quickly. I've already scheduled a rendezvous with Representative Vanderway and Senator Griffendorf to update them, as our legislative leaders, on the situation," Tuttle said. "Only God knows now it will be a mission of mercy to get Vanderway medical help as well, since he was with Senator DenBraber on that trip."

"Tuttle, I'm in no condition to do a briefing."

Tuttle sighed. "Nor should you do one. Your best position is here. In leadership. In the capitol. I'm due to leave for said rendezvous and briefing in"—he paused—"zero seven minutes, thirty-seven. I'll brief these folks and we'll check on the health of Representative Vanderway at the same time."

"What about Ham? Is he going to be OK? Do we know?"

"Governor," Tuttle said quietly but sounding like he wanted to yell. "We have Senator DenBraber at Sparrow right now being examined by the best people. That's low-hanging fruit. Let my people pick it."

"Sparrow?"

"Sparrow Hospital, sir. Yes."

Governor Bill stared at his desk, struggling to breathe. He leaned slowly forward, put his head between his knees, clamped his knees to his head, and studied the floor inside the kneehole of his desk. He let time pass, listening to the music from Tuttle's side of the conversation. Finally, he said, "Tuttle, Ham has to be OK. He's the one guy I totally totally lean on." The words were muffled, like he was in a box.

"Governor, the personal side of this, if I may say so, that's secondary for you at this juncture. Numero dos. Your state, Michigan and its people, are job one right now."

"They never clean under my desk."

"Governor?"

"The cleaning people. They don't clean under here; not very well, anyway."

"You're under your desk, sir?"

"Tuttle, why did you send him to Sparrow? Why not someplace bigger? Like in Detroit?"

"Honestly, sir, there are exceptional people at Sparrow. If they get in over their heads here, we'll move him. Besides, the family's nearby, sir, and for their sake…"

"Oh crap. Marci." Governor Bill said. He sat up too fast. The room spun a little.

"Mrs. DenBraber?"

"Yes. Marci. Geez."

"Informed," Tuttle said.

Governor Bill heaved a sigh. "I should have done that, I think."

"Again, low-hanging fruit, sir. She is under secure transport to the hospital right now."

"Their kids…"

"En route as well. From school."

"I should have called Marci," Governor Bill said, his voice rising. He stopped, and slapped his forehead. "Geez, and I have golf league." He looked at his watch and swore again loudly—too loudly. "Damn, Ham, why today of all days?" In the reception area, all eyes turned to look at him. Governor Bill swiveled his chair away to face the wall opposite his desk.

"Sir, if I may suggest, you're very emotional right now…"

"Yeah, I know. My mom was emotional, too. My dad hated it. Dad hired those consultants to work with me when I ran for governor. Emotion management—EM—they called it. They drilled into me their big fancy Emotional Skillset Training Module—the ESTM. Darn thing is, Tuttle, I can't remember a single thing from the eight-step EM checklist." Governor Bill laughed bitterly. "Probably because I'm too emotional right now." He forced a deep breath and exhaled loudly, slapped his palms on his desk, and pushed his chair back from it. In the outer office, Kelli was flat on her back on her desk, a wet paper towel covering her face, her legs dangling over the far side; the others, in a knot near the lone window, were chatting, shaking their heads, some were nodding, arms crossed. It looked like Kelli had some kind of virus, too. Governor Bill wondered how soon he would fall ill. He tried not to think about it.

On the wall of Governor Bill's office, in a framed black and white photo, Ronald Reagan sat on a horse. The photo had been a gift from his father on Bill's eighth birthday. There was a smile on the legendary president's sun-cracked face. Governor Bill studied the photo and silently read the inscription, although he had long since memorized it: *Young Bill—be tough, cowboy. Ron Reagan.* His dad hadn't smiled when he'd given the photo to him. His dad, Governor Bill's mom always said, was not a big smiler.

"Governor." Tuttle's voice sliced through Governor Bill's reverie. "Let's cut to the chase. I am proposing, as authorized by the constitution of the state of Michigan, to implement the defensive ops strategy as reviewed, you recall, last week with Senator DenBraber and Representative Vanderway in your office."

In the picture, Reagan didn't flinch; his eyes held fast on some distant point. Governor Bill's eyes held fast on Reagan. "The strategy was…"

"Preemption," Tuttle said. "We punch those Wisconsin bastards in the mouth before they launch a full-scale operation on us. Just like George W. Bush did in Iraq. You always admired George W., sir. Now is your chance to emulate him."

Governor Bill's eyes swerved from Reagan's. "I should have a picture of him—of W. Bush. We have a lot in common, him and me. You know that, Tuttle? He was the son of a pretty successful guy and the black sheep of his family. Sure, he'd done some coke. He lost years. People said he wasn't the sharpest knife…"

"All of that is good analysis for another day, sir. If I may…"

"Remember the rubble? With the bullhorn?" Governor Bill cupped his hands around his mouth. "'We will chase you down, you terrorist cowards.' That's what W. Bush said, something like that."

"He was a true leader in a tough spot, sir. On task. No wavering," Tuttle said. "As you should be right now."

"Damn straight, Tuttle." Governor Bill was pacing. "George W., they always underestimated him. But that day, he showed what he was made of. He knew what was happening. He knew what it was all about."

"The rubble, sir."

"The what?"

"What it was about. All of those people. The towers. The rubble."

"Really." Governor Bill frowned.

"Governor, look. The president, Bush the Second, he acted quickly to prevent any more attacks. You do remember the Bush doctrine, right?"

"I remember, Tuttle. You don't need a reason to attack. Just a suspicion."

"That's right. Or a tipping point."

"Right. We talked about that. A tipping point. A time when the weight of the evidence suggests the security…"

"…the security of your people is in jeopardy," Tuttle said.

"So, fine. Yes. Yes, Tuttle," Governor Bill said. He was suddenly weary of Tuttle. "Bush doctrine away. Go ahead. Light the, uh… Light the light. Or whatever."

"Excellent, sir. Excellent. Now the other major decision. How do we physically carry out our response? Option one was a strike using my state police troopers. But we ruled that out. Remember?"

"Of course I do, Tuttle," Governor Bill said, shocked at his own clarity, his firmness. Tuttle, like his father, tended to talk down to him. Governor Bill opened a drawer and pulled out the famous Sig Sauer. He had a brand new 9mm Glock in a shoulder holster, but the Sig was his go-to comfort gun. He'd used it at the state police firing range just the week before. It still smelled freshly fired. He loved that smell. Feet up on the desk, leaning back in his chair, Governor Bill aimed the gun at the ceiling, released the safety, racked the slide, squinted, and pulled the trigger. Click.

"Know what Tuttle? I can fight anyone," Governor Bill said. He eyed the window overlooking the street. Aimed. Click. "I can fight the unions. I can fight the media. I can fight a bunch of, like, rioters who tell me I can't cut their precious little minimum wage enough to help a few businessmen make a dime and create a job or two." A potted plant he hated, in a corner of the office. Aimed. Click. "I can even fight some certified nutjob cheeseheads. But I can't fight people who just don't believe in me and my decision-making ability. By your tone, I start to wonder whether or not you have any confidence in me at all. You sound an awful lot like my dad. I can do this job, Tuttle."

"My apologies, sir. I am just…"

"So, as I recall, option one was your state troopers do something to send a message to these Wisconsin infidels. But we nixed that. Right?"

"Yes."

"Option two was…" Governor Bill paused. "Option two was…"

"The private sector security firms."

So there it was. Governor Bill's stomach twisted. He pulled the chair close to the desk and put the gun down. "You mean hire my dad's paramilitary people or Benjie Teegarten's."

"Yes. And I know you had some resistance to contracting for our response."

"Some resistance? I had a lot of resistance."

"However, as requested by Senator DenBraber, this past week we did reach out to Teegarten's organization, just to discuss costs and availability."

"What did they say?" Governor Bill said, feeling increasingly irritated.

"Well, governor, as expected, Teegarten's outfit, Diamond Paramilitary, is not in our price range. On something like this, he will go market rate strictly. We tried to negotiate, delicately. No specifics on the op. But even talking in broad terms—even dangling the appeal of clear and present danger to people in his home state, it was a no-go. Not even, say, ten percent off on a couple of snipers at the weekend rate—if we wanted to take out a particular dangerous scientist over there. And they would mark up travel costs on that as well."

Governor Bill sighed. "So that leaves us where?" He knew the answer. He picked up the gun. He put down the gun. This situation was really pissing him off. Governor Bill grabbed the Sig Sauer and aimed at the elaborate ceiling light fixture. Click.

"Governor, sir," Tuttle said. "I've talked personally to your father. And he will work with us, rate-wise and otherwise."

The governor thought for a moment. He tapped the Sparky Anderson bobblehead with the barrel of the 9mm. Sparky bobbled crazily. Governor Bill stared at Sparky and felt something new—shame?—for having tried to call his father after Ham collapsed. Did George W. call his dad when the towers came down? Not likely. Because George W. wasn't his daddy's little boy, he was his own man. He'd called the shots. Oh yeah, he had. Governor Bill stopped tapping. He stared at Sparky. Everything, it seemed, was suddenly on his nerves. Stop fucking smiling, fucking Sparky. (He didn't even feel guilty about think-swearing; he was that mad.) Suddenly, irrationally, Governor Bill wanted to blow the happy goofiness off Sparky's face. He pointed the gun at the bobbling head, squinted, squeezed the trigger.

Click.

# Chapter Eight

Behind Tuttle, the music had segued to "Band on the Run" by Paul McCartney and Wings. The volume rose briefly then fell. Governor Bill twisted the gun so it was pointed at his face, closed one eye, and peered into the barrel. It was dark in there. He thought about the conversations they'd had about the Wisconsin threat. Thought about the suggestions he'd made. Everyone had ignored him. He was tired of being ignored, which was why he'd already made some decisions on his own. He turned and pointed the pistol toward the chair that sat across from him; the chair Ham would be sitting in if he hadn't collapsed and gone to Sparrow. Click.

"I think I talked about possibly working with some of the private militias to handle our little problem with our cheesy friends. Have you given any thought to it?" Governor Bill said. "You remember, I met a bunch of those private militia folks during my campaign. And my secretary—office manager—her husband is a member of one of those groups."

"Yes, and we had quite the discussion when you hired her."

"But Kelli, she's not a problem; she isn't a member. It's her husband. And he actually supports me. The militias, those guys love me."

"Yes, governor. I am aware. That's why we allowed her to work for you, but we're moving at extreme caution when it comes to the militia folks. If there was a net positive there, a worthwhile, proven upside to partnering with them, yes. But there is simply no there, there."

Governor Bill was confused when Tuttle talked this way. His father and Tuttle, Ham too, often wound him into logic knots he couldn't untangle. He closed his eyes and took a deep breath. He let it out slowly, opened his eyes, and stared again at Reagan on the wall. "Fine, whatever. I'm just saying the militia people are good at running their own little personal armies. When they get a guy like me in office in Lansing, someone who understands their point of view about the second amendment and about the guys in Washington taking away state's rights and, well, I think they might want to help us. I mean, these guys are dedicated to Michigan way more than you and most people realize." Governor Bill took a deep breath. "Which is why I think we should go that route, on this thing." He paused, wondering if he should confess the rest. *Screw it*, he thought. "Which is why I already sort of suggested it to Kelli."

"You what, sir?"

"I already asked her to check out the militia folks' interest, Tuttle. After you guys briefed me."

Tuttle didn't speak for several seconds. "Governor," Tuttle finally said, his voice as calm and persuasive as it could be, "you're really, if I may just say, really surprising us—me—here. That was a significant step—a breach of protocol—bringing an outsider into the ring of secrecy on this."

Governor Bill sat, swiveled away from his desk, and leaned forward, elbows on thighs. He froze, staring at the floor, the gun in his right hand. Shame and embarrassment lurked. He had become obsessed with the militia movement—supportive of it. And deep down, he knew it was because his father and

Tuttle and whoever else was always controlling everything in the state would not approve. But now he was struck again with the idea that he was in charge at a critical moment in history. It felt good to be him, making his own choices.

"I'm the governor. I certainly know all about protocols and breaching, Tuttle. Me talking to my secretary is not breaching."

Tuttle, after a deep sigh: "What did she say, sir?"

"They, the militia folks, were very interested. I think." Governor Bill swallowed hard. Now that he'd told Tuttle the truth, there was no turning back. "In fact, truth be told, they're ready. Just waiting for the word to help. I think. Pretty much."

From Tuttle, there was a long low groan. Governor Bill ignored it. "You just said yourself we can't use Benjie Teegarten for this. And it's probably some kind of conflict of interest to let my dad's people in on it. Right? Besides, I mean, how good is he—are they? Just for argument's sake."

"How good—who?"

"Dad's people."

"Well, most of the trade groups rate Silver Eagle at a strategic level—in terms of personnel and hardware and overall resources—the same as or a tick lower than Teegarten, at least in their core competencies. Number two globally but again, very much on par with the best."

"What would those be? Their 'core competencies.'"

"Well, I'd give them high marks in training, logistics, the tech side of things," Tuttle said. "But they're really in a superior position, exceptionally resourced, top to bottom. I mean, their hardware capabilities would put most of your third world militaries to shame. I personally can attest to that."

"Well, Benjie's people could handle assassinations and so on. You said you'd checked them on that. The militia can, too. Could Silver Eagle?"

"Yes, sir."

"Military, like, assaults? Could they do them? Militia folks can."

"Governor, your father's company is on par with Diamond and most of your small nation-state military forces. Unlike the militias, they are legal. Any conflict of interest can be explained and managed. So yes, they could get this done. Simply put. And in a very, very professional manner."

Governor Bill thought for a moment. He tapped the barrel of the gun against his nose. It hurt to do that, so he stopped doing it. His eyes were watering.

In the outer office, the Michigan State University mascot, Sparty—oversized foam-rubber fists on his skirted hips, gigantic, foam-rubber helmeted head tilted way over to the side to avoid scraping the ceiling, the big smiling face towering over the room—was talking to Kelli. Kelli, looking pale but in control, was seated at her desk. She had to lean back to look into Sparty's always-happy giant eyes; she was saying something about being reasonable.

"Damn. Forgot. We have a photo shoot today," Governor Bill said.

"Sir?" Tuttle said.

"With Sparty and the cheerleaders and, uh, the pep band. From Michigan State. A publicity thing for them."

"Governor you must not divert at this point. You cannot. You must focus on your decision. You'll absolutely have to cancel any other activities."

Governor Bill slumped forward and rested his head on the desk pad. He pointed the gun at the floor. Again, Tuttle with that tone; it was so, what was the word? Patronizing. Yes. Patronizing. "I am aware of that, colonel," Governor Bill said, his teeth tight. "I am aware of a lot of things. I am not a dummy."

"Yes, governor."

"And drop that, whatever you call it, that patronizing—that attitude," Governor Bill said. He sat up, the gun in his hand.

"Roger that, sir. But if I may say so, sir, we also need to optimize our time window here," Tuttle said. He hesitated, then added, "If we are going to contact Silver Eagle and get the ball rolling, we need to do that."

"I see what you did there, Tuttle. Trying to close the deal. Trying to ignore my order."

"Governor, if I may ask you to simply reconsider your position. Silver Eagle is the best option—no doubt."

Governor Bill stood and paced in front of the window, switching the gun from hand to hand as he paced, forgetting for the moment that Ham's body had been there not long before. He stopped pacing, seized by another thought. "What about other states?"

"States, sir?"

"You know, Indiana and so on. The rest of the country. I mean, I know we have to do this quietly to keep the federal guys out of it—we're going to catch it from DC when this is over—but how about our fellow states helping us?"

Tuttle made an airy whistling sound. "Sir, Wisconsin is a regional threat. I really believe our other neighbors will have our backs with Washington when this is over."

"Can we get some, like, military support?"

From Tuttle, a snort. "From who?"

"I don't know. Indiana maybe. Their state cops or whatever."

Tuttle sighed. "Sir, this was all part of our previous debrief."

"Rebrief it for me. The important stuff. Little it down."

"We go it alone."

"Not quite that little."

Tuttle let out a long ragged sigh. "Indiana, central and east, most of it is Amish. Or people who act Amish, farmers mostly. On the border around Chicago, gangbangers. Hip-hoppers.

Not reliable unless they're already on our side, which they aren't."

"Ohio?"

"Ohio may have the zeal, sir, but they're big people. Slow movers. And our U of M'ers won't stand for Buckeye involvement."

"But the Ohio governor; Smacker, isn't it? I, we, the wives and all met at a golf outing last year. Decent golfer. Good man. Smacker."

"There's homosexuality there, governor. Weakness."

"Smacker?"

"The name's Schumacher, governor. And no, sir, not him—in the family."

Governor Bill tick-tick-ticked his tongue against his teeth. "Yes, OK, right. I remember."

"A cousin. On his mother's side."

"You'd never know. Gosh, that man can hit a three wood," Governor Bill said. "How about Illinois?"

"Governor Hoeksma, let me bottom line it," Tuttle said. "The other states, they're back pocket at best."

"Back pocket? I'm good with that."

"Deep, deep back pocket."

Governor Bill digested this. "Tuttle, however we do this, we'll be hanging out there. All by ourselves."

From Tuttle's end there was a crash, then what sounded like a chicken squawking. The music was suddenly gone. Governor Bill plopped back into his chair.

"Tuttle?"

Tuttle's voice was briefly distant: "Governor, with all due respect…" There was more squawking, a grunt from Tuttle, then silence. When Tuttle's voice returned, it was at full volume; he'd taken the phone off speaker. "Listen, I learned this lesson early on in life. My dad was a tough, good-looking son-of-a-gun.

A construction worker. This guy sees him standing in line for beer at a Lions game once and asked him if he'd ever done any modeling. Gives him a business card. Turned out the guy was a big shot rep from one of the modeling agencies in Detroit. One thing led to another, you know, and pretty soon dad's doing modeling gigs, mostly for the car companies—truck ads and so on. He took a lot of heat from his buddies in construction for that. A lot of heat. But my old man didn't give a rip because he knew what modeling got him—what it got us. Cash. Cash to pay for cleft-palate surgery for my brother, who, it turned out—my brother I'm talking about—didn't want surgery and so he ended up running off to Utah with two Mormon cousins he'd met—another story for another day. Point is, Dad used that cash as a means to an end. It was cash for my mom to buy an extra pot pie or two to put in the freezer. It was a nest egg for my sister to go to college and get knocked up by a Pakistani professor; they're living in Istanbul now—again, don't get me started. You get the point. The modeling wasn't about Dad getting dressed up in clothes that weren't his and wearing makeup and, rumor had it, sleeping with every last woman with two legs in the modeling agency's portfolio. It was about the income. In-come."

Governor Bill frowned. "Which has what to do with what?"

Tuttle sighed. "Governor, when things get tough, you focus on the one most important thing. The end. The goal. That thing is what we professionals call 'the get,'" Tuttle said. "Your eyes need to be on that, sir."

"On the get."

"Yes, sir. You've got the chance to avenge what they've done to Ham and assure security for your people."

"Revenge for Ham and security for our people. That's like two gets—a double get. I thought you said focus on one."

"Focus on that, then—on your double get. Because then your head will be in the right place and so will the public's.

As George W. Bush would, I'm sure, tell you, sir, if you aren't focused on the objective then this whole notion of a preemptive attack becomes just attacking; it's like what common thugs would do. People need a good reason for doing this. So. Just. Please, governor, focus. On that, them, those gets. Let me figure out the best way to get them."

His eyes on the pistol still in his hand, Governor Bill thought about this. He thought about all the years he'd done what his father wanted, how George W. had probably done the same thing because, hey, that's how you get where you want to be. But what then? When you win, like, the governorship or presidency, what's the get after you've gotten that?

His head ached. The day was making him think way too hard.

From the outer office, he heard clanking. A flute—piccolo?—fluttered a scale. "The pep band is here. For the picture," Governor Bill said.

"Again, sir. That should not distract you right now."

Governor Bill took a deep breath and stared at the pistol. He felt powerful—more powerful than he'd ever felt. "You're right, colonel. No distractions allowed." He exhaled. Nodded to himself. "We're going alone on this. And when we go, we're using the militias, I think, Tuttle. Yes. Yes. Definitely." Governor Bill set his jaw. "Yes. We are. The militias, it is."

Tuttle sighed. "Shit."

"What's that, Tuttle?"

"Nothing, sir. Just spilled something."

# Chapter Nine

He'd done it. For the first time in his life, at least the first time he could remember, Governor Bill had taken the bull by the horns, the bullhorn by the handle thing you used when you were holding a bullhorn, and taken charge.

He pushed back from the desk, leaned forward, rested his forearms on his thighs again, stared at his shoes; the loafers were bouncing, the tassels dancing a random jig. Governor Bill felt wound up, amped, psyched. He worried about his heart and whether or not it was racing because maybe he was sick like Ham had been sick. He stared at the jiggling gun in his hand and vowed to have a complete physical and maybe try to get a run in today.

Tuttle was speaking. Governor Bill sighed. He was tired of Tuttle. "What, Tuttle?" he said.

"I said I can't overrule you on this, I'm guessing."

"Darn right you can't." Governor Bill tapped the gun barrel on the desk. His mind was running ahead, thinking of the militia people going into Wisconsin and attacking. In his imagination, they were moving toward the state capital in Madison, laying siege to the building itself. He saw the building in flames and heard people screaming in Wisconsin accents.

The image in his head made the governor uncomfortable. Governor Bill knew all wars ended up being messy—his dad always said that—but Governor Bill figured W. Bush's war had gotten messier because of the bad intelligence his advisors had given him. W.'s advisors had set him up with the whole "weapons of mass destruction" deal. Which was why Governor Bill now heard himself saying, "We're going to go in nice and easy, especially to start with, Tuttle. Understand?"

"Well, uh, sure. If that's how you want to play it." Tuttle took a deep breath. "The state police will stay on the home front here, hunkered in, and these private militias, I guess, will make the actual first strike." Tuttle's voice sounded stiff, tense. "That's your order, sir, as I hear it."

"You said 'first' strike."

"Yes."

"I think we need to keep this at one strike. Get in there. Make a statement. Hit them hard, you know, and then see where we're at." Governor Bill pointed the gun at the door to his office, closed one eye, aiming. Click. "We're not going to get tangled up in some kind of mess like a bunch of crazy people." Governor Bill didn't understand completely what he was feeling, but he was pretty sure it was the feeling a leader had when he did something leader-like.

"That's your choice, sir."

There was a long pause, both men waiting on the other.

The suddenly confident Governor Bill broke the silence. "OK, then. I'll let Kelli know. She'll let the militia people know. Then we'll get these people over there. Have them, you know, strike at them somewhere and then we'll see what happens."

Tuttle sighed. He decided to give it one last try. "If I may, governor, just remember, there's no shame in keeping the flame lit on our back burner. Not necessarily Benjie Teegarten's outfit, given the price, but I can envision a situation in which you might want to consider reaching out to, well, the other option."

"My dad, his team…"

"Governor, your father not only has the military capabilities, his organization is exceptional at managing the outgoing message. He has people who spin information very well. And he also has positive contacts in DC. I'm not personally saying we should ask your father's people for help. It will be your call, if we come to that. Entirely your call. But something to keep in mind."

Governor Bill turned away from the photo on his wall and felt a surprising rush of relief. An old, reliable part of him was comforted to imagine his father in the wings, waiting to help. He knew it would look bad to just turn the thing over to him now, but if things got out of hand, well. "OK then," he said. "We'll keep that in mind, Tuttle."

"Okay, then. Good. Good. Keep that back burner lit, sir."

"Roger that, Tuttle."

"And, governor, just one other thing before you set this in motion with your militia contacts. First, you need to make the ultimatum call."

"Right, yes. The call. The ultimatum call. Of course," Governor Bill said. He scowled and pointed the gun at the Sparky bobblehead. "What call is that exactly?"

"To Oleson."

"Right. Ahhh… Remind me. The message? To Oleson?"

"Ultimatum: three hours."

"Three hours and…"

"You tell him three hours and if they don't come clean, turn over their bioweapons, reveal the program, and Oleson doesn't resign as governor, well, then we will respond by whatever means we—you—deem necessary."

"Right. Not a lot of time is it, Tuttle?"

"No, sir, it's not."

Governor Bill put down the gun, grabbed a pen, and wrote *Call Oleson* on a Post-it. He underlined Oleson three times. He thought for a moment and wrote *Cancel golf*, before he said, "Shouldn't I make a, like a speech or something to the people?"

"Not advised, sir."

"Sure feels like this needs a speech. Media is all over the deal with Ham."

"On this part of it, on our counterstrike, we're black. Deep black. Total secrecy at this point. And you don't need to be out in public making speeches right now on any of it."

"But Oleson? Won't he talk?"

"He's in a bind, governor. Our bet is he'll keep this to himself; he'll try to wriggle free on his own. Whatever happens, we need no outside interference."

"Right. Roger. Roger that, Tuttle. Black." Governor Bill again underlined *Oleson* then added an underline to *Cancel golf*, studied the note again, and scowled. He added another underline to *Oleson*. Better. But not quite right. It bugged him.

"OK. I'm off to Griffendorf and Vanderway." Tuttle's voice faded away from the phone. "Concurrently, I'll be safety-netting the rest of our state leadership. Can't let them cut off the head of the snake." His voice faded back in, stronger. "I have undercover security in place, sir, for you; they have eyes on your perimeter. And I've just confirmed Lieutenant Governor DeWeerd is airborne."

Governor Bill sat up. He stared at Sparky Anderson, who seemed to be sneering at him. "DeWeerd. She can't be involved in any of this."

"We intend to keep it that way, governor. She is wheels-up to our secure site in the Upper Peninsula—the UP—for security's sake. Salted away for the duration. We're calling it a security drill; we have staff there to make it work. I can vouch for them."

Governor Bill felt a throbbing in his throat. He fiddled with the headset, opened his mouth to respond, closed his eyes again. "I've never dealt with anything like this before."

"Sir, remember," Tuttle said, "we have given these people—heck, let's call them what they are, terrorists—opportunity."

"Right."

"We have talked. Back channels. You know that."

"But are you sure they got it? We covered the cheese thing. Told them what we knew about the history of all this."

"Yes."

"The prairie dogs."

"Absolutely."

"The Hollywood tie-in. The El Chapo connection."

"Roger."

"And they, they…"

"Laughed…"

"They think we're making all this up or something." Governor Bill stood and squinted out the window. On the lawn below, two muscular men in matching T-shirts and sunglasses appeared to be watching his window. The two men were holding hands. "They think we're some kind of joke."

About thirty yards to the right of the men in the T-shirts, Donna-Deena-Desiree from media relations was standing on the sidewalk that led into the capitol building. She was shouting toward a uniformed maintenance man who was walking backwards, dragging a podium across the lawn. The maintenance man slipped and fell. The podium fell on his legs and he cried out as he kicked the thing away. The reporters who had been shooed away by Kelli were now walking from the capitol building toward Donna-Deena-Desiree as she scurried, stumbling in her heels and trying to hold the flap of her skirt closed, toward the fallen podium and angry maintenance guy. On the street, the sunglassed eyes of the T-shirted couple remained fixed on the governor's office window. Up the block, a white truck with a satellite dish, *News 8* emblazoned on its side, was trying to parallel park at the curb. The truck hit a parking meter. Red plastic exploded from a taillight. The group of reporters, Donna-Deena-Desiree, and the maintenance guy, who was now up and again wrestling the podium, stopped what they were doing and looked toward the satellite truck. Neither T-shirted guy flinched.

Governor Bill sighed and returned to his desk. Sparky Anderson bobbled, goofy-grinning, in a shaft of sunlight. "Who knows where this stops?" Governor Bill said.

"Well, sir, that is the question of the day," Tuttle said.

"I'll tell you where it stops, colonel," Governor Bill said. "It stops here. With the, the what did you call it? The get."

"We've got to get that get, sir."

"Got that."

"You'll make the calls then, governor?"

Governor Bill looked at the note on his desk. He picked up the pen and circled *Oleson*. He said, "Affirmative."

"Good, sir."

Governor Bill thought for a moment. "Again, what do I say, Tuttle? To him. Oleson."

"Sir, governor," Tuttle said with a sigh. "We covered all of this in our meetings on this matter. The PowerPoint should be in a secure folder there on your desktop."

"Oh, right. Yes. Of course. Sure," Governor Bill said. He twisted in his chair, tapped a key on his computer keyboard. The monitor flickered to life.

"I'll call you when I know what Oleson wants to do. And then I'll let Kelli know to set, uh, things in motion."

A long pause from Tuttle, another sigh, and then he said, "Again, governor, keep that back burner lit."

"Yes, I know. Right. I will, Tuttle."

"OK, then."

"OK, then."

# Chapter Ten

Her name was Babsy Witt. Tuttle, as he left his apartment for the rendezvous with Griffendorf and Vanderway, could not stop thinking about her. She'd occupied a preciously important corner of his mind ever since she'd walked out his door the night before.

When he first saw Babsy, in a bar, weeks before, he'd thought she was transgender because Tuttle believed he had an eye for men who became women, although he stressed that he wasn't attracted to them; his "eye" was more about police work and being able to know something about people just by studying them in, say, a dark, crowded bar. Babsy, since birth, had been female. She told him this over drinks, several, and he believed she was telling the truth, particularly after Babsy spent the night in his bed for the first time.

Theirs wasn't a particularly intense affair. In Tuttle's mind, they were just two unmarried mature adults who bonded over a shared love for the pop music hits of the 60s and 70s, a fascination with dressing up in disguises and an appreciation for efficient sex.

Then, yesterday afternoon, she'd said what she'd said.

"I'm FBI, babe, and we need your help."

When she said it, Babsy was feeding Tuttle's two live game hens by dropping food pellets, one at a time, through the holes in the chicken wire of their homemade cage. The cage was on his kitchen table, Babsy sitting next to it, Tuttle leaning against the counter at the sink and watching the sunlight play with the purple streaks in Babsy's graying hair; the two hens, happily clucking, were unaware that Tuttle had, until this moment, intended to wring their game hen necks for a romantic dinner with Babsy.

He was screwed. "I'm FBI" —well, that was something you can live with, like when a lover tells you he/she has twelve children from another marriage or once belonged to a cult that worshiped dead Rhesus monkeys—two situations he had nimbly managed previously. But "we?" "We" meant the lover wasn't a lover at all. "We" meant "setup." Like his love in Saigon, this love was not real. When Babsy—sweet, beautiful Babsy, who could tie a cherry stem with her tongue while humming anything, anything, by The Mamas and the Papas—said some large and powerful "we" needed his "help," well, Tuttle knew the affair was over and that he, a masterful law enforcement officer with CIA cred in his file, had walked into a setup, again, like a lovesick puppy.

The rest of her story flowed out of her as though she'd rehearsed it, because she had. The feds were worried about Silver Eagle and its owner. Guns, military equipment and "serious weapons" were flooding into Will Hoeksma's growing arsenal by a rate some at the Bureau considered alarming. His recruitment efforts were reaching into dark and sinister places around the globe, attracting people some at the Bureau deemed threatening to national security. More important, Babsy said in her calm voice tinged with an accent from her native Bulgaria, there were those in the Bureau who sensed Hoeksma was behind the crazy rumors floated in conservative circles about a conspiracy against Michigan governmental officials by Wisconsin cheese people.

Will Hoeksma had friends in Washington, Babsy said. He also had enemies there, quite a few of them. Benjie Teegarten, truth be told, had more of the former and fewer of the latter than Will had. Benjie's people had raised the red flag about Will and, in turn, had also raised a flag about Tuttle.

After several seconds of silence broken only by the contented rustling and clucking of the unsuspecting fowl, Special Agent Babsy Witt at last turned to look at Tuttle. Her good eye, the one without the black patch Tuttle found so sexy and mysterious, bored into his eyes with no trace of the love he'd thought he'd seen there just an hour before. Tuttle wanted to kill her. But before he did, he wanted to tear off the patch to see if she really needed it or if it, too, had been a lie. She seemed to sense his rapidly deteriorating goodwill so she bottom-lined the situation: Some at the Bureau wondered if Tuttle was aware of what Hoeksma was up to. The word was that this deal with Wisconsin might, unbelievably, blow up into some kind of armed confrontation. Given his position as the head of the Michigan State Police and as a close advisor to Will Hoeksma, Babsy said, there were those at the Bureau who expected to be updated on any and all things related to Silver Eagle that may be of a federally illegal nature, and that many of the same people did not trust him to do that. After reading the Bureau's file on Tuttle and learning of Tuttle's past and his seemingly intense loyalty to Will Hoeksma, she, Babsy, had come to not trust Tuttle either. That was why she'd been forced to approach him in "a non-traditional way." The affair had been her idea but now she was tired of it, tired of him, his breath, the fact that he bathed only once monthly, his habit of correcting her command of English, and his love for frozen tater tots. Her good (and brown) eye stared at him from a face that was suddenly a stranger's, the pink-lipsticked mouth telling Tuttle she'd been asked to remind him of his role in a 1971 cocaine shipment from Afghanistan that had disappeared while he, Tuttle, was supposedly transporting it for the CIA. Babsy said the kilo of cocaine she'd found, surprisingly, in his, Tuttle's, bathroom cupboard that very afternoon would certainly establish that he was still in the drug-running business and that would not reflect well on Tuttle's future if the existence of that cocaine were to come to light. Tuttle tried to think when she'd had time and opportunity to plant the coke and capture a photo of it. But Babsy, she just kept talking, destroying everything about the two of them and probably the plan Will had so diligently created. The Bureau, she said, expected Tuttle to keep them fully informed about all aspects of Silver Eagle's operation.

"Act like nothing has changed," she said.

"Don't upset the apple basket," she said, for the moment sounding very Bulgarian.

"Your cooperation with the Bureau in its efforts to monitor Will Hoeksma and prevent any illegal activity are expected and will also weigh in your favor should there be an investigation that indicates your culpability," she said. "Your lack of cooperation will result in charges against you for cocaine possession with intent to deliver." She then showed him the photo on her phone of the kilo in his bathroom, strategically placed next to a tube of prescription medication with his name on it.

She left then, and took the cocaine with her.

Now, as he headed for his rendezvous with Vanderway and Griffendorf, Tuttle couldn't get her out of his mind. He still wanted to kill her, in part because he knew in order to do so he'd have to see her again.

Tuttle's cell rang. He glanced at the SUV's dashboard screen. Will Hoeksma calling. Crap. He thought for a moment. He needed to play this perfectly. To begin, it was best to rip the scab off the wound. Will hated beating around bushes. He preferred cutting to chases. Tuttle took a deep breath and pressed a button on the steering wheel to answer the call. "We have a problem," Tuttle said.

"What kind of problem?" Will's voice boomed from the vehicle's speakers.

"Well, your boy wants to work with the militia nuts. Have them handle the state's response."

A long, poisonous pause, then Will said, "I take it you talked him out of *that*."

"Not, well, not exactly." Tuttle was thinking fast, trying to calm the response before it came. "He's actually already set them in motion, or at least he's doing that right now, but…"

"'Set them in motion'?"

"Well, yes, yes…"

"They're already active? They've been told to, what, *attack*?"

"Well, he's prepared them…"

In all their years together, Tuttle had never heard Will Hoeksma swear. Not so much as a "damn" or a "son of a bitch." But he let loose with a string of profanity so foul it was clear he was surprisingly fluent in obscenity. The torrent was aimed at Tuttle, Will's governor son, Will's governor son's assistant— Tuttle managed to squeeze in that Kelli had made contact with the militia groups—and everyone else who had "conspired against him," as well as the horses and various other animals on which they'd ridden in or who had participated in their conception (apparently forgetting, momentarily, his role in the creation of Governor Bill).

When Will paused at last to take a breath, Tuttle said softly, "This isn't as bad as you think."

From the speakers, there was just the black hiss of the telecommunications cell. Tuttle, tentative, finally said, "Will?"

"I'm here."

"Look. Listen. I know this is a prob… a challenge," Tuttle said. "But I really get the sense your boy will come back to us on this." Tuttle had no idea if what he was saying was true, but it felt good to say it. "He will come running at the first hint of real trouble."

"So you're going to sit there and wait while some uncontrollable idiots hijack this thing?"

"Well, actually…"

"Good Lord, Tuttle. You have no idea what they're going to do. None. You have no battlefield control and no way to communicate with them, do you?" Will added something that sounded like "fuck" under his breath.

"Will. Listen. We have a communications protocol in place. I'm to be directly updated on their progress and, if I may say, there is ample time here. This is manageable. Exceptionally so."

"Manageable? Of course it's manageable. By someone who knows what the hell he's doing, anything is manageable." Will laughed. "Walking on the moon is manageable. Getting monkeys to fly out of my ass is probably manageable. You want me to get monkeys to fly out of my ass, Tuttle?"

"I don't think that's very manageable, actually."

This time the silence, the hiss of it, sounded a little more ominous. "Are you trying to kill me, Tuttle? Is that it?"

"No, not at all. I'm quite good at killing, as you know…"

"Was there a list of things you were going to do today to try to get me to die and this was one of the things on the list? Because if it was, it was a mighty good list."

Tuttle bit his tongue, closed his eyes for a moment, and collected himself. "I should've had you make the call to him. You did say you wanted me on point, though."

"I was going to be in the shadows, Tuttle, you stupid bastard. I want no profile on this. None."

"Well, maybe if you took a little profile here now, well, maybe your direct contact with him would get this thing back on track." Tuttle was imagining Babsy, sweet Babsy, his wretched traitor, coming to him, asking for information, and he, her confidante, telling her the Hoeksmas had decided together to attack.

"So it's up to me now. That it? I have to do everything around here?" Will's voice was still quivering with anger. "I have half a mind to have my guys go after these militia nutballs and roll them up like a bunch of Middle Eastern terrorists. It would show them and you and that idiot son of mine what we could do."

Tuttle let the thought hang in the digital wind for a moment. "Think about that for a second."

"About what?"

"Well, you have a bunch of militia types riding into Wisconsin on a mission to attack the good people and government of that sovereign state. They have no provable ties to you."

From Will, silence. Tuttle took it as his cue to continue. "We know this whole Wisconsin scenario—granted, it's your baby—but it is based on a premise that not everyone has bought into, or will buy into."

"Tell me something I don't know, Tuttle. It was always supposed to be a little out there. Otherwise, the Tea Party types wouldn't have believed it. What's your damn point? We're on a running clock here."

"The point is that the current circumstances give you more wiggle, not less." Before Will could counter the argument, Tuttle pushed ahead. "You keep your people on standby. You play this right, you could look like the guy who saved Michigan or you could be the guy whose company saved Wisconsin from crazy militia freaks."

Another long pause, then Will said, "That's exactly what I was thinking, you jackass."

"Yes, yes, of course," Tuttle said, suddenly awash in relief. He thought again of Babsy. "So, so, ummm, as next steps…"

"As next steps…" Will stopped and thought. "As next steps, you don't do anything else to muck this up."

Tuttle allowed a small laugh. "Got it."

"And I will alert my people to be ready."

Will hung up.

Tuttle drove on, thinking of Babsy and what he'd tell her when the time was right. He imagined her pleased with him. He imagined killing her.

Governor Bill could not recall the action plan previously developed by Ham DenBraber and Tuttle, but he found the PowerPoint detailing the plan, after a frantic search of his computer. He read through the steps in the plan several times and then, sixteen minutes after ending the call with Tuttle, Governor Bill Hoeksma completed another call, this one to the governor of the sovereign state of Wisconsin. Governor Bill demanded that Governor Oleson acknowledge his state's attack on the sovereign state of Michigan, identify the locations of all viral agents currently being developed or stored in the state, and surrender all participants, including himself, involved in the attack. If he did not comply within two hours, Governor Bill told Governor Oleson, he could expect a military response from the sovereign state of Michigan.

Before Oleson could respond, Governor Bill, as he'd planned, hung up. He sat at his desk with bowed head. He closed his eyes. "Dear God," he said. He thought for several seconds. "Thank you this day for our daily bread." He paused, then said, "Amen." He sat up, sighed deeply, eyes open, jaw set.

"Governor?" It was Kelli's voice through the intercom.

"Yes," Governor Bill said. "What is it?"

"It's Governor Oleson, sir, calling you back."

Governor Bill felt a punch of panic. "What? Really? Already?"

"What was that, sir?" Kelli's voice had a frown in it, a trace of skepticism.

"Act like I'm not here."

"Governor, you just…"

"Tell him I'm off-site. In a meeting. Give him my cell number. Have him call that." Governor Bill took a shaky breath. "In a couple of minutes." He turned back to his computer screen. Now what was he supposed to say?

As a kid, Tuttle had often to come to the family dinner table dressed as someone other than himself. His mother, a pianist for the Flint Symphony, had encouraged the creativity. His father, a cop for the city, thought the costumes were "fruity" and tried to put a stop to "the nonsense." Tuttle's mom was a beautiful and frightening bisexual whom Tuttle's dad adored and feared. He allowed the costumes but privately seethed about them.

Tuttle had used his knack for disguises in many tactical operations during his military and security careers. Now, as he raced toward his rendezvous with Griffendorf and Vanderway, he used a small pocket mirror to admire the outfit he'd put together for the meeting. The costume was probably not entirely necessary. But Tuttle figured it wouldn't hurt, particularly if the shit hit the fan and their operation fell apart—he was going to deny he knew the details anyway, wasn't he?

Will's plan had all seemed so simple: scare people with a good conspiracy threat, convince the ditzy governor-son to ask for Silver Eagle's help; Silver Eagle would respond with a show of force and expertise. International news story, guaranteed. No blood had to be lost to make it work, but if blood was spilled, so be it. Silver Eagle would look strong and the Gunvernor would take the blame or the glory while the future of privatized armies, Will's as opposed to Benjie Teegarten's in particular, would be as bright as a napalm conflagration. Whatever the moral outrage that came from the head of one state attacking another, the Gunvernor would be to blame for that too.

Now, with another option on the table—Will chucking the original plan and instead using Silver Eagle to defend Wisconsin—things were getting awfully complicated. But Tuttle felt satisfied. He'd done what a good soldier does; he'd adjusted the mission to fit the situation on the ground. The fact that the Hoeksmas were taking charge, that was the goal—his get. He was just being a good soldier, following orders, he would tell Babsy. Those guys were in charge of the whole mess.

Tuttle turned up the radio, which was tuned to the 70s satellite channel. The familiar soul-pop of KC and The Sunshine Band's "Get Down Tonight" usually lightened his mood. Now, it reminded him of a recent date with Babsy; they'd gone to a karaoke bar on 70s night and then ended up at a twenty-four-hour shooting range where, buzzed on cheap Japanese beer, they'd talked music trivia and filled paper men with holes until 2 a.m. Babsy knew every word to every KC and the Sunshine Band hit. She was also a hellofa shot, a fact that should have raised a red flag. She'd claimed she worked as a barista at a Starbucks. In Tuttle's mind, looking back, Starbucks was not the type of place where good gun lovers worked; he should've figured she wasn't the person she claimed to be. He could feel the pain of her betrayal and the pressure of her demands. He seriously wanted to make love with her one more time. He really really hated her. He wanted to wring her neck after kissing it.

# Chapter Eleven

"No one gives a rat's rear about this place anymore," Hank said. "There's bird crap all over the picnic tables. No one's cleaning these things off."

"I'm shocked you care." Frances yanked a handkerchief from her stupidly large (her description) black purse and did her best to scrape away the dried droppings. She paused to give Hank a smirk. "I mean, hey, you're dying."

Hank grunted and tossed a manila envelope on the table. He unsnapped his holster, withdrew his sidearm, checked to confirm the safety was on, and put it on the table next to the envelope. "Oh, I don't care. It can all go to pot, far as I'm concerned." Hank took a seat and the table rocked; the side opposite him remained a couple of inches in the air. Frances sat, her weight squeezing the table to earth. "I told him 'MSU, just past the Sparty statue, at two o'clock.' Where you suppose he is?"

Frances twisted to look toward the old statue that stood sentry at the hedge-lined entrance to the campus. She sighed. "He's the head of the state police, Hank. You suppose he's got his hands full?"

"Like we don't? Two state officials here. One of us dying. Can't imagine what would take president here."

"Precedent," Frances said. She looked beyond Hank's glare to a young man and a young woman who were sitting on a blanket a few feet from the edge of the Red Cedar River; they were locked in a passionate kiss. "Young love blooms."

The table rocked as Hank turned. "Oh sweet holy Moses."

"Don't appreciate the public displays of affection?"

"You know what I don't appreciate. Some girl's going to have some explaining to do when she gets home."

"Which means you have a problem with her being white and him black."

"Most people would." Hank turned back to Frances. "Most people who haven't lost their minds."

"I've said it before: bigotry does not become you, Representative Vanderway."

Hank twisted back to the couple, now prone on the blanket, still kissing. "That's not bigotry. That's just wrong," he said. He was gripped by a coughing spell that left him wheezing. His color, which had seemed better than it had at breakfast—the fresh air and a morning of debate on the minimum wage had done him well—was now, again, not good.

Frances offered Hank her handkerchief. Hank shook his head and wiped at his nose with the back of a trembling fist. He looked old and fragile.

"Use your head. Get out of Lansing. Go let your wife take care of you," Frances said.

"I'll probably be gone for good next week. She'll be there for me then. No use putting her through the worst of it." He cleared his throat, a long, jagged performance that sent a flock of ducks at the river's edge into conversational panic. The young couple broke from an embrace and looked toward Hank and Frances.

Frances smiled and waved. "We're OK here, folks, just an old whale coughing up Jonah."

Hank, wheezing, shoved the envelope across the table, and tapped on it with a knuckle. Frances hesitated, then opened the envelope and reached inside. Across the way, the couple had parted; the guy was sitting up, lighting a cigarette; the young woman was standing, straightening her clothes. She adjusted the holster strapped under her left arm. She glanced their way. Frances smiled at her, and then dumped the envelope's contents on the table and began sifting through them.

"Governor, I just got to tell you, there's a guy doing one hellofa impersonation of you out there," Governor Oleson said.

Governor Bill, headset on, put down the pistol and stood from his desk chair. His right hand toyed with the cell phone in his pocket. He stared out the window at the increasingly busy scene on the grounds of the capitol building. A press conference was forming. The word about Ham had spread quickly. He felt dread in his gut, then reminded himself that he didn't do press conferences. He yearned to do a speech, though. Governor Bill liked giving a good speech.

"Whoever it is, this guy got hold of my direct line somehow," Oleson said. "We're tracking it down. He called me a second ago and told me you were—get this—asking me to confess to something or other or face some kind of attack. Sounded like it was all based on this nonsense your conservative friends have been talking about, concerning our monkeypox outbreak last month."

"Really?" Governor Bill flopped back into his chair.

"You have some kook loose over there today; someone sucking the wacky weed?" Governor Oleson said with a laugh. "Or are DenBraber and those conspiracy-nut friends of his playing with your head and mine?"

Governor Bill frowned, clenched his teeth, opened his mouth, clenched again. For an instant he thought whatever was ailing Ham had somehow rendered him unable to speak. Governor Bill cleared his throat. "It was no kook. No. It was me."

From Wisconsin, silence.

A duck waddled over and stopped near the picnic table. "Go on." Hank waved at it. "We've got no food for you." He shook his head. "Kids spoil the things to death, feeding them crap all the time. Go on." The duck stood its ground.

Frances was bent over two glossy photos from the envelope Hank had brought. "Let me guess," Frances said. "These things that look like factories are, ahh, factories." The duck looked at the two of them and quacked.

"Cheese plants in Sheboygan, according to the Google anyways," Hank said.

"Something tells me you're going to disagree with the Google," Frances said.

"It's actually a Wisconsin government owned compound. One building's for viral agents. The other's bio-research," Hank said. "The cheese thing is just a cover."

Frances said to the duck, "See what happens when you let cheese get away from you?" The duck opened its bill but didn't quack.

"We've got people inside at these places, Frances," Hank said, tapping the photos. "Not many, but some. And they're good. At these plants, our people are working maintenance. They got full factory access, first shift. See there, the loading dock? Our people took that picture during their break."

Frances squinted at the blurry photo, raised it to her face, and then held it at arm's length. The bracelets on her arm jangled. She shook her head and smiled. "Your pictures look like whoever took them was either drunk or just really really bad at picture taking." She gave the photo another long look.

"Still, I'd say that was a tractor trailer rig, which is exactly what I'd expect to see in a loading dock."

"Check out the parking lot."

Frances squinted. "The long yellow thing?" After several seconds, she smiled. "Where I come from, that's a school bus."

"Right again."

"Field trip?"

"Field lab."

"Come again?"

"A mobile lab. A laboratory. In an old school bus."

Frances chuckled. She looked at the duck. The duck took two waddles to the right and looked at something in the grass. Frances turned back to the photo. She squinted at it over the top of her glasses. This was getting ridiculous.

Hank said, "That bus is hell on wheels, courtesy of the people of Wisconsin."

Frances studied her friend's face. Hank was tired and sickly but very very serious. "You really believe these people, the whole deal. The cheese story. Everything."

The duck made a sound, half quack, half gulp—a qulp.

"Mobile Death Fac One." Hank sniffed. "That's what our guys inside call the bus. Mobile Death Factory Numero Uno."

The duck began pecking frantically at something in the grass.

"Number one?" Frances said.

"Oh, there's more. There are many more, my friend." Hank cleared his throat, cocked his head toward the duck and spit at its feet. The duck froze, stared back, bill open. Frances closed her eyes. *Dear God*, she prayed.

"That was you, Hoeksma?" Governor Oleson of Wisconsin said.

"Roger," Governor Bill Hoeksma of Michigan said.

"Roger?"

"You know, I confirm it."

Governor Oleson's laugh started as a snicker and rolled into a full-blown chuckle. "Hoo boy, Bill. Good stuff."

"Good?"

"Funny. Very. Funny funny funny. I mean, hey, I get it."

"I'm not sure you do—you did." Governor Bill frowned, closed his mouth, picked up the pistol, poked the Sparky Anderson bobblehead, and then opened his mouth again. "I'm not sure you get anything."

"Of course I do. I'm not the ninny those guys at the Governor's Conference think I am," Oleson said.

"I didn't say that." Governor Bill stared down the barrel of the gun at Sparky Anderson and again imagined shooting Sparky off the desk. This made him smile, not unlike Sparky, who also was smiling.

"I get a joke as well as the next guy. And I just got to say your timing was unreal. The Lord sure works in mysterious ways; I tell you that. It's been a rough one over here." Oleson's voice wobbled. "I needed a little, a little bit of lightheartedness, you know?"

Governor Bill scowled at Sparky. "Why do you say that?" Governor Bill said.

"Oh it's nothing, really," Oleson said, choking on the words. "Listen to me, I'm crying like a baby." Oleson fell silent for a moment. "Bill, could I call you back?"

"You think this is so they can make viruses," Frances said.

"Weapons," Hank said. He stuck out his jaw.

"Viral weapons."

"Exactomundo."

"And these spies of ours, they confirm all this? You trust whoever is telling us this?"

Hank didn't respond. His eyes were fixed on the duck. The duck was looking toward the couple by the river.

"Why wouldn't they just go to the police? I mean, if they're making illegal weapons, it's, uh, illegal," Frances said.

"Yes, and it's the government and the government means the cops are in on it. Get real, Frances."

The duck made a strangled sound, whirled, waddled toward the river, stopped, hesitated, and then came back. It looked up at Hank and quacked. Hank sneezed, sniffed, and wiped at his nose.

"Who told—who gave you all this stuff?" Frances said.

"Ham, some of it. And Parker and this guy on the—the guy from the Internet. Clayton Store. The one that does the blood test."

Frances drummed her fingers on the pile of papers in front of her. She studied the duck. "Who are these guys, the ones inside the plants? Who are they exactly?"

"Trustable people. Loyal to us."

"Ham. He trusts them?"

"Ham hired them."

"That I can't figure."

"I can. Ham gets it. Ham's a patriot."

"So this is about patriotism?"

"What kind of question is that?"

"Seems to me it's a good one. You've got a bunch of weirdos making poison to kill people—if you do and right now that's a big if—well, that's a criminal thing. You get the FBI or ATF involved if you have to," Frances said, her voice rising. "You don't start making it some kind of creepy vigilante crusade disguised as loyalty or some kind of weird patriotic thing." The duck was jabbing at its breast, shifting its weight from one foot to the other. "Seems to me you're being unpatriotic—else why wouldn't you tell the federal people what you have here? Truth be told, your radio friend and these others have been spreading the story about Wisconsin and it's so bizarre half the country thinks we're totally nuts. Why not tell them what you got here—if it's real?"

"I don't care what the rest of the country thinks. This is real and our state's got a right to defend itself. That's constitutional. But there's no getting the feds involved in this, in any way," Hank said. "Not with that crowd that's in there now."

"Crowd."

"This president and her people. They'd sooner have a cup of tea with a terrorist as shoot one."

"Which is why you're packing heat these days, like half the other people around here?" Frances nodded at Hank's gun.

"I tell you what, open or closed carry, any kind of carry, is the way to go with someone like that living in 1300 Pennsylvania Avenue," he said. "Not that it matters for yours truly anymore."

Frances sat up, tucked her chin, and frowned. "So. This is about politics? All of this?"

"Everything's about politics. These are socialists running the federal government. A bunch of left-wing peaceniks with an agenda to gut the military and they have ties to the Muslims and other radicals right here that aren't pretty. We're, all of us, everyone in every state, way less safe since they've been running things in DC like some kind of hippie commune. No wonder this happened with that lefty Oleson in Wisconsin and all those cheeseheads."

Frances closed her eyes to think. When she opened them, she tried her best conciliatory housewife-from-Grosse-Pointe voice. "You know, dear, this whole 'Wisconsin Threat' conspiracy has been a big deal with you and some of your friends, but it has not caught on nationwide. There's a reason for that. There's a reason everyone thinks it's crazy." She reached across the table and patted Hank's hand. "Because, dear, it's fucking crazy."

Hank pulled his hand away. "It may be crazy, but it's also true," he said, nearly shouting. He swallowed, cleared his throat and lowered his voice. "I wouldn't be surprised if your girlfriend in the White House has been pressured to suppress this thing."

The duck quacked. "Stupid bird." Hank waved a limp hand at the duck. "Go on," Hank said. The duck didn't budge.

"Hank," Frances said. She leaned toward Hank and gripped her friend's shoulder. "Smart, good men can lose perspective. And women, too. But look around. Seems like half the state carries guns these days. You guys have got everybody jacked up on paranoia. Take a step back. Listen to yourselves. You're all believing, actually believing, some warped story about cheese and Denton McAllister and on and on. And the ironic part is you're out there like Bush's guys before Iraq," Frances said. "You notice how it's just like that, right?"

"Like what?"

"It's like Colin Powell making the case for the invasion at the UN. It's like someone scripted this to sound, I don't know, like it's real. Even though it's not."

Hank gave the duck a long stare. The duck held his gaze for a moment then, again, started pecking at something in the grass. Hank cleared his throat and shifted his gaze to Frances. "I understand you could give a shit about me but I'm shocked you have so little regard for your little family's safety."

Frances clenched her jaw and looked squarely at Hank. "Look," she said. "My better half and I, and the dogs, love it here. We have friends and family across the state. If there is something bad going on, we have a lot to lose. And right now the thing I'm most afraid of is that you, my friend, have gone from being a good, strong conservative who drives me crazy to some kind of zealot who sees demons everywhere and wants to make some kind of statement."

Hank's bloodshot eyes stared out from under drooping lids. "I'll tell you straight. No good comes from you debating this.

We need to be united. Trust the truth. Get with the program. Or get out."

"You threatening me now, Hank? We come to that?"

"No. I'm not threatening." Hank coughed. He turned and held the duck's gaze. "I'm just saying; you watch your attitude. And your back. This situation matters to some powerful people."

"Who?"

Hank and the duck stared each other down. The duck shifted his weight from one foot to the other. Frances studied Hank's haggard face, searching for an answer she already should have known. Finally, her thoughts landed on the obvious. "Oh," she said. "Oh. Hold on." Frances felt a wave of embarrassment. She chuckled and looked at the gray sky. "Sorry, God. I haven't been thinking too clearly lately. This is about the big man. The big cheese." She looked again at Hank. They stared at each other. The duck looked away. Hank wiped his nose with his fist and scowled.

"He's done more good for this state than you ever have. Any of us have," Hank said.

"In a vengeful, mean-spirited, self-absorbed, make-my-son-the-governor-so-I-can-keep-control sort of way."

"He's a good Christian man."

"If he's a good Christian man, and I think he's a narcissistic, manipulative, war-profiteering, mercenary bastard, what does that make me?"

Hank kneaded his forehead with the tips of his fingers. "Let's not debate this right now."

Frances looked at the duck. The duck avoided her gaze. "You're trying to go to war or something here and there's a man back in the shadows of this who is pushing this"—she looked to the sky again—"this propaganda."

"It's true. All of it," Hank said with a sniff.

"Yes, and it's also true that Will Hoeksma owns a company that's essentially a bunch of killers for hire, his own private army, that would stand to benefit."

Hank stared at the papers and photos on the table. He rifled through them, found several sheets stapled together, licked a thumb, and flipped through them, stopped, folded several pages back, and tossed the document in front of Frances. "Look."

Frances studied it.

"From some scientific equipment catalog. See here, this, what's circled; they found a bunch of them inside the plant." Hank jabbed at the picture of a device. Frances frowned and squinted at it.

"It's a centrifuge," a deep voice said.

Frances turned. A man, long-haired and bearded, wearing sunglasses and the green coveralls and matching baseball cap of the university maintenance department, stood behind her. He was holding a rake.

"Excuse me?" Frances said.

"An RD-Eleven for military use," the man said, stepping forward. He leaned the rake against the table. "May I sit?"

"Sit," Hank said. "Sit. Sit."

# Chapter Twelve

Governor Bill, gun in hand at his side, peeked into the outer office. Kelli and Sparty the MSU mascot were mopping her desk with paper towels, Kelli holding in one hand a Starbucks cup with no lid. Sparty, that huge head of his too huge to allow him to stand without bending way way over, was kneeling on the floor. "I'm sorry, geez, I'm sorry," Sparty said in a muffled voice. Everyone else was gone. The governor's cell trilled as Kelli swore at Sparty. Governor Bill shut the door, pulled his phone from his pocket, hurried back to his desk, sat in his chair, tapped the phone screen, and swung it to his ear. "Hoeksma," he said.

"Bill, sorry. I, well, I, we had a death in the family today," Governor Oleson said, his voice thickening. "I'm not myself."

Governor Bill's throat swelled. In his head, he saw Ham, heard the sound Ham had made falling to the floor.

"Bill? Governor?" Oleson said.

"Yes. Yes," Governor Bill said. "Who?"

From Oleson, sobs. Governor Bill felt a surge in his chest and, unexpected, tears burned behind his eyes. He swallowed and thought about Ham and the possibility he would die.

Governor Bill chewed, in vain, on the inside of his mouth; the tears escaped anyway.

A full minute passed, Governor Bill's forehead softly thumping against his desktop. From Governor Oleson, Governor Bill heard crying or sniffling or laughing? Governor Bill didn't care what he heard. All he could think about, for the moment, was Ham. How could he do this?

The man sat on the picnic table next to Frances, took off his baseball cap, and tossed it on the picnic table. His hair slid an inch or two over one ear, revealing bald head above the other ear. The beard was an unnatural red and didn't match the askew hair. The mustache appeared to be coming unglued.

"Colonel?" Hank said.

The man held a finger to his lips.

"Tuttle?" Frances said, and despite the circumstances she started to laugh. "You're in disguise?"

"Continue, congressman," Tuttle said, nodding to Hank.

Hank pawed through the papers with gusto. "Hold on. Wait. Here. Receipt for"—he stared at a yellow sheet—"centrifuges. You ever seen a centrifuge used for cheese?"

Tuttle snorted. His hair slid another inch off center but he seemed not to notice. "These folks aren't about cheese."

For several seconds, Frances sat, thinking, tapping the picnic tabletop with a badly chipped pink-polished fingernail. She prayed again, silently, for wisdom. From the direction of the couple on the blanket, a tinny tune floated.

"'Brandy,' by Looking Glass," Tuttle said. "1972."

"Huh?" Hank said.

"A great song. One-hit wonder, Looking Glass. But they made a good one. That's quite the ringtone for a younger person to have," Tuttle said loudly toward the couple. The guy was answering his phone. "Wouldn't mind that one myself." He smiled and pressed a thumb against the flapping edge of his mustache; the tinted eyes stared off for a moment, as though he were remembering something.

Finally, Frances looked at Tuttle. The state police commander's gaze swung to meet hers. Frances contemplated Tuttle's stare. "So you tell me. How much does this have to do with one man and whatever his crazy agenda is here? And you know who I'm talking about. Who started all of this nonsense?"

Tuttle smoothed the mustache with a thumb and forefinger, and turned to Hank. "Someone still doesn't get it."

"No," Hank said, his throat sounding thick, the words coated. "Not at all."

"Representative Griffendorf," Tuttle said, "you're an important person in this situation. We've trusted you with a lot of very classified information because, frankly, your state needs you. We think—thought—you would see the risk and help drive public opinion when the time comes to do that. Make no mistake, this is a critical moment. We're in serious danger. I have every reason to believe that strong and powerful people based in Wisconsin mean to harm officials in our state government. I believe they represent a clear and present danger to each of us and to the citizens of this state. I have every reason to believe that they're a danger to neighboring states as well—even to their own people."

"Hold up there," Frances said. She looked at Hank and nodded toward Tuttle. "He's talking in a southern accent?"

"He is undercover," Hank said.

State police commander Tuttle sneezed. The wig slid forward; the hair was in his eyes. With a trembling hand, he shoved it all back into place.

Frances couldn't help herself. She laughed and laughed hard. It was a hearty, raspy laugh deepened by years of long-abandoned smoking.

Hank's fist hit the table and cut Frances's jag short. "I can't believe you. All day I'm spilling my guts about the danger we're in—the danger I'm in—and you won't listen. Instead, you ridicule. Now you bring up the same old crap—the nonsense about Will Hoeksma having some kind of deal on."

"If it walks like a duck." Frances smiled and shrugged.

Hank wiped a line of foamy spittle from his lips. "Well, I tell you this, my friend, I for one welcome having Will Hoeksma as a constituent. Will Hoeksma's the best damn thing that ever happened to this state. His uncle built his first washing machine right there in a garage in Zeeland. Amerispin Dual Force Automatic, they called it. Just your average guy out of college after serving his country and he invents practically a whole industry. Will took it from there. And once he made his bundle, he could've gone off and fished but did he?"

"No, Hank." Frances closed her eyes. Longed for a cigarette.

"My goodness no. He helped keep more people from getting terror-attacked the one way he knew how."

"By making money off the fear of it?"

"By starting a paramilitary company that could make Americans secure wherever they go," Hank said. "People can talk all they want about Benjie Teegarten at Diamond Security; Will Hoeksma built Silver Eagle by the sweat of his back. And that's the truth."

"Brow. Sweat of his brow."

"What?"

"Never mind."

"I'll tell you something else about that man," Hank said. "He takes care of every person who ever worked for him. And never once did Will, Sr. fail to put his family or his church first. Sent every one of those kids through goddamn Christian school. Little Billy gave him hell but look now. Governor."

"There. That. What you just said," Frances said. "His kid's the governor. What got him there? His intellect? His powerful capacity for politics?"

"Be careful," Tuttle said.

Frances turned to look at him. "Are you threatening me now, too?" She thought for a second. "And, by the way, you're sort of sounding Canadian. The accent. If I was straight I might find that kind of attractive."

"You're talking pretty poorly about the governor of this state," Tuttle said, now sounding German.

"He's also a poor excuse for a leader, put in power by a bunch of movers and shakers with an agenda." Frances stopped herself. She could see Tuttle's eyes narrow.

"You listen to me, Frances," Hank said. "You know the way the world works. Guys doing what Will Hoeksma does, they get the benefits. That's the deal. You see anybody who's gotten a job from him, anybody working in a public building he donated the money to build—well, ask them if they think it's fine Will Hoeksma gets to make things go his way once in a while. If that includes helping his kid get into office, so be it. All's fair."

"So, what Will Hoeksma wants, Will Hoeksma gets?"

"The man earned his clout."

"OK, so what does he want now?"

"What do you mean?"

"Wisconsin, I mean. Market share? That it? This is business?" Hank looked away.

"You OK, governor?" Sparty said. The voice was a girl's. Governor Bill, shocked, realized she'd been saying this to him—"You OK, governor" or some form of it—several times. Governor Bill lifted his own head to see this girl Sparty's giant helmeted head, that big chin and confident stare oddly comforting, thrusting through the open door into his office. This girl Sparty was kneeling in the bulky costume, staring at him. "Sorry, your receptionist, she, she went to get more paper towels and I heard you, well, crying," the girl inside Sparty said. She stood, the helmet ducking, that goofy body entering.

He'd always figured Sparty had small holes through which he—she—looked at the world. Governor Bill cocked his head and studied the mascot's sideways face, searching for the holes. "I'm fine," Governor Bill said. "Absolutely fine." No holes that he could see. Weird. "Yep. Yes sirree, I'm okey-dokey," Governor Bill said with a sniff. With his free hand, he picked up the pistol. He took several seconds to examine the Sig Sauer logo on the grip, hoping all the while that Sparty would leave. Finally, he looked up. Sparty was still standing there, head twisted, gawking down at him.

"Governor?" Governor Oleson said from the phone. Governor Bill was clenching the phone in his left hand but somehow had forgotten it.

"Oh, I'm—hold on, governor," Governor Bill said. With a sniff, he swiped at his nose with the back of a fist and gestured with the pistol for Sparty to leave. Sparty hesitated. Governor Bill pointed the gun at the big head with no obvious eye holes, smiled, and said, "Get along there, cowboy," in his best John Wayne voice. Sparty obeyed.

Tuttle shuffled through the stuff on the table. He found what he wanted. "Look here." It was another photo. "This."

"A house?" Frances said. "With, oh wait, a school bus in front of it."

"McAllister's house. In Hollywood. Mr. Rodriguez Related to El Chapo."

"Denton McAllister. We're back to that, to him." Frances studied the grainy photo through half-open eyes. Her silent prayer had turned to pleading. *Help me God. Now. Please. I'm begging you.* "For crying out loud. It's a school bus in front of some house," Frances said.

"McAllister's got no school-age kids," Hank said.

"No need for buses," Tuttle said.

Frances stared at Tuttle. She thought about how stupid he looked.

Hank managed a grim smile. "Now you've got it."

Frances's gaze snapped back to Hank. "Got what?"

"How onimous this is. This is onimous as hell."

"Om-inous," Frances said, the word sticking to the roof of her mouth.

"What I said. Onimous." Hank sat forward, dropping his voice. "This thing's gone way far, Frances, too far. We've got to act before we get acted on worse. I can't think what would happen if Oleson unleashes some of this crap on more of our people, then turns on an Iowa or Minnesota. Look what it does to you. Look at me, Frances. I mean, fine, don't look. I don't care. Seriously. I don't care about me. I care about the others that might have to suffer like this," Hank said, and he coughed for emphasis. "McAllister, he's—he's Hollywood, for gosh sakes. I don't like his eyes. He's got that foreign look. You can just tell. He's up to no good..." If he gets hurt for whatever he did, that's fine by me. It's the innocent people I'm worried about.

Frances closed her eyes briefly and began kneading the skin of her forehead with her fingertips. "Dear God. Take me now," she said.

"Governor Oleson?" Governor Bill was alone again in his office. He'd put the Sig back in his desk drawer and had returned to a position he found surprisingly comforting: sitting, forehead resting on his desk, staring at his loafers. He was wondering if the position was healthy. He was wondering how long Sparty had been a girl. He was wondering what the deal was with Governor Oleson and the crying.

"Yes. Yes, I'm here." To Governor Bill, Governor Oleson's voice sounded crooked.

"Someone died. You said—a death," Governor Bill said.

"Yes. Sure."

"But who?"

"Well, as if it was any of your business, my wife."

Governor Bill coughed. "What? You—your—no way."

"Oh yes."

"Oh, I'm... really? I'm s... sorry." His wife?

"Well, yes, it wasn't pretty."

"What—what happened?"

"Cancer. Horrible. The chemo. The hair falling out. Weak."

Governor Bill sat up. "This just happened."

"Nope. Took three years, four months, twelve days from diagnosis. Quite a spell, actually. My gosh, the woman took forever."

"I mean she just died?"

"Depends on what you mean by 'just.' It took a while actually; I mean, it ended this morning but this had gone on for quite some time. My dad called to let me know she'd gone—when was it?—oh, ten, 10:15 I guess."

"You weren't there?"

"Where?"

"At the hospital."

"Hospital." Governor Oleson snorted. "Oh my goodness no. We wouldn't have had her in the hospital, not with healthcare costs the way they are."

"So what did you—where?"

"At my folks' house. They've got a hide-a-bed right there in the family room. My mom's eighty-three but she gets up and down good still."

Governor Bill stood and walked all the way around his desk, one hand in a pocket, the other pressing the phone to his ear. He stopped next to his chair, closed his eyes. "You're not even—a second ago you were crying," he said.

"Hoeksma, listen, my dad always had a saying in the cheese business. 'Never moo over curdled milk.' That's what my dad always said. I mean, look, I suppose there will be a funeral and time for grieving. And I'll have to phone the kids but that can happen tonight. All in good time."

Governor Bill walked to the window, stopped, and looked out. "Your mom, she took care of her and you weren't even there."

"Governor, I prefer to forward-think; the bright side, know what I'm saying? This was a very unfortunate situation, but truth be told I'm all about the future, looking ahead to how I can help the people of this great state."

Governor Bill's thumb trembled over the red button that would end the call.

"What can I do you for, governor? Oh that's right, you're going to attack." Oleson laughed. "When's that going to happen, sometime today I hope?"

Governor Bill ended the call.

In Wisconsin, Governor Oleson smiled. "Who's yanking whose chain now, governor?" he said. He paused, suddenly aware the connection was dead, shook his head, smiled, thought for a second, and then speed-dialed his perfectly healthy wife. She was going to love this one.

Governor Bill sat for a moment, stunned, his brain chewing hard on the situation. Finally, he picked up his desk phone and pressed the button to ring Kelli's extension. His eyes were fixed on Ronald Reagan's. Governor Bill imagined himself on a horse.

"Commander, Commander Tuttle." It was the young man by the river. He was thumbing off his cell phone, slipping it into his pocket, running toward them. From a pocket of his cargo pants, he pulled a gun and held it stiffly at his side. Behind him, the young woman was slinging a backpack over her shoulder and scooping up the blanket.

From the street, a siren bloomed. Hank, startled, half rose, lost his balance, and fell back onto the picnic table bench. Frances held onto the table to keep from falling off. "What the hell?" Hank said.

"Game on, sir. I repeat. Game on." The young man reached the picnic table and tried to help Tuttle to his feet. Tuttle slapped at his hand. The young man recoiled and knocked over the rake. "Game most definitely on."

Behind him, the woman was talking into the wrist of her sweatshirt. "Bluebonnet, this is T-Ray, subjects are in hand. Repeat. Vanderway and Griffendorf secure."

Her sleeve squawked a muffled reply: "Roger T-Ray."

"You're sure about this?" Tuttle, now standing, looked at the young guy. "Affirm with password."

"Affirmative, colonel. Scarecrow raped the Tin Man. I repeat. Scarecrow raped the Tin Man."

Tuttle ripped the false mustache and beard from his face. "God in heaven," he said in an accent that sounded, to Frances, Spanish. "Remind me next time to under-glue." He handed the fake facial hair to the woman, took off the cap, peeled the wig from his pink scalp, and faced Hank and Frances. Gluey, hairy residue marred the sheen of his head. A tuft of his real mustache was gone. Blood, matting the salt and pepper whiskers left behind, was trickling down his lip.

"If I may," Tuttle said to Hank and Frances, "let me introduce state police officers Langdon and Smertze."

"Smith, sir," the young guy said.

"And Dunkel," the young woman said.

"Sorry. Yes. That's right. Smith. Smith and, and…"

"Dunkel, sir," the woman said.

"My apologies."

"That's all right, sir."

With his lower lip, Tuttle sucked some of the blood from his mustache, making a sissing sound. "This is black ops team nine. They are…"

"Ten, sir."

"S'that?" Tuttle sissed more blood.

"Team ten. Nine is Baker and Nofsprig."

"I thought Baker and Nofsprig were thirteen."

"Negative, sir."

Tuttle huffed a sigh. To Smith, he said, "I assume we're proceeding on the first vector?"

Smith frowned.

"He made the call?" Tuttle said. "And the declaration? Scarecrow did?"

"Scarecrow?" Hank said.

"Governor Hoeksma," Tuttle said with a Latin-hued siss.

"Yes, sir," Smith said.

"We are engaged?" Tuttle said.

"Imminent, sir," Smith said. "Scarecrow punched—"

"Raped," Dunkel said.

"The Tin Man…"

"Yes, sir."

Tuttle touched the hole in his mustache and winced. He stared at the blood on the tip of his finger. Governor Bill Hoeksma had apparently contacted his office assistant who, in turn, would have contacted her husband in the militia. "Surprised Oleson would let it come to this," Tuttle said.

"We need to move, sir. Vector one," Dunkel said.

"Well, it's his hell." Tuttle wiped the blood on his pants, and then looked at Smith. "Transport?"

"Inbound." Smith jerked his head. A large black sport utility vehicle, headlights flashing in a crazy syncopation with a red and blue light bar on its top, was making its way across the campus lawn toward them. Its siren whoop whoop whooped. Students, some covering their ears, were running, stumbling to get out of the way. A black Labrador with a green collar chased a duck, the duck's wings flapping, across the truck's path. Smith waved at the vehicle, pointed to his ear, then made a dramatic slashing motion across his throat. The siren choked and stopped. The SUV turned, plowed over a plastic green-and-white trash receptacle and headed toward them.

"Where are you taking us?" Hank said.

"To make history, congressman." Tuttle sissed blood from the wound in his lip. He had drawn a gun from a concealed pocket in his coveralls and had dropped his accent.

"Where?" Hank said. "Where, Tuttle?"

"Secure location," Tuttle said and looked at Hank. "We'll have medical care for you there." Tuttle sighed and patted Hank on the shoulder. "We'll do our best for you."

"Someone want to tell me what just happened?" Frances said. The SUV had stopped a few yards away, engine running. The black Lab circled back and trotted toward the vehicle, nose low, sniffing. Tuttle and Smith opened the doors. Dunkel gestured for the two politicians to climb in. Hank complied. Frances held back. "What's going on?"

Smith looked at Tuttle. Tuttle nodded. Smith turned to Frances. "There's been a casualty," State Trooper Smith said. "Senator Den—"

"Ham?" Hank leaned out the open door. "What happened?" The black Lab, seeing the opening, jumped into the car and scrambled across Hank's lap onto the unoccupied portion of the middle bench seat.

"What the?" Hank sneezed and sniffed. "Who the hell's dog is that?"

The Lab, still standing, bent and nudged Hank's hand with its wet nose. Hank slapped at the nose. The dog, flustered, circled twice before sitting in the middle of the seat, facing forward, panting.

From near the river, a young man with long hair ran toward the vehicle, yelling, "Barney, Barney." The dog, now identified by its owner, still seemed committed to stay.

"Shoot that animal," Tuttle said to Smith. "We don't have time for this nonsense."

"Sir?" Smith said.

"Baker, I said shoot that animal," Tuttle said.

"Baker? I'm Smith, colonel," Smith said. "Baker's on maternity leave."

"What happened, Tuttle?" Hank said.

"The damn dog jumped over you, into a state vehicle." Tuttle racked a round into his gun's chamber and stepped toward the car. "Get that mongrel out here, congressman."

Frances lumbered around to the open passenger door on the other side of the car, reached in, grabbed the Lab by the collar, and gently led the animal out of the vehicle. She let go just as its owner, out of breath, reached her. The Lab grabbed a crushed paper cup from the grass and began strutting circles around its master, who grabbed it by the collar, shot a look back at the SUV, and hustled away. "You people are f-ing nuts," he said.

Frances stepped up and into the vehicle. She slammed the door. "Dog problem solved, colonel," she said, looking across Hank to the clearly irritated Tuttle. "Now what were you saying about DenBraber?"

Tuttle reluctantly slid the gun into its holster. He held Frances's stare. "He collapsed."

"The pox," Hank said. "Oh my goodness."

"Yes," Tuttle said.

"Ham's dead," Hank said, his voice a raspy near-whisper inside the car.

"Ham. What?" Frances felt the world wheel and turn.

"Not dead. Collapsed. Very very ill," Smith said.

"DenBraber? We're talking Ham? Correct?" Frances said.

"Yes," Dunkel and Tuttle said together.

Frances shot Tuttle a raised eyebrow. "You're not saying this is…"

"Oh, he most definitely is saying," Hank said.

"Yes. Our adversary has been given the opportunity to surrender…"

"Surrender?" Frances said.

"Yes, and the window for that opportunity has closed. By order of the governor, we are now in full response and protect mode," Tuttle said. Tuttle pulled his phone out of his coveralls. He got into the SUV. He swiped the phone on and looked at its screen. A photo of Babsy, dear purple-streaked and eye-patched Babsy, stared back at him. Tuttle felt a pang of anger and lust.

PART TWO

# It Takes A Militia

# Chapter Thirteen

Miky Spike's dad, whose name was Harnan but who went by Rub for reasons no one could or would explain, was not a big fan of carnival rides—your zippers, your wipeouts, your double Ferris wheels—due to inner ear issues related to his war wound. Her mom, Colette, loved the rides. So Colette went on the tilt-a-whirl at the Berrien County Youth Fair alone. Colette had no way of knowing her decision to do so would be the reason the date—August 9, 1981—was etched on her tombstone. Relieved to avoid the ride, little Miky and her dad headed to the pig barn to pet the piglets. They were equally oblivious, never imagining the distant thunder they heard was not all that distant and was out for blood. Miky was just three years old with a tiny palm poised over the cute baby stage of what would one day be prize-winning pork when a 100-million-volt bolt from heaven-turned-hell struck Colette's steel seat in mid-whirl and made Miky a half-orphan.

Rub had the inner toughness to help him and his daughter weather the lightning strike that killed Colette. Rub's mom and dad had died in a methane explosion on the family farm when Rub was six. Raised by an uncle whose right arm and sunny disposition had been taken by the same explosion, Rub grew up tough as stale jerky. He was a high school football star—a running back who, legend had it, led his team to a state championship despite his dislocated hip. Rub was a hunter, a bare-knuckle fighter. He was a bandage-it-with-duct-tape-and-let-it-bleed man. He enlisted in the Marines the Monday after he graduated from Berrien Springs High School. In Vietnam, he slogged through a hellish tour of duty he relished—"Some guys are cut out for this shit," he told his buddies. He was poised to re-enlist when he caught some shrapnel from a Viet Cong mortar on what was supposed to be his last week in uniform. Rub came home from the war with a Purple Heart in his rucksack, honorable-but-unwanted discharges in his file and his left eye, a ringing in one ear that came and went and, swear to God, made him think of the first weird chord of "Summer in the City" by The Lovin' Spoonful, and a chip on his shoulder. By the time he walked out of the VA hospital in Ann Arbor, Rub had swapped the eye infection for a fake eyeball and the chip for a simmering anger at someone and something nameless. He was home not two weeks, standing straight and tall in his flattop haircut and camo fatigues at a Kmart, trying to cock his head to discreetly check out the cute cashier in the next aisle with his real eye while compensating for the damn ringing in his ear, when a long-haired guy flipped him the finger and mumbled something that sounded like "baby killer." Before his brain could decipher why, Rub knocked over a candy display and grabbed the long-hair by his tie-dyed T-shirt. The only thing that saved the guy's face was the cute cashier, who quick-pulled the .38 she kept with the chapstick in her Kmart smock and got off an ear-thumping warning shot that blew away seven ceiling panels, wounded a roof-top air conditioning unit, earned her a swift and immediate dismissal, and won Rub's heart. Rub came away from the incident with a new reason to be angry and a woman, "Colette," the plastic name badge on the smock said, with whom to share his nagging, low-grade rage, at least until a stormy summer evening in 1981.

In the early years of their marriage, Rub and Colette ran their farm together, and it took most of their time and a great deal of their considerable combined energy. During lulls in farm life, both relished the freedom of hunting and fishing, riding their twin Harleys or, when the winter storms blew in off Lake Michigan, their Arctic Cat snowmobiles. Downtime was, above all, reserved for guns; they spent hours at the shooting range, at gun shows, and at swap meets.

The idea of having children came up only occasionally, and then the discussion inevitably returned to Colette's bloodline, which included a white uncle / Latina aunt combo. Colette swore adding another limb to a mixed-race family tree would bother Rub. Rub swore it wouldn't. He loved Colette, after all. So what if his kid wouldn't be as white and European as the rest of Rub's family?

For the most part, they stayed away from the "kid talk," as Rub called it, until it returned like a bolt from the blue at a gun show in Grand Rapids in 1976. Colette was debating with Rub the price on a mint condition Colt AR-15—his take was the price didn't matter; they just didn't need another AR-15—when a boy of about six caught her attention. Brown-eyed with black hair cropped in a flattop like Rub's, in jeans and a black Jackson Five T-shirt, he seemed both tough and vulnerable. He was standing alone in front of a display of weapons, holding a Ruger Mini-14 with both hands, treating it like it was a semiautomatic egg, a look of unmistakable love and awe on his face. When she realized she was staring at the kid like a love-choked teenager, Colette put down the Colt without another word. She scuffed like a zombie through the remainder of the displays—for the first time in a great while she didn't buy a thing. Colette couldn't shake the thought that their baby, if they had a baby, would look just like that boy.

After the show, the evening's Tigers game was already underway and Mark "The Bird" Fidrych was pitching, but Rub turned off the radio in his battered Ford F-150. Instead, he drove home with Colette in silence, munching fried pork rinds from a bag trapped between his overalled thighs, taking an occasional break to lick each of his fingers and drink from the bottle of Fresca he'd jammed in the blue plastic cup holder that hung from the rusty driver-side door. He'd driven half of the seventy miles back to the farm before he finally glanced at her. Colette was staring straight ahead, the sun through the windshield sparking flecks of gold in her brown eyes and the wind from the window whipping her long brown hair. Damn, he loved the way she used just the tips of her fingers to brush the hair from her face. Damn, he loved Colette.

"Sorry about the Colt, honey," Rub said. "I just thought…"

"You ever think of having a baby?" Those brown eyes turned to hold his gaze.

A horn honked. A tiny corner of Rub's brain registered it. His eyes remained a heartbeat, maybe three heartbeats, too long on Colette's—his mind jumping like a drunk toad between the idea that she was serious and the hope that she was playing some kind of game that would lead to sex when they got home. When he reflexively swiveled to cast his real eye on the car in the other lane—what Rub would call a damn Jap-scrap rustbucket Datsun—Rub veered completely into the wrong lane, everything going into slo-mo, not unlike when he'd been wounded in 'Nam, the long-ago event melting for six horrible seconds into this one. There was an explosion but not really one; it was more heat than sound. Then a gush of panic and fear and rage followed by just a whisper, a nanosecond, of thought that said, *Screw it, I was going to die someday, anyway*. Then it was over.

They were lucky. The other driver had braked and veered enough to minimize the impact. Colette, like the driver of the Datsun, was unhurt, other than a slight case of whiplash for which she spent three irritating weeks in a neck brace. The doctors said it would take six months, minimum, for Rub to fully recover from his ruptured spleen, broken leg, and various other injuries.

The doctors didn't know Rub.

After three weeks, he pried the cast from his leg with the aid of a long screwdriver, a rusty hacksaw and a couple of long pulls from a fifth of Southern Comfort. He was back to work on the farm full time within six weeks, sporting the limp and chronic pain that would be with him till the day he finally relaxed his steely grip on this life enough for him to pass into the next one.

To Colette, the car crash was a message from heaven. Life was shorter than you could ever imagine, she told Rub. Everywhere you turned these days, there were assholes like the driver who had hit them. Besides, didn't he want someone who could take over the farm?

Forgotten was the worry over the family tree.

Rub agreed. Colette stopped taking birth control.

Nothing happened.

At first, they tried with frequency and enthusiasm. Inevitably, their sex life became less a joy and more a job. Colette remained spectacularly unpregnant.

Colette's gynecologist confirmed the problem wasn't her. She shared this with Rub, who spent a week or longer drinking that insight away. When he came out of the binge, he told her he wouldn't give up and that she should think again if she even thought he was going to go to some "dick doctor." Colette expected as much.

Rub grew bitter, secretly angered at the possibility—in his mind, the *probability*—that he was "shooting blanks" due to exposure to Agent Orange, "the chemical shit the geniuses who ran the war used to kill the jungle" in Vietnam. He grew to desperately desire a son; the failure to produce one played into his already considerable distrust of the federal government, distrust that had festered and deepened as he'd watched veteran buddies struggle with life after the war. He nursed the notion that the government was going to rob him not just of one eye but also of fatherhood.

Rub began spending hours at the tiny Berrien Springs library researching Agent Orange and the federal government's lies during the war. When he'd exhausted that library's limited resources, he began combing through the shelves and microfiche at the main library in Grand Rapids. His buddies began tagging along. Their reading took them down a wild warren of rabbit holes. The commute gave them time to think and debate.

Soon, Rub and his small circle of friends accepted a number of conspiracies as facts: the Kennedys, killed by Hoover and the FBI with help from the Mafia and Fidel Castro; the moon landings, faked; Elvis, quite possibly alive. Over time, they came to believe a shadowy cabal of east-coast elites dictated the results of presidential elections, the makeup of the Supreme Court, and the performance of the stock market; the US was, as Rub described it, "the Wizard of Fucking Oz gone bad."

All of these ideas, heated by a paranoia each had nurtured since the war, stoked their anger with the government and society they felt had betrayed them or at the very least taken them for granted.

When Colette at last conceived, Rub was thrilled and surprisingly disappointed. He was forced to put at least one evil genie, Agent Orange, back in its bottle, if only temporarily.

One night several months into Colette's pregnancy, Rub was at his favorite bar—a place named The Shamrock for the Berrien Springs public schools' athletic nickname, The Fighting Shamrocks. He was relaxing, nursing a Stroh's, playing pool and bragging about his soon-to-be baby boy (this being the pre-ultrasound era, Rub was guilty of premature gender determination; Mickey became Miky shortly after Colette delivered their unexpectedly vagina-equipped child three months later). One of the pool players that night was a Greyhound bus driver from southern Ohio whose name Rub could never remember but whose conversational thrust struck Rub as hard as the shrapnel from the life-threatening VC mortar.

"You bring a baby up in this world today, and you best just lock and load, my friend," the bus driver said. He stopped and squinted at Rub through a haze of cigar smoke. "There's a war or something brewing out there, a war against the law abiders, the honest, good regular folks." The guy jabbed the smoky cigar, gray ash flicking to the faded green felt of the pool table. "And I tell you what. It's not the cops or the Federal Bureau of Insubordination or the CI-fucking-A what's going to protect you and that family of yours. No. Because, guess what, they got their own agenda, they and the international monetary bankers and the radical left. They are all about keeping the boot on our necks, making sure we stay in line and don't call them out for their policies and their lies. You can bet your sweet ass that the first thing they're coming for is A, your guns and two, your other guns. You got a wife and a child, well, that ratchets it all up. When it comes to our families, it's all going to come down…"

"…to you and me," Rub finished the thought with him.

"Damn right. Back where I'm at, in Ohio, we started our own militia, see. It's constitutional, you know. Constitution says, first of all, you got the right to bear arms and you got the right to assemble what's called an unorganized militia."

There it was, out on the table with the cigar ash: a remedy for a need Rub had had since he'd returned from 'Nam. This guy

123

had founded a group of like-minded, like-valued people that would do something if something needed to be done.

The guy and Rub ended up talking till the place closed, the idea of forming a local militia settling into Rub's belly with the Stroh's and a whiskey shot for the road. As he drove home in his new old Ford F-150, John Fogerty and Creedence singing about a senator's son on the radio mixed with the eternal ache from Vietnam and the long-hair who'd flipped him off all those years before; the fantasy image of his baby boy and young wife looking to him, relying on him, to protect them—all of it danced in his head and in the moonlight on his cracked and bug-splattered windshield. When he got home, he awakened Colette—being uncomfortably pregnant, he figured she wasn't fully asleep anyway—and told her of the night and the militia and the threat he could sense, could feel, in the country he'd fought for. He was willing to fight again, he told her, but on his own terms. With his own army. Colette could see the passion in his eyes. She could feel it as Rub paced in the moonlit bedroom, as surely as she could feel the burden of her not-boy child on her bladder. So she got up to go to the bathroom, before Rub could finish.

Weeks later, when Colette gave birth to their daughter, aided by a midwife, on the kitchen table of their farmhouse, Rub was surprised twice: first, that the baby was female and second, that he was instantly, breathlessly, head-over-steel-toed-work-boots in love with her. Colette, for whom the delivery was difficult partly because the salt shaker fell and rolled under her arched back during her final pushing, would later tell friends that the bond between father and daughter formed "before I had a chance to deliver the placenta."

It was clear from the start that the two passions in Rub's life, Miky and the militia, would be forever linked.

# Chapter Fourteen

Rub and Colette officially formed their militia three months after Miky was born. Membership, at first, was limited to a few buddies and their families. The group gathered monthly for family cookouts and target shooting. The mood was festive. Baked beans, babies and bullets. But it wasn't long before Rub became impatient; he felt called to a cause, not to a supper club.

"What 'cause' specifically?" Colette asked one night. Rub was pacing the living room floor, Stroh's in hand. The baby was upstairs in her bassinette, sleeping. Colette, on the couch, flipped through the new issue of *Guns & Ammo* magazine and waited for him to come around to his next thought. The old house groaned in the wind-washed wake of a receding rainstorm. From upstairs, a soft cry. They froze. Then, nothing. Miky was a good baby, as sweetly disposed as her mother. Rub's attention turned to the elk head mounted on the paneled wall. He looked into the brown glass of the dead animal's eyes. "I feel like nobody gets what this thing is all about. Except me and you."

Colette put down the magazine, unwound herself, and stood. As a baby present, Rub had treated her to some new ink, the name "Miky" on a heart, one for each foot. Rub had always thought her feet were sexy. Now they were sexier. Colette wriggled her hand into the right pocket of her jeans. She pulled out a pocketknife, sat again, crossed her right ankle over her left knee, pulled the right foot toward her, and began cleaning her toenails with the knife. Without looking up, she said, "If the rest of the guys don't get it, it's because you haven't told them what to get. You need to write it down—make up a, like, a constitution."

She looked at him then, like she was testing him, those brown eyes of hers reaching out from under her bangs.

"You know I could just jump your bones right now," he said.

"Keep your pants on, mister," she said, returning to her toenail cleaning. "Soon as I'm done here, I'll get a pen and paper; you start thinking what we want to say."

On a sheet of typing paper, Colette wrote *Constitution*. Then, for forty-five minutes, they debated the group's name. It was a frustrating discussion, Rub stuck on "Silver Snake Militia" and Colette fighting him over it.

Colette finally took a break to check on Miky. She was quietly seething as she climbed the stairs. Rub liked Silver Snake because he pictured the militia as a slithering, mysterious group of warriors that would sneak up on you in the night; besides, Silver Snake had been his platoon's nickname in 'Nam. Colette didn't like it because the name reminded her of Kenny "The Snake" Stabler, who'd played quarterback for the Oakland Raiders, a football team she'd always hated.

On her way downstairs, Colette looked out a window at the red sky; the sun was setting. In her head, she saw the words *Red Sky* typed on paper and decided God wanted the name of the militia to be Red Sky. At least, that was how she argued it to Rub, knowing there was no way in hell he'd disagree with God.

Red Sky Brigade it was. They added "Brigade" because Rub liked the coolness factor.

Once they agreed on that, things really got rolling. Rub spewed his thoughts and Colette figured out the wording, writing with a teeth-scarred blue-ink Bic pen, the sheet of paper on a copy of *Field & Stream* in her lap. When they were done, Colette cleared a spot at the kitchen table, grabbed a few more sheets of the typing paper from the junk drawer in the kitchen and typed the constitution on the old Royal typewriter she'd inherited from her father. Colette loved the feel of the Royal's keys on her fingertips, the ding it made when it reached the end of the line. It made her think of her dad and the angry letters he had written on the machine—letters that threatened payment-demanding utilities and his kids' stupid teachers. She loved the opportunity to write. Colette had dropped out of junior college after a big breakup with a bad boyfriend but always had figured she'd make an amazing journalist or maybe a novelist.

It was nearly 2 a.m. when she finished. Rub had fallen asleep on the couch, mouth open and drool running across his scruffy face, empty cans of Stroh's scattered on the floor beside him. Careful not to wake him, one ear tuned for any sounds from the baby, Colette clicked on a lamp, lit a cigarette, and sat on the floor next to an overflowing ashtray. As she smoked, she read through the Red Sky Brigade constitution carefully, feeling a rising sense of pride and what she would have called "destiny," had the word not eluded her. She was proud of the words she'd chosen and how they sounded in her tired brain. She'd dictionary-checked all the spellings she wasn't sure about. She was satisfied. This was good shit:

*Because it's a fact that it's permitted in the Constitution of*
*the State of Michigan and the one for our federal government*

*itself that right-thinking patriots can and should organize "an unorganized militia" to protect their rightful property and families against the criminal immigrant and other undesirables, robbers, foreign countries, and deviant people (sexually) plus the more important and BIGGER threat of the kind of TYRANNY that throughout our nation's history has been committed against private citizens by the Veteran's Administration, FBI, CIA, and THE MILITARY-INDUSTRIAL COMPLEX and ESPECIALLY to protect us from the people and politicians who would take away our rights under the SECOND amendment, we declare ourselves members of the militia organization to be forever and always called the RED SKY BRIGADE, the Red Sky symbolizing the dangers on the "horizon" and it also is what we are defending: the red sunsets over Lake Michigan that are so identified with the land we call home, that being western Michigan. Our organization is open to all races except any ones that would do us harm. It is not open to people who don't share our opinions on things. You must be a citizen of Michigan, USA, you have to take an oath that says all Americans have a GOD-given right to own arms and defend their personal property with those guns—no matter who the defending is against and whatever the weapon is you choose. Also, you have to be ready to fight threats BOTH FOREIGN AND DOMESTIC who don't respect our values, our troops, or our flag and—if necessary—to survive with our families in the state of Michigan's wilderness until such time that we can safely return to our homes. Also, it is strictly banned for members to engage in anything sexual or of a romantic nature while at a militia event (unless it is considered after hours and in the personal privacy of personal accommodations such as your own tent, between consenting heterosexual adults, or alone). The consequences of not following our rules, or of failing to keep to the values of the Red Sky Brigade, is immediate discharge. All discharges will be voted on by the Red Sky Brigade leadership. Once that vote is decided, there is no appeal.*

# Chapter Fifteen

In the years following Colette's death, late at night when Miky was in bed, Rub took out the document Colette had typed. He sat on the front porch of the old farmhouse, smoking a cigar and sipping a beer, classic rock drifting through the rusty-screened windows from the kitchen radio. He read the Red Sky constitution and heard her voice speaking the words, emphasizing what mattered—the good parts about freedom and what the militia, their militia, was going to do. He always liked the part about sexual relationships. He'd wanted to make that section more graphic but Colette had toned it down.

Such late-night episodes were rare. Rub was no fan of nostalgia, sentimentality, or, worse, self-pity. The way he figured it, God dealt you the cards and expected you to play the hand. In this case, he'd gotten a hellofa raw deal, sure, but Miky needed to see the value of sucking it up and moving on.

He figured Miky couldn't miss the mom she didn't remember, so Rub made darn sure Colette's photos and feminine touches disappeared quickly from their lives; he stuck them in cardboard boxes and in a place deep in his heart. The boxes, he stored those in the barn where he also kept the pesticides. Mice and bugs wouldn't dare touch them.

Rub poured all of his substantial heart and cast-iron strength into his daughter, his fruit farm, and the militia movement. Until Miky was old enough to be in school, Rub kept his daughter on the tractor, in his pickup, or in the barns and packing sheds with him as he worked. When someone volunteered to babysit, Rub refused. He saw fatherhood as his duty. He sat with Miky at breakfast, lunch, and dinner. He read the Bible to her after supper and classic children's stories to her at bedtime, mixing in the occasional militia leaflet or militia-recommended book. Once she entered school, he devoted his evenings and weekends to her. He raised her to be a good Christian woman, taught her to trust God in all things but to remember God had a special place in his heart for those who helped themselves. He began feeding her these truths matter-of-factly along with her gummy bears and Cheerios, when she was just in elementary school. As she grew older, he repeated them and also quietly communicated other absolutes about the sanctity of marriage between a man and a woman, the beauty of sunny, dew-kissed mornings in the north woods, and the advantages of any Sig Sauer over the Glock 19. Members in good standing of the First Baptist Church of God in Christ of Pokagon Township, Rub and his girl also worshiped at the less ethereal but, to them, equally sacred altars of Bob Seger, Ted Nugent, and the Detroit Tigers.

Miky's first gun, a well-used Henry Lever Action .22 Rub bought at a gun show, was his present to her on birthday number six, which fell on a Saturday. Miky bounded down the stairs from her bedroom, still in her desert camouflage pajamas, and found the rifle on the kitchen table, wrapped in the previous day's edition of the *Detroit Free Press*.

"Can we try it out?" she said after tearing through the wrapping.

"Sure can. Let's get breakfast first," Rub said, figuring on their usual Saturday menu: bacon, eggs, grape juice, and brown-sugar-cinnamon Pop Tarts. Before he could ignite the burner under a cast iron skillet, Miky had filled two yellow plastic bowls with Froot Loops and was reaching into the old Whirlpool refrigerator for milk.

By 8 a.m. they were at his favorite shooting spot on what Rub called the "back fifty" of the farm. There, in a meadow carpeted with wildflowers still wet with dew and framed by a hearty stand of decades-old maples and oaks, sat a small junkyard of rust-eaten farm implements. Rub balanced a couple of Vlasic pickle and Smucker's jelly jars on the corroded seats of a long-retired John Deere and lined up an emptied six-pack of Stroh's cans on the haggard remnants of a twice-broken-and-repaired trailer.

Kneeling behind her, he wrapped his arms around the apple of his eye and helped her aim at a target and squeeze the trigger.

She was a natural.

That muggy summer of her seventh year, Miky and Rub practiced four or five nights a week. She became so skilled, he occasionally let her shoot his favorite Remington. The first few times, the rifle's kick knocked Miky on her butt and bruised—damn near broke—her shoulder. With the aid of an ACE bandage wound tightly around and over the shoulder, she learned to protect her skinny body against the recoil. Rub stood in the amber light of summer evenings, watching pretty, gritty Miky and saw Colette. This made him as close to happy as he could be.

The Red Sky Militia's get-togethers—as Rub had hoped—became full-scale training events, designed to prepare each family for combat and survival whatever hit the fan.

It was unwritten militia doctrine that you left your kids out of the training until they were able to handle it; nobody wanted a bunch of tag-playing yard apes lollygagging around a gun range. When Rub brought Miky at age eight to her first summer bivouac, a weeklong outing held each August on a militia member's private property near Imlay City, it was a shock to no one.

She was ready.

That week, Rub's little gal collected and carried firewood, searched for edibles in the woods, and showed grownups how to spear fish with a spear she'd made from a tree branch. For good measure, she stood at the adult distance and shot the heart out of paper targets nailed to trees—the makeshift shooting range.

She was, in short, the apple-very-near-the-tree everyone figured she'd be. "You done awfully right by that girl" was the oft-repeated sentiment.

Miky went on to win her militia Rifleman Junior Grade badge at age nine. By the time she was in a training bra, she was a level three rifleman—"riflewoman" or "riflegirl" had been banned as "PIHS" (politically influenced horseshit) by Rub. Level three meant she was capable of handling a full military-style operation while leading a team. Rub's little girl was a princess in camo. A ponytailed badass.

Teenaged Miky managed the farm's books and the seasonal staff of about twenty-five workers. She took Spanish in school so she could translate (and often referee) when Rub had a run-in with one of his Spanish-speaking migrant workers.

Rub made it clear she was his voice and ears in all things agricultural and paramilitary. The workers and militia members didn't resent it. Miky was an easy kid to like.

At school, Miky was also popular; she carried her late mom's good looks and her own natural athleticism well. She had a blunt, sarcastic, down-to-earth attitude that was partly from the genetic shadow thrown by Colette, and was also the byproduct of Rub's parenting style. Sex, periods, boys, girls, bowel habits, all were fair game at the Rub-Miky dinner table. Girls loved her attitude. All the guys (and not a few girls) thought she was hot. No one wanted to piss her off.

In high school, she found her equal. Or, more appropriate: she at last noticed him.

It was the fall of their freshman year. The first day of cross-country practice. Miky shot a white-hot smile and an impish wink at Bernard "Bo" Watts as they laced up their trainers in the gym. Bo, the sole offspring of Willy and Shirley, one of Red Sky's founding couples, felt his knees buckle, gathered himself, and stuck out his tongue.

And they were off.

A lifetime of cold weather militia campouts and survivalist training weekends prepared them well for distance running. They soon found themselves alone together in the drudgery and pain of long training runs—teammates couldn't keep pace.

By their senior year, Bo and Miky were both school and regional record holders. Bo, running in his trademark camo knit cap, finished his career as individual state champion and Miky was girls' runner-up. In the crush of three hundred runners at the championship race's start, a trailing runner stepped on Miky's left heel and tore off her shoe; she ran the final two and a half miles with one bare foot and lost by three seconds to a foreign exchange student from Germany who competed for a small Catholic school in suburban Detroit. This fed Rub's always-simmering frustration with "the system," the vast, nebulous governing infrastructure that he and the other militia members believed worked diligently against the hard-working Middle Americans who funded it. He filed a grievance with the Michigan High School Athletic Association, arguing that the foreign student should not have qualified for the event since she, the foreign student, was, well, foreign. Rub's ten-page, handwritten complaint disappeared into the MHSAA bureaucracy. Rub wasn't surprised.

Miky quickly shook off the disappointment of losing the race. By this time, she and Bo were headed to Central Michigan University together, on athletic scholarships. And they were in love.

# Chapter Sixteen

Rub always imagined he'd die in a smoke and fire hell storm ignited by government agents or, maybe, at the hands of a punk trying to steal his guns. So it came as a surprise when, on a chilly day in his forty-eighth year, as Miky and Bo were enjoying their junior year at CMU, his windpipe became hopelessly blocked by a bite of a bratwurst. He was at a militia training event miles from any hospital. The Red Sky militia had banned the Heimlich maneuver due to what Rub and others saw as its "suspicious Jewish origins," so Rub gasped and gagged—his face taking on a blue-gray hue—as other militia members took turns pounding on his back. Eventually his gasping and gagging stopped, the brat stubbornly stuck. So it was that Rub exited this earth, lungs starving, legs twitching, The Lovin' Spoonful echoing in his head, on a half-frozen patch of sandy soil in the Allegan Forest.

Miky and Bo competed for the CMU Running Chippewas until Rub's death, but both found that juggling classes, eighty-mile training weeks and part-time jobs was nearly impossible once grief was added to the mix. So they quit their teams.

For several months following Rub's death, Miky could barely get out of bed. She always did get up, willing herself to class and work. Friends suggested she "see someone," but Rub's girl would have none of it. She hated the depression almost as keenly as she felt the dark weight of it. Finally, after one particularly brutal night in which she slept exactly twenty-two minutes, long enough to dream about her father and, for the first time in years, her mother and a never-before-imagined kitten her mother had adopted named Mr. Buckles, Miky quietly declared war on the brutal, gripping sadness. She went for a run through campus in her pajamas and a pair of bunny slippers that belonged to one of her roommates. Her stunt drew the attention of a concerned campus policewoman. The local television station got wind of the story and ran a feature piece portraying Miky as an ex-athlete dealing with tragedy the one way she knew how. She became a minor campus celebrity and Miky, literally, ran with it. She began running in all types of goofy gear, in all weather, at all times of the day and night: a bikini during a cold fall rain at sunrise, a parka at noon during a summer thunderstorm, a gorilla costume in a late-afternoon January snowstorm. She became a campus legend, a freak, or a joke, depending on your perspective. All Bo knew was that it seemed to help. The fog began to lift. Miky spent less time in bed or wrapped in a comforter in front of the television.

With cross-country and her father no longer in her life and depression retreating, Miky moved in with Bo and threw most of her energy into earning a teaching degree. She volunteered as a coach at a local middle school. Bo majored in mechanical engineering until his growing jones for illegal narcotics forced him to rethink and major instead in the scholastically less challenging agricultural engineering. They threw epic parties in the old Victorian they rented. That they kept their relationship together, spent most weekends with the militia, and stayed in school was a testament to Miky's work ethic and Bo's ability to study while stoned.

They graduated, Miky with honors and Bo barely. She landed a job as a high school teacher and cross-country coach at Three Rivers Public Schools, a medium-sized district in the southern part of the state. Bo struggled to find work until a militia member put in a good word with a guy who knew the assistant product manager for the Frosted Flakes brand at Kellogg's, in Battle Creek. The position was in the maintenance department, and Bo was overqualified, but he knew how to fix stuff and was not highly motivated. It was the perfect gig.

Miky and Bo bought an old farmhouse just south of Kalamazoo. There, parties weren't as frequent and were a lot less notorious—she had an example to set for her students and runners.

Bo ditched the drugs, except for the occasional joint, and became a very sober and sought-after speaker and writer. His blog and podcast, "Diary of the Mitten Maniac," had several thousand followers. He and Miky were often invited to national militia events, usually so Bo could give a talk. He was widely known for his views on illegal immigration and what his PowerPoint presentation called "The Bastardization of the American Dream." Critics called his tone racist. Bo blamed "illegal immigrants, left-wing bleeding hearts and their sympathizers in Congress and the media" for the characterizations.

The Red Sky Brigade was now one of more than a dozen militia organizations statewide. Organized by geography, leaders of the individual Michigan militias met regularly and joint operations were common. Well-built (he was a weightlifter), fit (he still ran), and handsome, Bo was the unquestioned and respected leader of Red Sky, known for his passion and his grasp of the issues. Miky was the increasingly reluctant militia princess.

"You're like a zealot's zealot," Miky told him. It was the week before Ham DenBraber's collapse. They were in bed at home, spooned together in the dark, fading to sleep after a weekend militia campout. Bo's weekend had been spent leading strategy sessions and combat-like maneuvers. Miky had done some shooting, gone for runs in the woods, and tried to play her militia role while fighting the creeping realization her love for the militia movement had died with her father. She felt more like a teacher and coach now than a freedom fighter.

"A zealot's zealot. What's that supposed to mean?" Bo said, his voice brittle.

"You see the world through militia-tinted glasses, babe," Miky said, trying to sound conciliatory and critical at the same time, which wasn't easy.

They twisted away from each other, onto their backs.

"Here we go," he said with a sigh.

"Traffic is bad on your way to work, you say it's because liberals spent more money on social stuff than they did on infrastructure. If the neighbor's dog craps in the yard, it's a violation of personal space and lack of respect for personal property. If the Internet is slow, hackers could be launching a cyberattack or the NSA could be eavesdropping," she said, her voice rising. "I just don't buy all that. Sometimes dogs just shit where they shit."

They were quiet for a moment, both trying to keep the conversation on the knife-edge of civility.

"Wow, that ratcheted up quickly," Bo said.

"Well, this shit's been bugging me."

"Do you even get it anymore—what it's about?"

"I get it." She didn't get it.

"Well, you sure don't sound like you do." He knew she didn't. She knew he knew.

"I do. I really do. It's just, look, you guys fester on this stuff—on the path America is on, on your rights being, like, under siege, and it all starts sounding maybe a little like paranoia. Now there's this thing, this deal with Wisconsin."

Bo was suddenly out of bed, pacing in the dark. "It's not paranoia if it's real. If they're coming for us and no one has our backs, someone better be ready to step up."

"Listen to you. Now who's ratcheting up?"

Bo stopped in front of a bedroom window, his muscular profile backlit by a streetlight. When he spoke, his tone had dropped a notch. "You're a hellofa shot and field cook. You could survive a blizzard outdoors in the UP. Heck, you could clean your weapon in the middle of a blizzard then shoot the eye out of a sparrow at a hundred meters. You used to be as hardcore militia as they come. I can't imagine what your dad would say if he could hear you right now."

She took a moment before responding.

"You're right, babe," she said at last, "but my dad always worried about guys getting caught up in pure emotion. He used to say emotion was part of the militia deal, 'but you best watch…'"

"'…you don't get yourself drowned in it,'" Bo said. He reached inside his boxers and scratched himself. His hand lingered, jammed down the front of the shorts. "This is different. This is legit. Emotion warranted, I'd say. Rub would too."

"No, this is what dad was worried about—a bunch of guys getting so amped they're ready to, like, attack Wisconsin or some shit."

"The Gunvernor is our man, you know. He's one of us. A straight shooter—emphasis on shooter. He says Michigan needs us, well… I think your dad would approve."

"Don't hang this on Dad. Don't even start with that." Miky's voice was sharper.

"Maybe you don't know everything you think you know," he said, coming back to the bed. He sat, his broad naked back facing her in the gloom.

"Now what does that mean?"

"Never mind. It's too late anyway. Wisconsin's a done deal."

"Done deal? You don't even know for sure what the deal is."

"Me and the other militia heads already took a vote. It was unanimous. We take action against Wisconsin. I volunteered Red Sky to spearhead. The Windwalkers in the UP, they challenged me on that. But they only have nine guys, three women, and a couple of pit bulls. I told them we were way better equipped; besides, we would be locked and loaded, just a quick drive away from the southern border of the conflict zone, via I-94 and the Indiana toll road."

"Please tell me you're kidding."

Bo stood again. He turned, looming over her, half of him washed by the light from the windows. His expression told her he wasn't kidding.

"But how... When?"

"When we get the word from the governor's office, we launch our communications protocol, and we head up the attack. Call for reinforcements as needed. The Windwalkers will cover the northern frontier and be ready to move south if called upon."

Miky sat up, pulled the sheets around her; the house was cold. "After that, what's your strategy?"

"We'll figure it out," Bo said, walking toward the open bedroom door.

"Bunch of dudes all jacked up on the thought of a war. You have no battle plan. And it's all based on some bullshit story."

"I need a beer," Bo said from the hallway.

"Make it two." She flopped back on the bed.

# Chapter Seventeen

A week later, Ham's face met the floor of the governor's office in Lansing, and the call went out for militia support. But Bo and most of the rest of the Michigan militia members (including all of the Wolverine Windwalkers) were at a former church camp near Tulsa, Oklahoma, attending the annual national militia assembly. The place was rustic. Phones were forbidden. Bo and his fellow Red Sky members were deep in militia nerd-dom and could not be reached.

As dictated by the previously agreed-upon protocol, the call to arms went out from the governor's office to Bo's cell. When Bo didn't answer, the highly placed militia contact (Kelli Alexander) used a disposable, untraceable phone to call a friend of Bo's, Dan Dyke, a militia sympathizer who owned a hog farm near Niles. The phone call was just long enough for Dyke to hear the code word "Cheesus." He hung up and then called the cell of a long-time militia member, a guy he knew only as One-Thumb Jack, and said "Cheesus." One-Thumb Jack had two fully functional thumbs and he used both of them to send a text message—*Cheesus*—to four different numbers. As planned, only one of those numbers, answered by a sympathetic former Methodist minister in Sault Ste. Marie, was for an active phone.

The ex-minister drove his rusty Ford F-150 to a payphone in a strip mall, where he called a number he'd written on a scrap of toilet paper. This phone was answered by a woman who ran a carwash in Sturgis. When the minister whispered "Cheesus," she frowned and repeated the word loudly. The minister also repeated the word. The woman repeated it as a question. This alerted Elizabeth Gurney, another militia sympathizer, who was standing next to the carwash owner. Elizabeth was supposed to have answered the carwash phone, but had been distracted by an intense text conversation she was having with her weird sister, Diane. When she heard "Cheesus," Elizabeth stopped texting. The owner hung up the carwash phone and muttered something about "stupid prank calls." Elizabeth trusted her gut and speed-dialed a number in Paw Paw. That call was answered at the Paw Paw camp by the Red Sky member nicknamed Zooker, who was ex-US Army and an unemployed former co-worker of Bo's.

"Cheesus," Elizabeth said. And Zooker smiled.

Miky was on spring break from school and hadn't gone to the conclave in Tulsa. They'd fought about it, she and Bo had. She figured the time away would do them both some good. So she'd stayed home and he'd headed to Oklahoma in his pickup and a huff.

Miky had come to Paw Paw for some target shooting at the Red Sky camp. Instead of the usual army boots, she wore an old pair of Asics running shoes. Underneath her sweatpants and long-sleeve T-shirt, which was emblazoned with *CMU Cross Country*, she was wearing running shorts and a running top. She planned to get in about six miles after the target practice.

She had hoped she'd be alone at the camp, but there were two other vehicles in the gravel parking lot. The big, silvery pickup truck belonged to an asshole they called Spud. Spud ran an archery shop in Muskegon. He'd probably driven down for a few hours of munitions practice. Spud liked to blow shit up, Bo said. Now, given the percolating Wisconsin situation, Miky figured he might be getting his chance to do it for real. The thought made her stomach dance.

Spud's truck was parked well away from the only other vehicle, a rusty, used-to-be-yellow El Camino she recognized belonged to a guy she knew only as Zooker. Zooker was a friend of Bo's Miky barely tolerated.

Miky was parking in the spot next to Spud's, getting her Jeep Wrangler as close to the truck as she could without hitting it— this would annoy him; Bo and Miky loved to annoy Spud— when Zooker came running from the direction of the camp's barn-like bunkhouse. Miky shoved the Wrangler into park and hit the button to lower her window. Zooker, wheezing, slowed his run to a determined walk, his combat boots crunch-crunch-crunching on the gravel, that gray ponytail of his bouncing, his tobacco-stained Fu Manchu contorted by a mouthful of unspoken words. He waited until he was a few feet away to let the words spill: "The call, Mik. It came. The call." He managed to get out the key information: They were to be the boots on the ground, spearheading the attack on Wisconsin. Now.

"You've got to be kidding me."

"Shit you not, girl. This is the real deal. We got to move." He turned to run.

"Whoa whoa whoa, big guy. How do you know? How did they…?"

Zooker stopped. His back to her, he looked to the sky for a moment, flopped his arms, and then slowly turned around. His face was flushed and he had a bulge in his right cheek. He squinted and then shot a squirt of tobacco at the back tire of her Jeep. "Some chick just called. Had the code word."

"What chick?" she said. "Wait. There's a code word?"

"Chick's part of our, like, network. And she knew the code. Soon as I talk to Spud, I make the return call to confirm, then we're all set to go and we move out."

Zooker turned and began jogging clumsily away. Over his shoulder, he shot another stream from his chaw. "Get ready to move. It's just the three of us so we are gonna have to be ready for some shit here, girlfriend."

Miky sat, stunned, picking through the ramifications of her current situation like a crow inspecting a particularly putrid carcass. This was bad, that she knew.

But she couldn't just sit here.

She punched open the door, stepped out, jerked open the rear door and started pulling the gear onto the graveled ground. As she packed what she'd need into an army-green duffel bag, she could hear Rub's voice, ranting over a long-ago supper table, talking about how private citizens, not the "guys in the suits in Washington-f-ing-DC," had the "God-given right and responsibility to protect their homes, their state, and their G-damn country." One day, her dad swore, trouble would come. And with it would come the call for all right-thinking people, people who had prepared their families to protect themselves, to rise up.

Miky had never wanted to be part of the rising up. And she was fairly sure Rub would be pretty much not OK with the current situation. But he would've expected her to keep her head straight, to play out the crisis.

So here she was, trading the sweats and long-sleeve T for camo pants and top—what the guys called "BDUs" for "Battle Dress Uniform" and sniffed with importance when they did, as though old US Army fatigues they'd picked up on eBay made them real freaking soldiers. It felt a little weird, but she kept her running gear on under the BDUs. Wearing the army stuff, just putting it on, made Miky feel stupid. The running stuff against her skin felt like a little bit of sanity.

Miky took a deep breath and closed her eyes. They were planning to shoot Americans. People from Wisconsin. And for what? For whom? The whole prairie dog thing was just another crazy conspiracy theory. Everyone with half a brain knew that. She imagined her dad's hand on her shoulder, telling her one of his conspiracies, and she realized his presence in her subconscious was not always an asset. She saw Bo's face, the fire in his eyes when he talked about the movement and how they'd be ready when whatever what was going to hit the fan, hit the fan.

The call had come. The damn, long-worried-over call.

Something twitched in her gut—dread?—her rapid heartbeat boogying it up a notch. She swallowed and prayed it would go away. She tried to focus on logistics, reminding herself to email a week's worth of lesson plans to the school administration office—she was going to need a sub for a bit. Who knew how long this would take?

She wished she could go for a run. She looked at her running-shoed feet and laughed. The Asics and camo were definitely not a match. Oh well. She wasn't about to put on boots.

Miky took a deep breath and ran through her checklist again.

# Chapter Eighteen

Three hours after Zooker confirmed the call—while Governor Bill was worrying over the impact of his decision, in Lansing— Spud was hunched behind the wheel of his mammoth Ford F-350. They had navigated the heavy traffic of Chicago and were in enemy territory; the Welcome to Wisconsin sign, long past, had launched Spud into a spasm of fist-pumping, window-pounding, and war-whooping, but Zooker had told him to "calm the F down" because he, Zooker, wanted to avoid "getting arrested just for driving a big-ass Ford into a Prius." Things had quieted after that. Miky, riding shotgun, was sipping water from a heavily scuffed Nalgene bottle and punching the buttons of the truck's radio. Zooker was sprawled in the extended cab's back seat, chewing tobacco, occasionally shooting smelly squirts of it into an empty McDonald's coffee (large) cup. They were dressed in BDUs and Kevlar helmets and were checked out in full gear, some of it on them, the rest in the truck's cap-covered bed. Each had an M1 and a hundred rounds in mags or stripper clips, a gas mask and canteen, a compass, a poncho with a liner, a flashlight with both red and blue lens covers, fifty feet of parachute cord, a sheathed knife, a medicine kit, a cleaning kit for the rifle, toilet paper, water purification tabs, and waterproof matches. They also had a small kit of personal hygiene supplies; prepaid, disposable cell phones (all but one, Miky's, was turned off); and the Red Sky Brigade's current handgun of choice (a point they debated every six months or so), a Smith & Wesson M66 .357 Magnum with a four-inch barrel, and a stash of ammo for it. The only things missing from their standard combat gear checklist were a camp stove and handheld CB radio. And reinforcements.

"You guys do Arby's?" Zooker said.

"Kind of early. Just had lunch," Spud said. "You suddenly losing your memory, old man?" Spud's thumbs were jitterbugging on the top of the steering wheel.

"No. I mean you like it. Arby's."

"Burger King," Spud said. "That's what I do. Burger F King."

"Miky?" Zooker said.

Miky frowned. She was in no mood for conversation. "I prefer, like, Subway. Try to stay away from the fast food burger crap. Try to eat right."

"Listen to you, all 'Subway.' Can't handle a Whopper, apparently." Spud snickered and glanced in the rearview at Zooker, who stared out the window like he hadn't heard the comment.

"I'm sure you get your hands on one as often as you can," Miky said. Miky knew Spud well and wished she didn't.

Zooker, still staring at the Wisconsin countryside, spit into his cup. The spitting made Miky want to throw up. She took a swig from the Nalgene. "Just saying, we're going to need to plan for chow. Got no camp stove," Zooker said.

"Got no radio neither," Spud said.

"Dude, that's why we got the burners," Zooker said. They'd been over this.

"Yeah, turned off. What good's a phone if you got it turned off?"

"The orders are that we just keep mine on," Miky said. "I am on point for contact. They need to call us, they call my burner.

Likewise, I will call the contact number if we get into something we don't want to be into. Otherwise, for security's sake and the sake of staying focused on the mission, you guys are blacked out for now. Which leads me to ask, are you absolutely sure you have your phone powered off?"

"You are way over-worrying the phone deal," Spud said. "I know what to do, had the same training as you."

"Dude knows," Zooker said.

"I know he knows," Miky said. She fiddled with the radio. The two men stared at the scenery.

"Someone's all on edge," Spud said. "Must be that time of the month."

Miky swallowed a surge of rage. Guys like Spud were a dime per dirty dozen in the militia. Rub and Bo had been blind to the way they treated women. She'd learned on her own to ignore them—usually. Now she focused on the task at hand. "There are others coming, right?" she said. "I mean, the call went out everywhere? It's not like—not everybody went to Tulsa."

Neither man answered.

Zooker coughed and spit into his cup.

Spud sniffed. "Don't go doubting our capabilities, Miky."

Miky sighed and shook her head. "This is messed up." She closed her eyes and pictured the three of them trying to fight an army of Wisconsin state cops and national guardsmen. "All I heard for the past month was how there was trouble and, when it hit, the call would go to the Paw Paw camp because it was the closest to Wisconsin and that's where most of us come to train. So now it comes and there were only three of us. I got no idea what we're supposed to do—what the mission is." She opened her eyes and twisted to look at Zooker. "I mean, if we're supposed to do something big, we're going to need help."

Zooker was studying a barn in the distance. Miky imagined the family who owned the barn. She saw them as red-cheeked, happy people. She wondered if Zooker could kill them and realized he could. "Zook. You called in others?"

He finally looked at her. "You know the deal. I'm sure someone did call someone. And if they didn't, well, we're in this to send a message to the cheesers."

"Message is?"

"We defend our home against disaster, crime, invasion, terrorism, and tyranny," Spud said.

"'Zactly," Zooker said.

"And it don't say in there anything about how many of us there needs to be to do the defending," Spud said.

"Spudman's got it." Zooker stared at Miky and gave her a wink and a wry smile.

"Damn straight, I do. And it was the hand of God we all three had full gear stowed at Camp Pee Pee," Spud said. "You ask me, seems like the three of us is meant to do this. What if we hadn't been there? What if we had nothing but our side arms with us, or what if we never met each other? Know what I'm saying?" Spud paused for a moment. "Right place, right time. I mean, wow." He surveyed the highway ahead, pounded the steering wheel with a meaty right fist, and let out a whoop.

Miky sighed. She was playing out the scenario, trying to figure what to do, trying to think, and Spud wouldn't shut up. "I don't even want to talk but you're just forcing me to so I get a minute without hearing your voice."

"Whoa. The lady scores," Zooker said.

Spud didn't seem to feel the jab. "Amped is all. Can't help it. Get this way when I'm going to fucking war." He pounded the wheel with gusto.

"My dad would be wringing your neck about now," Miky said. "Always told my mom she couldn't let emotions get the best of her. That's what he told me."

"Your folks are legendary, man," Zooker said, nodding, his manner grave. "Seriously. Legendary."

"So since she's second-gen militia she's an expert on everything. Cell phones and emotions and so on," Spud said.

Miky rolled her eyes. "You just need to calm down, that's what I'm saying." She twisted to look at Zooker. "So the guy or whoever called gave you the word and just hung up?"

"Yep."

"Who'd you talk to on your call-backs?"

"A man, then a woman," Zooker said. "Guy was called Cobra."

"The other?" she said.

"Chick named Pinkie."

"And they…?"

"Both confirmed. Word for word," Zooker said. "This is the real deal."

"But what deal is it? I mean, what are we supposed to do here, exactly?" Miky punched the dashboard. Anger bubbled in her chest again. Anger at Bo for being gone and anger at Rub and her mom for being dead—anger at all of them for leading her down the path to this fucking moment.

"Saw this coming, you know," Zooker said. "The cheeseheads jumping in like this."

"The one I can't figure is Denton McAllister," Spud said. "That almost seems, like, made up."

"Loved that dude in *The Deer Hunter*," Zooker said.

"*The Deer Hunter*?" Miky said.

"Yeah, the movie, you know."

Miky sighed. "That was Christopher What's-his-name," she said, momentarily relieved at the diversion.

"No, it was him. McAllister," Spud said.

"Walken. Christopher Walken," said Miky.

"Swear to God it was McAllister," Spud said.

"This works out, you can ask him yourself," Zooker said. "Figure we'll run into him."

"Prairie dogs," Miky said. "Which supposedly don't even live here, in Wisconsin, by the way."

"Someone brought them in just for this, way I heard it," Spud said.

"True that, my man," Zooker said. "Brought into a pet store."

"In Madison, think it was," Spud said.

"Yeah, story was they told everybody the dogs was brought in to be, like, exotic pets," Zooker said. "The same pet shop s'posedly had some fancy rat imported from Ghana, over in Africa, that was infected with monkey whatever."

"A pouched rat," Spud said. "Or pooched. Maybe it was 'pooched' or some shit. Weird name is all I remember."

"Yeah," Zooker said. "It s'posedly got mixed in with the prairie dogs in this pet store and infected them with, guess what?"

"Monkeypox." Spud was nodding like a goofy monkey. "It was a big news story. Only they made it sound like the whole thing was an accident."

"Yeah, really it was a test of this, like, biological weapons program the government was working on in labs and shit. Them and the, like, cheese industrial whatchacallit."

"Cheese industrial complex," Spud said.

"Exactly," Zooker said. "This was a trial run. Original plan was families would buy the infected prairie dogs and get sick. Governor and his buddies all wanted to see how it would work. Problem was, instead of selling them to families, some dudes bought the whole bunch of them and let them loose out in the country. Bunch of people got sick. The governor and them made up the whole thing about the pooched rat as a cover. What I heard, anyway."

"Poached, I think," Spud said.

"Whatev…" Zooker said.

"You realize none of that makes any sense," Miky said.

Spud acted like he didn't hear her. "Last week, up at Interlochen? I was talking to this guy we call Wazy about this. Wazy said he heard this pox or whatever could drop a man in, like, three days."

"You know Waze?" Zooker said.

"Absolutely," Spud said.

"Waze and me go back," Zooker said.

"Him and me and a couple others were up at Interlochen on an overnight," Spud said. "Target shooting and some patrol tactical shit."

"He hung out with Nichols, you know that?" Zooker said. "Terry Nichols, I'm saying. Mr. Oklahoma City Co-conspirator Bomber himself."

"Absolutely. Waze knew Terry and James Nichols both," Spud said. "Back before the O-K City bombing, of course."

"Both?" Zooker said.

"Waze says to me, get this, says one night he was over at James Nichols' farm and Terry showed up. Then some guy called and James answers then gives the phone to Terry. Terry suddenly gets all weird on the phone, talking code," Spud said.

"Who was calling?"

"Tim-o-thy McVeigh," Spud said. "This is like a month before the Oklahoma City bombing and the guy who did it was talking to the Nichols boys. Wazy was there, swears it's true."

"I would have left that house right then. Those guys were certified. C-R-A-Z-Y," Miky said. She ached again to go for a run—to pause this thing and let her mind float away for a while.

"Go easy, girl," Zooker said. "Watch who you're putting down, now."

"Yeah, don't even start," Spud said.

"Bite me," Miky said.

"You wish," Spud said.

"You're a moron," Miky said. "McVeigh was a baby-killer. I don't appreciate baby-killers."

"You want baby-killers, what about Janet W. Reno and William 'B.J.' Clinton?" Zooker said. He'd put the cup down and was leaning into the space between the front seats. His breath was sour.

Miky swallowed and turned to look out her window. "So you honestly believe it was OK to blow up a building filled with everyday people and babies—babies."

"Who said McVeigh and Nichols did it?" Zooker said. "Who even ever proved they were the ones—the only ones—that did the Oklahoma City bombing?"

"Oh, so your fallback is that McVeigh and Nichols were somehow framed by who—every single department of the federal government, the same federal government that owned the building?"

Spud frowned and stared out his window. "If it was just McVeigh and them that did it," he said, "why were all the ATF and FBI guys out of their offices in the federal building right when the bomb hit? They worked in the building. But all of them were out when the bombing happened."

"I don't know that that's true. If it is, it was a coincidence. Maybe they were just out. People go out."

"They had to be tipped off," Zooker said. "Someone told them."

"Maybe they went to get lattes," Miky said. She wished they would drop this. Sometimes it seemed like the militia was just a bunch of paranoid guys who liked guns and beers and talking conspiracies. Dudes, thinking they knew insider stuff no one else knew, getting worked up till one of them got the nerve to do something. She sighed. "It was 1995. Ancient history. Who knows anymore? What does that have to do with us today, with the three of us—what, starting some kind of war?"

"Face it, Miky, those federal dudes knew to be gone that morning," Spud said. "They were tipped off. That's confirmed all over the Internet."

"Yeah, and you know about the six explosions?" Zooker said, flopping back into his seat. He wrestled his coffee cup from the cup holder.

"Four," Spud said. "I heard four."

"Some people that was there heard six," Zooker said. He spit in the cup. Miky's stomach squirmed.

"Point is the story got to just 'one' awful fast," Spud said. "Mainstream media wanted McVeigh as the mad bomber in the truck to be the story."

"Who tells you this stuff?" Miky said.

"Oh, it's certified true," Spud said. "You gotta lay off the porn and read the good stuff online, Miky." He snickered and sniffed, shot a glance in the rearview, and then glanced back to the road.

"There was an extra leg found in the rubble," Zook said. "You know about that? The severed leg with the military boot on?"

"Oh, yeah. Oh, most definitely yeah." Spud wiped spit from the corner of his mouth. "They couldn't match the leg to any other body in the rubble."

"Heard it was an Arab leg."

"Exactly," Spud said. "Tell you what. I think the government blew up their own building. Or let, you know, foreign types do it. Some Middle Easterners."

"Makes sense," Zooker said.

"All's you do is set delayed charges in your critical spots way ahead of time and get the H-E-double-hockey-sticks out. Tell you what. I could do it," Spud said with a snort. "I could do it easy. Feds can do whatever they want and make it look like whatever they want."

"There was a flipping truck filled with flipping fertilizer…"

"S'posedly," Spud said with a snort. "You got proof, Mik?"

"It was there. On the news. In pictures."

"Surprised your mommy and daddy didn't tell you the truth on all this, Miky," Zooker said. "Seriously."

Miky gritted her teeth. "My mom was dead, so that would've been hard. My dad, well, I used to argue with him about this all the time. You guys like to get all festered up about this shit and sometimes, it just is what it is—no conspiracy, just a baby-killing maniac with a grudge." She looked out the window at the countryside and felt a familiar tightening in her chest. "You act like he's some kind of militia hero. McVeigh, all those guys, weren't even in the militia. They made us look stupid. Evil. I'm not in this to be evil."

"McVeigh had connections to the militia movement, feds were getting worked up about us—the militias. McVeigh was in the area, so they took advantage of him," Zooker said. "He was, what you call it, a prawn. Like in checkers or chess or whatever."

"Pawn," Spud said. "It's chess."

"Yeah, a prawn," Zooker said.

"Like Lee H. Oswald, Junior," Spud said.

"Nichols was a prawn too," Zooker said.

"Terry," Spud said.

"Both, I guess," said Zooker. "Both of them."

"They were pawns of whom?" Miky said.

"Of whom else? The mainstream media, the government, everyone who wanted to make the militia look bad," Zooker said. "Unless you haven't noticed, Miky, the federal government is not a big fan of the militia, which is kind of the point. They might consider an armed citizenry a bit of a threat. They want us to understand that."

"What matters is, soon as that building went down, we knew it wasn't one of our own, wasn't McVeigh or Nichols or nobody. It was them—the government—their message got sent," Spud said.

"Absolutely," Zooker said.

"Clinton, Reno—big on messages back then," Spud said.

"Just ask David Koresh," Zooker said. "Branch Davidians compound, 1993."

"Oh wait, can't," Spud said. "Dead."

"Ask Randy Weaver's wife," Zooker said.

"Nope, can't," Spud said. "Dead. Ruby Ridge, '92. Killed by the ATF. The federal gov-er-ment."

"Guys. Look. I know," Miky said. "I was raised on this, remember? I remind you, once again, that Tim McVeigh was not a militia member. He was an Aryan racist asshole; yeah, I know there are guys like him in the movement, but we try to weed them out. My point is, your whole theory isn't worth shit. It's just jacked-up overthinking and it's typical. It's what got us in this situation today."

Miky felt Rub urging her to take a deep breath. To just breathe for a minute before she said anything more. She stared out the windshield at a vapor trail high in the blue sky. Rub would've called it a "chemtrail," would've said it was the government, poisoning the climate or something. Finally, unexpectedly, the truth tumbled out of her. "I just don't know that I buy all of this, this paranoia. This militia true believer garbage. Never really have, I guess," she said softly, then added, "Guess I should learn to worry more. Or something."

The truck seemed to gasp. The men, for once, were speechless.

# Chapter Nineteen

"Is it 'Michiganian' or 'Michigander?'" Governor Bill Hoeksma said. "I never can figure that. For the life of me."

Deanna Weatherbury, media relations officer for the state of Michigan, was sitting in the governor's chair, typing at the governor's computer. She bit her lower lip and stared at the screen. "Well, sir, as I said, speechwriting is not my primary expertise."

"Nonsense. You're doing great, Deenie." Governor Bill stood behind her. He kneaded her shoulders. Deanna cringed. The governor angled his head toward the office door. "Kelli? Michiganders or Michiganians? I forget. What do we call ourselves these days?"

From her office, Kelli Alexander said, "Gander, I think, governor. But if you want—" She walked to the open door, took a bite from the almond biscotti she'd had the intern Tammy get from Starbucks, and said, "I can have one of the interns research it." Kelli's face was blotchy from crying; she just didn't feel well and Ham's condition worried her. She couldn't shake the feeling she might be pregnant.

Governor Bill thought about this. "Do we have anyone available who could do it?"

"Tammy could," Kelli said. She sniffed, turned, returned to her desk, sat in her chair, and picked up her cell phone. "Or Orvella."

"I thought Orvella was guarding the elevator downstairs, keeping those media guys down there till me and Deenereeno get this speech ready," Governor Bill said with a nod and a wink at Deanna.

"No, sir, we just had them police-tape the entrance. No one can come up."

Governor Bill frowned. "The whole entrance? Of the building?" He glanced toward the window. Kelli froze, the cell inches from her ear, her pretty pink mouth poised to accept the last of the biscotti, which was an inch away from her extended tongue. "Seems a little drastic, don't you think?" Governor Bill said.

Kelli thumbed off the phone, tossed it to her desk, and threw the biscotti at the wall. She swiveled in her chair and started to stand, sat, stood, and took a step toward the open door to the governor's office. Governor Bill smiled out at her and waved. "Never mind, Kell-ster. You're good. Better no one should come up here right now."

Kelli took a deep breath and returned to her chair. She looked at the list of baby names she had scrawled on a notepad. Tears blurred her vision. Quietly, she read each one. "Hammy, Hammick, Hammond." The names had become a comforting, distracting litany. "Hambone, Hamboreen, Hambonita, Hamjean, Hamifer." The office phone rang and Kelli jumped, a squeak escaping her throat. Flush-faced, she glanced to the governor's office. Governor Bill was still standing behind Deanna, reading from the computer screen. Kelli snatched the receiver from its cradle as it rang again.

"State of Michigan, the governor's office," she said.

"It's me." Will Hoeksma sounded terse, maybe a little irritable.

"Hold on," Kelli said. She put the receiver down, spun away from her desk, stood, closed the door to the governor's office, returned, and picked up the receiver. "Why haven't you called me?"

"Listen. I know how tight you and the hubby were with DenBraber."

"It's not just that and you know it." Kelli pushed back from her desk, kicked off her shoes, and planted her bare feet on the desk. Her emotions—anger, frustration, sadness, and something that felt like fear or excitement or both—boiled through her chest like caffeine from three too many cups of coffee. "It's weird here right now." For an instant, she also thought of the biscotti, now in pieces and crumbs on the floor.

"How's he?"

"Who he?" She scowled at the biscotti.

"Your boss."

"He's gotten all funny."

"Funny how?"

"Like, I don't know. Earlier he was sad and confused like you'd expect after"—she paused to swallow an unexpected sob—"what happened with Ham, with the senator. But now, now he's, like, play acting, you know? All confident and assertive."

"How?"

"Taking charge. Issuing orders. Playing with that gun of his. And being all, like, nice at the same time."

"George W. Bush."

"He's mentioned him. Several times."

"That's who he's acting like, I'm betting. His idol. He's been that way ever since some reporter compared the two of them and he took it as a positive. No wonder he's making my life hell right now. And I suppose you're now part of it."

"Part of what?"

"He talked to you. About your husband. About the damn militia."

Kelli froze. "How do you know that?"

"I know everything." His voice had an edge.

Kelli took a deep breath. "Yes. Yes I… He did ask me to reach out…"

"And you did. You reached out to the damn militia and didn't inform the man who's been paying you to keep him posted on what goes on in my son's little world." His tone had turned menacing. "Now, Lord knows what will happen."

"Well, I certainly don't know what will happen," Kelli said, feeling out of control—like she was sliding down a very dangerous water slide, maybe the one at Michigan Adventure she'd gone down last summer the day her husband shot their cancer-riddled twelve-year-old corgi, Pepper; the slide had taken her mind off Pepper but only because she'd gotten enough water up her nose to be more miserable about the water than the death of her dog. She swallowed a wave of nausea. "I don't care," she said, letting emotions drive her, ignoring Will Hoeksma's stature and a nagging memory of Pepper needing two bullets because Taylor had dropped his beer when he took the first shot. "You came to me and asked me to keep track of what your son was up to and not a couple months later all of the sudden he's in here talking about that crazy deal with Wisconsin and how Taylor and the militia could help. And next thing I know, today, Senator DenBraber is hauled out of here looking dead and Taylor isn't here but I'm supposed to call and 'set the ball in motion with the militia.' And I have no clue what is going on but I'm not supposed to whisper a word to anyone about this…"

"I'm not just anyone. As I remember, I paid you to keep me on top of whatever he does. Turns out, you haven't kept your end of our bargain."

"First, I don't care that you paid me. I have no idea why you've been paying me, why you just don't talk to your son directly. He's your son, after all. Your son... Plus, there's Colonel Tuttle, who's in touch with both of you all the time, as far as I can tell."

"I don't trust Tuttle," Will said. "I told you that. Don't. Trust. Tuttle."

"There's something really bad happening here, isn't there?" Kelli said. "And it started with you calling me and asking me to be your little spy, and Taylor, well, he's always told me 'don't trust the Man.' And sure enough, now Senator DenBraber is maybe dying or something, the stupid reporters and the cops are on my last nerve and the governor, he's in here working on a speech acting all cocky and full of himself while my husband is off somewhere." The thought of Taylor engaged in real warfare or worse stopped her. She had to remind herself that he was in no condition to fight, not now, not with him in that back brace ever since a moron at work, a ponytail-wearing ex-con named Jerry Plannenberg, had backed into him with a forklift. A lawsuit was pending and their lawyer had said he needed to keep the back brace on and lay low at home until a settlement was reached. The back brace was good luck, really; it was the only reason Taylor was home and not at the stupid militia conclave out west somewhere. And it would most definitely keep him out of what-the-heck-ever was happening with Wisconsin. But she didn't care. She'd had her fill of this nonsense and this day.

"A speech?" Will Hoeksma was talking. "He's writing a speech."

"That's what I said."

"On his own."

"No. I said she's helping him."

"Who?"

"Deanna Weatherbury."

"Just the two of them?"

"Yes."

A long sigh. "I told Tuttle no speeches."

Kelli sighed. "You think I'm making it up?"

There was a long, tense silence. Finally, Will, his voice shaking with what Kelli took as probably fury, said, "You must, must, put a stop to this."

Kelli sat up. "Don't tell me what I need to do or not do, not anymore. I don't like the way any of this smells. Because, on top of all this, swear to God, I'm sick and pregnant," Kelli said, sobs now threatening to overwhelm her words. "I am pregnant and something horrible is happening here and the father of my baby, Taylor, my husband, is now caught up in it…" Through her tears, she saw the alert flashing on the desk phone's screen. How long had it been flashing? The whirr of the ringing line, why hadn't she heard it? "Hold on," she said. "Hold on." She put the first line on hold, took a deep gulp, sniffed, and answered the other one. "State of Michigan, the governor's office. How may I help you?"

"It's Governor Oleson. I need to speak with Governor Hoeksma. Now."

Kelli closed her eyes. "Yes, sir. Hold please." By rote, she punched the keystroke combination to put Oleson on hold, opened her eyes, took a breath, then punched the combination to pick up her call with Will. "Look," she said. "I don't know what's happening here right now for sure but I do know it looks like danger or something close to it and yes, you've paid me a small retainer, but now you owe me way more than you pay me. It's not just him and me, Taylor and me, anymore. It's us. Me and Taylor, and maybe, I guess, a baby—oh why, why on earth we took that cruise and I let him talk me into champagne…"

Kelli caught herself, the night in the cabin of the cruise ship playing out in her mind as wonderful, not at all like this day. She swallowed more tears and took a deep breath, resolving to be strong or to at least sound strong. And to never drink champagne again.

The door from the governor's office creaked open a few inches. Governor Bill stuck his head through the opening.

"Was there a call for me?" Governor Bill said.

She swallowed. "Sir?"

"I said, 'was there a call for me?' I heard it ringing." Governor Bill said.

"Ummm." Kelli felt sick to her stomach.

"Hello?" Governor Oleson said.

Governor Bill pushed the door open and took a step into the room. "You OK, Kellster?"

In Kelli's ear, there was the wrong voice, the wrong call. This was Oleson. Could she have picked up the wrong line? Yes. Yes. Oleson was saying, "...really think you need to let me speak to the governor. Unless of course you're speaking for him. And if you are speaking for him, well then you have some explaining to do. Or he does. Or both of you."

Governor Bill, standing there, his lips moving, talking to her. "I was wondering if my dad ever called."

Kelli tried to open her mouth but her jaw was locked.

Oleson, in her ear, said, "I don't know what kind of funny business you have going on over there. But let me be very clear, young lady. Very very clear. I need to speak with the governor of the state of Michigan, and I need to speak with him right now."

Kelli could not open her mouth. So rather than talk she held her hand up, palm out, to Governor Bill Hoeksma, which had the desired effect of stopping him in his tracks. Then Kelli woodenly, robotically, pressed the combination to put Oleson back on hold, looked up at Governor Bill, forced a tight smile to her scarlet cheeks, and nodded toward the phone.

"That him?" Governor Bill said.

Kelli thought for a second about who "him" was. Finally she managed to speak. "Yes. Yes, sir. I mean no. No. It isn't."

Governor Bill frowned.

"What I mean is, this one, it's Oleson. Governor Oleson. He wants to talk," Kelli said, pointing to the phone. "On the phone, to you, for you. Oleson."

Deena had stood and wandered over to the window. Governor Bill scuffled by her and plopped into his desk chair. "Could you excuse me a sec, Deen-o?"

"Certainly," Deanna said without looking at him. She turned to leave.

"No, no. Stay. I just need to take this a second." Governor Bill picked up the office phone and nestled it between his ear and shoulder. "This will just be a minute." He stabbed the pickup code. "Oleson? Listen." On the other end of the line there was a sharp intake of breath. Governor Bill rolled his eyes. "Listen to me," Governor Bill said, "and listen very carefully. I am not going to listen to apologies or explanations or this or that. So if that's why you called, you can just forget it."

Her back still facing him, Deanna grabbed her purse from the table by the office door. She took a peek over her shoulder and gave him what she hoped was an apologetic smile. Governor Bill frowned at her, held up an index finger, and mouthed what she thought was "Hold on," although Deanna wasn't sure; she sometimes overthought mouthing. She smiled anyway, mouthed, "Bathroom," opened the door, grinned at him nervously over her shoulder, and stepped carefully into Kelli's office, closing the door behind her.

Governor Bill scowled, shook his head, and took a deep breath. He thought about what it meant to be the leader in a situation like this one. He pictured George W. Bush on the flight deck of an aircraft carrier, wearing a flight suit. This was a leader's time, he thought, and even though he usually didn't like being in these situations, here he was. He sat in his chair and put his feet on the desk. Into the phone, he said, "Listen to me. This awful, horrible decision I've had to make, well, you know what? You made it for me. Your hand was in it. So the blood, if there's blood that has to be, like, bled, spilled, shed—whatever—then, well, you might as well have done the shedding, the spilling, the blooding—bleeding, I mean. It's your fault is what I'm saying. Not mine. Mine fault. My fault. You hear me?"

"What are you trying to tell me? Do you even know—"

Governor Bill hung up. For a second he frowned. Governor Oleson's voice had sounded like his father's.

In the outer office, Kelli was picking up the phone again. Deanna gave her a smile and hurried toward the bathroom.

"I'm not a bitch, you know. You think I am but I'm not," Kelli said.

Deanna stopped. "I didn't say you—" She cut off the response. Kelli was talking to the caller, not to her.

"What are you looking at?" Kelli said to Deanna.

Deanna gave her a look and hurried off.

"Ms. Alexander, I have no opinion about you or your relative level of bitchiness. What I do care about is that there is a situation in my state that I believe may involve your office, the governor's office, and it needs to be explained," Governor Oleson said.

"Governor?"

"Yes," Oleson said, his voice shaking.

"Hold on. Oh my gosh. Governor? Oleson?"

"Yes?"

"Oh. I'm. Sir. Hold on. I have my lines messed up, crossed."

"No, I absolutely won't hold on. I—"

Kelli didn't hear the rest of what the governor had to say. The receiver still in her hand, she sat back in the chair. That was the position Deanna Weatherbury found her in moments later—receiver inches from her ear, mouth open, and a peculiar smile on her face—when Deanna returned from the bathroom. Deanna started to walk past the odd tableau—in the bathroom she had swallowed two Xanax, left a voicemail with her therapist, and vowed to herself in the mirror she would not behave the way typical civil servants behaved in times of crisis; in short, she would not give in to her emotions and become an angry, ranting idiot to her idiot boss. This was no easy vow for Deanna to make or keep. Deanna's parents, Baptist missionaries to New Guinea, had been killed when she was an infant; their minivan, crammed with donated fuel oil, was rear-ended in an airport parking lot in Sydney before it could be airlifted to Papua, and Deanna had been raised by a wealthy agnostic aunt who had put her through Yale and who saw the slightest glance at the golden rule as weakness. Even so, Deanna often found herself enveloped in the genetic vapors of her parents' sensitivities to their common man. Now, as she strode by Kelli, who was blotchy-faced and oddly immobile, she stopped. "Are you OK?" Deanna heard herself say. Deanna could feel the Xanax working and sensed a creeping wave of happy apathy that made it all—the collapse of the senator, the business of the speech and Governor Asshole (it was the Xanax calling him that in her head) rubbing her shoulders and talking to her like she was some chick he'd met in a sorority at U of M—seem wonderfully moot.

"I'm getting my period," Kelli said. One plump tear rolled down her cheek.

Deanna stared at Kelli for a moment, trying to think of something to say. The warm mist in her head was making it difficult. To think. Finally, she heard her voice saying, "I get periods." This must have been funny because Kelli began to laugh, which led Deanna to add, "And I hate them," which caused Kelli to laugh so hard she slammed the telephone receiver on its base and stood.

"Want to go get a drink?" Kelli said.

Deanna thought hard. There was an obligation somewhere. And this Kelli woman, her gut told her, was someone she didn't particularly like. But. "Sure," she said. Then she remembered what the obligation was, pondered it, and said, "I don't like speechwriting anyway."

"Great," Kelli said, picking up her purse. "But I'll need to make a pit stop on the way out."

# Chapter Twenty

"You don't know if you buy what we're doing here?" Spud said, spitting the words at Miky. "You, Bo's special lady and the daughter of the founders of Red Sky, question this? You keep talking like that and we'll be dropping you off right here by the side of the road. Or worse."

Miky glared at Spud. "Really?" she said, the heat rising in her chest. Then she imagined Bo giving her a look similar to what Spud was giving her. That cold, blue-eyed stare from Bo made her shiver. She was afraid of her own husband? Yes, sometimes she was.

"Hold on, Spudster. No one's doing nothing like that," Zooker said, his voice soft and reassuring. He laughed, a peacemaker's laugh. "Everyone just chill here a second. Mik is just letting off steam. Just like us. Just, you know, talking shit."

Spud clenched his teeth, opened his mouth to say something more, glanced at Zooker in the rearview and thought better of it. He returned his attention to the highway in front of him.

Miky caught her reflection in the window, in a helmet, looking like GI Jane, like someone from a movie. Despite everything, she felt the urge to laugh. Here they were, thundering through the state like some fuel-injected, high-horsepower crusaders on a holy mission and it was unclear what the mission even was. She shot a glance at Zooker, then turned away, more to hide her smile than to stare again at the countryside. She was with two hardcore militiamen dressed like GI Joes, blindly hurtling toward some potentially violent and certainly criminal confrontation started by who knew, and it all seemed like an insanely stupid joke. Even if they figured out what the heck they were going to do, the chance of success was nil. Zooker had experience in battle; he had that going for him. Spud, he was just a weekend soldier buzzed on a drug he didn't understand. He and Zooker were lost in an intense conversation now, Spud glancing in the rearview, then back to the road, gesturing with one hand, the truck's cruise set on a healthy 79 mph. Miky wanted to laugh. She wanted to scream. She wanted to stop the world from rotating for a few minutes so she could get her bearings.

"What gets me, we all pretty much figured this day was coming," Zooker was saying to Spud. "So today, the call comes and this chick, Pinkie——the one that confirmed us for action?—she heard it was Hoeksma, the Gunvernor himself, giving the orders, like the state government wanted us to be first into Wisconsin."

"No shit?" Spud said.

"I would not shit you."

"Unbe-freaking-lievable," Spud said.

"Yeah, there's just no way," Zooker said.

"Wait. What?" Miky said. She immediately regretted joining in but she couldn't help herself.

"What I'm saying is, we're willing to do this because he supports, like, the militia. But I don't buy that he ordered it."

"Absolutely," Spud said.

"First off, this Pinkie, no way she's got any idea who made the first call," Zooker said.

"Yeah," Spud said. "That shit's all communicated double black blind."

"Double black…?" Miky said.

"…blind. Absolutely," Spud said.

"Which means?" Miky said.

"It means total fucking secret," Spud said, talking to some point out beyond the hood of the truck.

Spud reminded Miky of some of the high school kids she coached; all emotion, no self-control, no common sense. The kids had the excuse of puberty. Spud was just dumb. She swiveled to Zooker in the backseat. He eyed her over the top of his disgusting coffee cup. Miky frowned at him and said, "But we all heard, most of us anyway, the governor wanted our help. That's what Bo said. You know that. Everyone knows that. I mean, it's been no secret, right? I mean, it's totally logical the call came from him—from, like, the governor's office."

"Why we call him that, you suppose?" Spud said.

"Call who what?" Miky said.

"Your man? We all call him 'Bo.' Call everyone else their militia, like, nickname. Except you and Bo."

"On account of because he's Bo," Zooker said. "The real deal, you know. That guy is. The real f-ing deal. Miky here is his lady. No nicknames needed."

"He don't impress me all that much," Spud said.

"If you're trying to get a rise out of me about Bo, think again," Miky said, her teeth clenched.

"Oh, I know about getting a rise," Spud said.

"Spud. Dude," Zooker said.

Spud laughed. He kept his gaze forward, avoiding eye contact with Miky, who was glaring at him. "You, me, Pinkie, the man in the moon—no one's got no idea who made the call for us to attack 'cept the dudes in the shadows," Spud said. "That's how this shit works."

"You're spot-ass-on there, Spud. Lots of sinister shit at work here." Zooker spit.

"Sinister fucking shit," Spud said, shaking his head.

Miky let her helmeted head fall back against the headrest. She was sinking in the quicksand of stupid—Rub's expression—and this could get very dangerous very fast. "Look," she heard herself saying, "like I said, we all heard the rumor that the governor was going to ask us for help. It fits the way that dude is, doesn't it? He's all Rambo, all George W. Bush, strutting around. He wants to be in the fricking militia. Isn't that obvious?" She felt herself getting shrill, which pissed her off, which made her sound more shrill. "Besides, does it really matter who called us? We're here and that's what you want, isn't it? Isn't it?" She let a dry laugh escape and she shook her head. She felt so helpless. She hated helpless. And shrill. She wanted to punch someone. Or go for a run. Or punch someone and then go for a run.

Zooker spit into his cup. Spud stared down the highway. Finally, Zooker said, "Had a frigging spine on him, that George W. Rumsfeld, Cheney, all of them, solid Americans."

"His being Skull and Bones never bother you?" Spud said.

Miky groaned. Round and round; this was how it always went.

"Who, Bush?" Zooker said.

"Who else we talking about? Bush was Skull and Bones. And John Kerry and all. Both of them," Spud said. "Whole bunch of them are."

"You heard of Skull and Bones, Miky? Secret society at Harvard?" Zooker said.

"Yale," Miky said. She sighed. "It's Yale. If you're going to talk nonsense, get it right. Bush went to Yale."

"Same difference. Started as smugglers way back; that's where the name comes from," Zooker said. "Skull and Bones. Bush One was in it. Like Spud says, bunch of them in it."

"Most secret organization in the world. I mean, maybe next to us."

"What does that have to do with anything?" Miky said. She wasn't sure why she needed to intervene. But she felt like screaming and figured that wasn't an option.

"We're just saying, there's more going on behind shit than you know, Miky." Zooker said. "Really scary fucking sinister shit at play."

Miky couldn't stop herself. "You two are waaaay losing me. We're talking about a war here between Michigan and Wisconsin based on some craziness with prairie dogs. How about let's focus on the insanity at hand. If any of this crap we're involved in—this great cheese conspiracy—is true, it's got nothing to do with some grotto-meeting secret society Dick Cheney and Lord knows who is a member of," Miky said. "I mean, call me crazy."

"Zook?" Spud looked in the mirror.

"You're crazy," Zooker said.

Both men laughed.

"Problem is, Miky, you need to stop thinking and start listening," Spud said. "It's all connected."

"Alllll," Zooker said.

"And the minute you get that is the minute you realize the government—state or federal—would never ever…"

"Never ever ever," Zooker said.

"They'd never reach out to us for help for nothing."

"Right."

"The day they did would be the day the Pope himself shit in the woods," Spud said. He stared off for a moment, then said, "Unless they were trying to screw with our heads."

Zooker considered the point. "Oh, I got ya," he said. "I mean, if it's the state wanting us to think it's the state, could be A, they want us *not* to do anything to help or B, they want us to do something and fail on purpose—they figure that's what we would do if we thought it was them," Zooker said. "So their objective would be a negative, like, outcome, either way, basically."

"Right. Exactly."

"Well, that's certainly all crystal clear," Miky said.

They rode in silence for a bit, Miky numbed speechless.

"Course, could be someone closer to us that made the call," Spud said. "You think about that?" He glanced in the mirror at Zooker.

Zooker squirmed in the seat and spit in the cup, wiped his mustache with his hand, then wiped the hand on his pants. "Yeah. I been thinking about that a little."

"If it was someone else, then the rumor about it being the government, well that could be their way of telling us it's not the government," Spud said.

"But who do you think—who would do that?"

"Someone other than the government that wants us to think it's the government so we'd figure it's not," Spud said.

The truck hummed. Miky closed her eyes and waited for the next gold nugget of wisdom. "More I think about it, that's got to be the deal," Zooker said.

"Which?" Spud said.

"This has got to be coming from someone who wants us to think it's not the government. Like, like maybe it's guys like us only they can't do it themselves," Zook said.

"You thinking deep-cover militia, maybe northern Upper Peninsula?" Spud said.

"Oh sure, absolutely. That would have to be it. Upper UP. But I got no idea who," Zook said. "There are secret groups up there nobody, not even Mr. Bo, knows about. They'd have to be the ones making contact like they're the governor."

"Why do you say that?" Miky said.

"Because they're secret, that's why," Spud said.

173

"No. Why would it have to be a militia we don't know about, from the UP?" Miky said. "Never heard of such a thing."

"You know nothing, lady? That Bo keep you in a shoebox?" Spud said.

"If it happened during cross-country season I missed it; that's what he says."

"Cross-country?" Zooker said.

"You coach?" Spud said.

"High school boys and girls," Miky said.

"I was a heckofa runner," Spud said. "Back in the day."

"UP's heckofa dangerous place," Zooker said.

"You bet your UP loving ass it is," Spud said.

"Always been the breeding ground for just about every major, like, violent occurrence that goes on in the lower forty-eight," Zooker said. "Nothing new there. Always been that way. Common knowledge."

"Qualified for states my junior year. Ran 16:52," Spud said.

"Charles Manson and his crowd started there, up around Iron Mountain," Zooker said. "Back in the sixties."

"Charles Manson. Come on," Miky said.

"Charlie Swastika-Head himself."

"Honest to Pete. Sirhan Sirhan came in the country at Sault Ste. Marie," Spud said. "Right?" He glanced in the mirror at Zooker. "And the 9/11 guys supposedly had a connection up in Marquette?"

"Absolutely. Militia guys up there got their hands full with crazies and rumors," Zooker said. "That's why they keep in the deep black background and shit. They smell something like this deal with Wisconsin going bad, they'd let people know, but most likely stay out. Even the Wolveriners got no idea who's up there in the shadows, know what I'm saying?"

"So some secret group up there might want us to think the government wants us to do this," Miky said. "And they think we'll guess it's not the government, so we'll go ahead and do it?"

"There you go."

"Give the lady a prize, Zook. See, Miky, you gotta think this shit through."

"But you're still saying it's possible you're figuring it all wrong," Miky said.

"Could be," Zooker said. "Maybe is the government after all."

"Right. You gotta trust your gut at this point," Spud said.

Zooker said, "Gut says, this is militia guys way up north want everyone in the whole dang world to think the government wants us to come here and do their dirty work."

There was a long pause.

"Unless it's not," Spud said.

"Right. Unless it's not," Zooker said.

Miky made a sound she didn't expect—half groan, half laugh.

Spud stared out at Wisconsin, his jaw jutting. "In which case, gut says this comes down to our core values—you know, liberty and freedom and protecting our own and whatnot."

"Got that right, Spud," Zooker said. He sniffed, spit, and stretched. They both chewed on this for a moment.

"In which case we need to send our friends from the cheese state a message," Spud said.

Zooker suddenly sat up. "You got that right, Spud man. You got that abso-fucking-lutely right."

# Chapter Twenty-One

Miky churned over the logic, or lack of it, in the men's debate. She thought back to the morning, when she'd had a good, clear bead drawn on this day. She'd seen it as an opportunity for some alone time to sort through her feelings about the militia and—this part was tough to admit—about her husband. But somehow, here she was, in the middle of her worst-case scenario.

"All I can say," she said to no one, "I wasn't planning on this today."

"None of us was," Zooker said.

"Why we're here. To react," Spud said. "First line of defense. Go when called. Drop your life and grab your gun."

Miky sighed, opened her mouth to speak, but Zooker cut her off. "In Gulf One, I was blowing dust out of my nose on the road to Kuwait City before I'd barely said goodbye to my lady," he said. "Call-up was fast, I'm telling you; caught all of us off-guard. Course, I'd been in Granada before that—back in the eighties. That was a fast call-up too."

"You were in both?" Miky said.

"Absolutely. And there was no one asking me if it was a convenient time, I'm telling you that."

"Damn straight," Spud said with a laugh and glanced at Miky. "Nobody checking in to see if you were OK with it."

Zooker belched, swallowed, and stared out the window. "Story of my life," he said. "My dad left for LA five minutes after I hit the doctor's catcher's mitt. Guess you could say I was born being on point."

"You were reserves, right?" Spud said.

"No, regular army. Twenty years."

"Twenty years? You don't seem old enough," Miky said, genuinely intrigued by Zooker's biography. It was a nice diversion, if anything. "I guess that's a compliment."

Zooker laughed. "I quit high school and enlisted. Quit during metal shop. Literally. Walked out and went down to the recruiter."

"Seriously," Miky said.

"Yeah. See, Brian Boal and I was trying to make this, like, little pipe bomb; it was fourth hour metal shop with Mr. Diekema—'Toad,' we called him, because that's what the guy looked like, a toad—and somehow Toad got wind of it and come back where we was and asked to, you know, see our project. Wasn't much of a deal, the bomb wasn't. Mr. Toad, he comes back and asks to see and next thing I know Brian's, like, talking about this thing being my deal and him not wanting his mom to get called and him needing to stay eligible for track. Next thing I know Brian Boal's got his hands cupped over his nose and blood is gushing down his shirt and my knuckles are bloody but I'm, like, laughing and shit at old Toad, who's hopping around to get paper towels and telling the other kids to go get the principal, Mr. Rosenau, 'real quick,' and I'm walking away saying something about he can call my mom because I'm fine with it. On my way out the door I see the whole class like 'whoa' fading back out of my way, only Sandy VanKalken is smiling and giving me a fist pump. To this day I regret two things: forgetting to grab the bomb we was making and not sticking around long enough to see where things could go with ol' Sandy. Waltzed down to the recruiter office and got the paperwork. Mom signed it for me that night." Zooker paused and sighed. "Had no idea Reagan was going to go diving into South America 'bout when I finished basic."

"I'm sorry but that's just dumb," Miky said.

"He was a kid. Give him a break," Spud said. "Seriously, you on the rag here? That it?"

Miky ground her teeth and fought back the urge to grab Spud by the throat. She pictured herself going all Sandra Bullock in *Speed*, opening the door to the truck, wind whipping her hair and her clothes, crawling to the roof of the cab, and miraculously hanging on while another pickup driven by Bo pulled alongside, matching Spud's 79 mph exactly, Bo's face looking for a minute like Keanu Reeves' sweet face, that face stern and focused but those eyes of his saying, "C'mon babe, you can do this," she timing her move, jumping into the bed of Bo's truck and landing just so, doing a tight little roll, Bo and her veering off-road, spewing dust, heading west, west, west, the truck become a dust-trailing dot until it drilled an escape hole into the horizon.

"I just didn't expect to be handcuffed to you two in a situation like this." Miky sighed. "Even if I thought this made sense, this attacking Wisconsin deal—it doesn't—but we need, like, a plan and lots of people to carry it out, you know? Only one of us has combat experience. That's it."

"We're tip of the spear," Spud said. "Nothing wrong with that. The rest will catch our backs when they get back from Tulsa. They'll come in a hurry, once they hear what we done."

"Tip of the spear sounds fine if you've got a spear," Miky said. "I mean it's one thing to be confident. It's another thing to realize your operational deficiencies and take a step back."

"Listen to you, talking all 'deficiencies,'" Spud said. "If you need me to show you what kind of spear I got little lady, I'll be more than glad to."

"Dude, Spud, c'mon. Watch your step," Zooker said.

"What I need is for you to start thinking less with what little manhood you have and more with your brain," Miky said. "We're talking spears and nonsense and no one—no one—in this vehicle is planning what we're going to do."

"Someone's sure as hell all antsy now, Zook," Spud said. His eyes flicked to her, to the road, back to her, back to the road. "If you want to try those handcuffs you mentioned previously, I'm game. Might be a good way to calm you down." Spud snorted a laugh.

The business end of the gun's barrel was pressed against his temple before Spud's brain could translate Miky's move—the unsnapping of the holster, the quick draw—as a threat. "You got about five seconds to reconsider your approach." Miky's voice was hot in his ear.

The truck swerved onto the shoulder, tires grumbling on the rumble strip. Spud wrestled the wheel back into his lane, the tires grumbling again about the strip. "What the fu…?"

"Mik," Zook said.

Miky held her position for ten seconds—she clicked off all ten in her head the way her daddy had done it for her when she was chewing her food as a little girl, "one-daddy's-soldier, two-daddy's-soldier, three-daddy's-soldier"—then pulled the gun away, eased back; she was still gripping the ridiculously large pistol, the gun still aimed at a spot just above Spud's right ear, her head tilted as though she were toying with the idea of firing off a round for fun (she was). Spud glanced her way and said, "You're crazy. You know that? Crazy."

"You owe the lady an apology, my man," Zooker said.

"She needs to holster her weapon," Spud said.

Miky cocked the hammer.

Spud glanced toward Zooker. "You see this?" His voice wobbled.

Zooker spit in his coffee cup.

Spud, eyes on the road, swallowed hard.

"The way I see it: If I shoot, drop, and grab, I can steady the truck before we crash," Miky said. "Gonna be messy, though. And awfully loud. Right, Zook?" She glanced toward Zooker, who laughed this time as he spit.

Spud was frozen, face forward, his eyes stealing quick side-glances. "You put your sidearm away, and I'm good."

"Good and what?" Miky said.

"Sheezus," Spud said. He looked at her.

Miky jabbed the weapon toward him.

"Sorry. Fine. I'm sorry," Spud said.

Miky eased the hammer out of the cocked position, flipped on the safety and holstered the gun. "Good-daddy's-soldier," she said to herself.

After an awkward silence, Spud said, "Didn't mean anything by it."

"You're a pig is what you meant by it," Miky said.

They rode in silence for several miles, the tension simmering. Zooker finally spoke. "Whereabouts you from, Spud?"

"What's it to you?"

Zooker laughed. "Someone's got his BVDs up his crack now."

"Born in Des Moines. Raised there. Moved to Muskegon as a grownup—for a job. And since you're going to ask: dad was a urologist, mom was a mom," Spud said.

Zooker thought for a moment. Then he said, "Pee doctor? Your dad?"

"Yep. Spent his life with his finger up asses, especially his own. What my mom said, anyway. They weren't exactly on good terms," Spud said.

"So you had money," Miky said.

"Yeah, a bit," Spud said.

"Could've spent some on an education, seems like," Miky said, her eyes shifting away.

"Why we call you Spud, then? Figure you'd be Pee-boy or something," Zooker said.

Spud laughed.

"Listen," Miky said, "the state line was a ways back. Now, this sign says 'Beloit' right there. See it? Beloit." She gestured at a green and white highway sign. She looked at Zooker. "If you guys are all so big on doing this, let's do this. I mean, since it's just three of us, we're not going to launch some major operation anyway, right?" she said.

"I stole a truckload of potatoes once. Me and a friend of mine," Spud said. "Where the nickname comes from."

"My plan was to head to Madison, Mik. But given the situation, I hear you. We're s'posed to 'engage hostiles.' So we don't have to go all huge here, what with it just being us three," Zooker said. He looked at Spud. "You stole a truckload of what?"

"But why no sense of urgency? Why not just get it done?" Miky was thinking through options that didn't end in death or jail. "We could just, like, call in a bomb threat to a mall. Make it as, like, a political statement. 'Defending Michiganders' and all that."

"Potatoes," Spud said.

Zooker laughed. "What were you smoking that day?"

"It was all about some serious issues with my mother and father is what the shrink said. That and what they call 'poor impulse control,'" Spud said. He laughed. "Always was kind of quick on the trigger, except in the sack, if you know what I'm saying." He shot Zooker a look. "Course, between you and me, that day, there was a bottle of MD 20/20 involved."

"How old?" Zooker said.

"The MD?"

"No," Zooker said and laughed. "You."

"Oh, about the same as you when you did the pipe bomb," Spud said.

"Seventeen?" Zooker said.

"Something like that," Spud said. "Sixteen, seventeen."

"Freedom and self-protection bullshit aside, is there a specific objective once we, like, attack someone?" Miky said. "An end game?"

"Packed me off to military school after that. After I got off probation," Spud said. "Course, it backfired."

"How so?" Zooker said.

"Any idea who the 'hostiles' would be?" Miky said. In her head, she saw chubby-cheeked people with Green Bay Packers gear. She pictured Aaron Rodgers and Brett Favre. She didn't think she could shoot them.

"Wisconsin people. That's our objective," Zooker said, sounding irritated. "This thing is really up to us, I guess." He tapped Spud on the shoulder. "How'd it backfire?"

Spud shot a glance at Miky. He waited for her to speak. When she didn't, he said, "My mom wanted me out of the house; I think she figured I was the problem with, you know, their marriage and all. My dad basically hated my guts by then. Always talking about how I had 'no ambition' and shit. I mean, totally ashamed of me. I was a real tool, you know. Don't know what the deal was, looking back at it. Always felt like I was born to the wrong family, is what I told the shrink my old man sent me to. Dad, he just wanted me to go rot somewhere—be miserable. So to show him up, I really, like, committed myself to doing good in military school. I mean, I flat-out loved it." Spud stared out the windshield. "They were divorced within six months of me leaving home and I laughed my ass off."

"C'mon, guys. Listen. Let's think about this together. OK?" Miky said.

Neither man spoke.

"What's our objective?"

"Just told you," Zooker said. "We're s'posed to engage and then it's pretty much our call. Need to tell these assholes and everyone else that we're not gonna be messed with."

"But what's the plan?"

"Listen to you," Spud said. "Little Miss Plan."

"You're ducking the question," Miky said.

"OK. How about this? How about we just find someone to shoot? You want that? Because I can do that." Spud's face was turning dangerously red. He jerked the truck into the left lane and gunned it to pass a minivan. Spud waved at the driver, a pretty girl of about eighteen. The girl frowned. A woman in the front passenger's seat—Spud figured it was the girl's mom—leaned forward to get a look at him. A crooked smile cracked Spud's face. "This van here. Looks hostile to me." The woman's face went from inquisitive to alarmed. "Definitely hostile; don't think they like us wearing all this gear." He cut over, forcing the girl driver to break and swerve.

"Leave 'em, Spud," Zooker said with a chuckle, looking back at the girl. She had a panicked look on her face, but managed to get her vehicle back under control. "There's better fish to fry than a chick and her mommy."

"Gotcha." Spud glanced in the rearview and slowed the truck. He drove in silence for several moments, and then glanced at Miky. "The mission here, you ask me? It's to kick ass," he said. "Kick. Ass."

Zooker laughed. "Miky, listen. It's not like we're knocking off the government—just us three. But we're s'posed to get noticed."

"What I said, exactly," Spud said.

Zooker smiled at Spud. "Way I see this, it'd be way cool to capture the what-you-call-it. The bioweapons. The shit they been making. That's the big goal right there." Zooker sniffed and spit into his cup. "But one thing I learned a long time ago, you got to adjust to what's happening in the field. With three of us, this isn't gonna be like a full-scale invasion or some shit. That being said, we got lots of room here. We could drive to Madison and take over the capitol building…"

"But the bioweapons is what it is; what we got to get, ultimately," Spud said. "This prairie dog thing and who knows what all else there could be."

"Monkeypox," Zooker said.

"Right, but I'm saying they could have other stuff. We got to get that too," Spud said. "Somehow."

"And all this stuff is at the state capitol? You know that for sure? They have some building with a big sign that says 'Bioweapons'? We're gonna waltz in and blow it up and kill, like, half of Madison in the process?" Miky said.

"Spud does like to blow shit up," Zooker said.

Spud smiled. "Tru dat."

"Really?" Miky felt the heat again in her chest. "Really? Forget the fact we're, like, totally outmanned. Now you're talking like terrorists."

"We're Americans," Spud said.

"What's that got to do with it?" Miky said.

"We aren't a bunch of jihadists blowing up shit and killing people just to do it," Spud said. "That's just not in our nature. Terrorist ain't in us."

"I don't even know where to start on that comment," Miky said.

"Relax. We got this, Mik," Zooker said. "We're just out in front of all the, like, thinking and shit."

"This kind of shit's always best handled that way," Spud said.

"Without thinking," Miky said.

"Kind of, yeah," Zooker said.

"Spud's highly qualified for that," Miky said. She sighed. "Perfectly qualified not to think." She looked out her window. "Lord help us." She leaned so she could watch the minivan recede in the side-view mirror. She had always assumed and hoped life in the militia would never come to this. She wanted to go home, which made her feel ashamed, which made her want to cry, which made her angry.

Spud said, "Miky, you keep thinking so hard you're going to end up dead or worse."

"Yeah, we're all trained at level three. We know what to do," Zooker said.

"Damn straight. I re-certified last month," Spud said.

Miky closed her eyes. Rub had hated bullshitters like Spud. Bo was all for strategy and knowing the objective, avoiding the loss of innocent life. But she could also imagine Bo and her dad, God rest his soul, getting caught up in the moment—this moment—and just jumping in, guns first. "I feel like I'm going to puke," she said to her reflection. Her reflection looked like puking was an option. "I think we just need to do something here and get it done."

Zooker sat up, leaned into the space between the front seats and stared through the windshield. Well ahead of them on the divided interstate highway, an impossibly green Hummer was swerving from lane to lane. "Would you look at that?" Zooker said; he gave Spud's shoulder a tap. Spud glanced at Zook then at the Hummer. He leaned on the gas. "Easy, Spud. Go in easy," Zooker said.

"Zook?" Miky was staring at Zooker, mouth open.

"Steady up, Miky. You're the one who wants some action," Zooker said. "Wisconsin plates on that thing. Makes them fair game."

"Are you sure? I mean, you said Madison was the objective, right?" Miky said, realizing she was reversing her previous opinion concerning Madison. This made her feel stupid and a little like a ninny, but she couldn't help herself. The Hummer was an ugly green reality; Madison was a foreign city she'd seen only in pictures. "We let that minivan go, you know."

"Orders were to 'engage hostiles.' You said it yourself—we could just do something right here, right now, to get a little attention." Zooker had leaned back in his seat. He unloaded the wad of tobacco into the cup with a hard spit and unsnapped his holster. "These guys look hostile to you, Spud?"

"Definitely. Absolutely," Spud said, a note of glee in his voice. "Hostile."

"Hostile as hell," Zooker said.

"Whoa," Spud said. Ahead, the Hummer veered hard to the right, the big vehicle tilting wildly, then it left the road, jounced into the deep ditch and rolled up onto a grassy area bordering some pine trees.

Zooker looked at Miky, then slapped Spud on the shoulder and said, "I don't need no sign from God. But if you do, that's it, right there. Go get them, Spudster."

# PART THREE

# War is What You Make It

# Chapter Twenty-Two

During one of his five otherwise ill-spent years at Northwestern University, Benjamin Nighthorse III had a brief, enlightening affair with a professor of English Literature, Dr. Marci Hunt. Benjamin was a Potawatomi. For generations, his family had lived happily among the 10,000 lakes of the land which, for the past 175-ish years, had been called "Wisconsin." Dr. Hunt had what she described as a "smidgen" of Navajo blood and a deep reservoir of passion. What began as a full-throttle physical relationship led to a pillow-talk bond over the long sad history of the American government's treatment of North America's natives. Before she dumped Benjamin for a quieter, less drunk graduate assistant from Sudan, Dr. Hunt ignited in Benjamin a pride in his heritage and suspicion of the government that became both admirable and tiresome.

"Don't call me Native American," his standard rant began. "I'm not some contrived demographic descriptor dreamed up in a politically enlightened age. I am an American Indian of the Potawatomi tribe. Proud and red."

Strangers who heard Benjamin's description of himself as "Indian" found it fascinating; most had long since trained themselves to use the "Native American" label, believing it demonstrated an enlightened disapproval of the "Indian" term's inaccurate and unseemly origins. Acquaintances, friends, and family, and there were plenty of them in his hometown of Back Prairie, Wisconsin, mostly understood Benjamin's point: America's natives had been called "Indians" for the better part of four centuries; the name had, by all accounts, stuck. Changing it to something more accurate wouldn't change what the Europeans had done to Benjamin's ancestors—the raping, killing, seizing of land, and so on. Yes, it was a valid point. The problem was, Benjamin kept making the point. Benjamin liked to drink. He liked to talk. He did plenty of both. It got on nerves.

It didn't help that Benjamin was an extremely intelligent, stupidly wealthy, spoiled, narcissistic asshole, according to most who knew him, including his mother. He was a classic example of messenger soiling message.

Benjamin's family had owned Back Prairie's Blue Indian Baking Soda Co. since the firm's founding, in the late 1800s, by Benjamin's great-great-uncle Johnny, whose likeness still considered the baking public with proud scorn from each (blue) box of Blue Indian. The company was the state's first American-Indian-owned business and long had been the nation's third-ranked baking soda in terms of annual sales volume, this despite the efforts of Benjamin's frenetic father, Benjamin Jr., who, in the late 1980s, attempted to rouse the brand from decades of mild profitability and relative stagnation with a brand extension to the health-and-beauty segment. Blue Indian Antiperspirant Paste not only failed to nudge repeat-sales figures, it gave several thousand first-time users of the Extra Dry formula a blistering underarm rash; the market's reaction temporarily dropped Blue Indian to sixth place and may have contributed to Benjamin Nighthorse Jr.'s premature death, in October 1988, of a self-inflicted gunshot wound. Benjamin Jr.'s successor, Benjamin III's brother

Jonathan, guided Blue Indian Baking Soda back to the comfortable third position in the highly competitive baking soda marketplace. This was well received in Back Prairie, a company town where ambition was considered sinful and the status quo was embraced with reserved gusto. For Benjamin, his father's demise and his brother's rise combined with a sense of entitlement a co-inherited fortune couldn't satisfy. Benjamin was unhappy and bored. He was also smart, passionate, and had a great capacity for alcohol and women. In the three years since leaving Northwestern, he had been spending his share of the family fortune jetting the world in his private Lear, hooking up with and discarding female companions at a what's-your-name? rate while partying with an aimless, roving band of similarly disconnected celebrities, near-celebrities, and hangers-on. Everywhere he went— *everywhere*—Benjamin would drink and talk, talk, talk.

In Back Prairie, where Benjamin frequently returned to rest, dry out, and play devoted son to the mother whose waning tolerance he needed both emotionally and financially, the non-American-Indian locals bristled at Benjamin's outspokenness. But they were mostly polite Lutherans keen to see the good in people, and so, when asked about him, they typically pointed out that Benjamin was a smart young man with a gift for conversation and a way with the ladies. These were his talents, they'd say accurately with a smile and a wink. Those talents explained why the twenty-six-year-old half-drunk, bleary-eyed American Indian, who was at the wheel of his custom-green Hummer on a remote section of Wisconsin highway, could so profoundly affect his companion, Sassy Bones—she most recently an employee of The Lazy Ladies Gentleman's Club in Windsor, Ontario. Sassy was seemingly mesmerized by Benjamin's good looks and gift for gab—truth be told it was his not-so-subtle display of a seemingly endless supply of cash that held her attention—and this was unfortunate. Because, had Ms. Bones shown less regard for Benjamin's ramblings and right thigh—she was alternately massaging and squeezing it with a long-red-fingernailed left hand—Benjamin might have stopped his self-absorbed speechifying long enough to see the black truck approaching in the rearview mirror. And if he had, who knew? Benjamin may have placed a figurative ear to the ground, heard the approaching hoofbeats of trouble and made a move to avoid them. At the very least, Benjamin might have kept the Hummer moving down the highway. But Sassy's enchantment was enhanced by alcohol, quite a bit of it—they had been drinking peppermint schnapps from a paper-bag-protected bottle since their last stop, at a convenience store on the Indiana toll road just east of Chicago—so she needed to "tinkle."

"That's the fourth time you've mentioned the bathroom," Benjamin said, knowing she had, in fact, said it no less than seven times.

"C'mon baby, I really got to wee," Sassy said. She chewed her bottom lip and looked at the countryside flashing past. "I'll go anywhere."

"Perhaps you could pucker."

"I can't. Not anymore."

Benjamin hit the brakes and palmed the wheel hard to the right. The Hummer teetered on two wheels, bounced back to four, took the ditch in a bounding, contorted leap, and growled up the knoll that separated the ditch from a grove of pines. Somehow, Benjamin manhandled the Hummer to a stop before they hit one of the trees. "How's this?" he said, and turned to flash her a smile, but squealing tires from behind them snapped the smile to a frown. Benjamin shot a glance at the rearview as Sassy threw the door open and ran for the trees.

\*\*\*

"We did it, Zook. Damn. We did it," Spud said.

"Good effort," Zooker said. He and Spud were standing over Sassy Bones and Benjamin Nighthorse; both were face down in the soft bed of pine needles, arms tied behind their backs, about two tree-rows into the grove.

"Went down like a sack of taters," Spud said. "One punch to the noggin. And her—you even touch her?"

"Just grabbed her arm and she fainted," Zooker said. He toed Benjamin Nighthorse in the ribs.

"He's coming around. So's she," Spud said. "She's a hot one, isn't she? And him—he look Indian to you? I mean, like, feather Indian not dot."

"Dot?" Zooker said.

"You know, that dot thing the other kind of Indian wears on their forehead," Spud said. He bent over to study Benjamin Nighthorse. "Sure looks Indian." He thought for a moment. "Feather. Not dot. Native American."

"You didn't give them a chance to just, like, surrender or anything," Miky said. She was several yards away, crouched, her back against a tree. "Aren't you supposed to do that? At least let them surrender?" She was trembling. "Listen to me. 'Surrender.'" She snorted. "For what?"

On the expressway, an SUV approached from the south. Miky crawled three rows deeper into the grove and settled against another tree. The SUV sped past, buffeting the tall grass in the ditch. "May I ask you geniuses what the plan is if another vehicle stops?"

"They can't see us up here in the trees," Zooker said.

"They can see our truck and for darn sure his Hummer. That's some kind of green."

"You'll be fine," Spud said. He toed Benjamin Nighthorse's leg and leered at Sassy. Benjamin kicked out; a tassel-loafered foot caught Spud's ankle. Spud stumbled, tried to regain his footing, arms windmilling, his helmeted head bouncing off a tree as he went down.

Zooker took three steps back. "Whoa now." He laughed. "Not your best landing there, Spud." Zooker looked at Benjamin. "Dude's got some fight in him."

Spud stood—too fast—stumbled, and fell to one knee. Benjamin Nighthorse growled and struggled to roll over. Sassy Bones lifted her head; eyes wild, she spit dirt and pine needles and tried to speak, but all she could manage was a strangled "Benny?"

"Here," Benjamin Nighthorse said.

"What the hell?" Sassy was bucking, twisting. "Who are you idiots? What makes you think—"

"Hold on," Benjamin grunted; he twisted his torso to get a look at Sassy. "Careful what you say."

Spud scrambled to his feet as Zooker helped Benjamin roll over. Spud drew his weapon, walked to Benjamin, stopped, gripped the gun with two hands, and aimed it at a spot just below a lock of hair on Benjamin's forehead. Blood trickled from Benjamin's nose; some was smeared on his cheek.

"Let's get one thing straight. I'm an Indian. And I'd advise you to address me that way," Benjamin Nighthorse said to Spud. "I'd also point out that you cold-cocked me like some punk outside a bar." He sniffed and looked at Zooker. "Not sure what's up with all the GI Joe gear. But I'm guessing you want money."

Spud said, "I'm guessing you want to be the first casualty of war."

Miky, eyes on the road, stood and walked carefully toward Sassy. Another car approached and rocketed past.

"Put the gun away, Spud." Miky knelt and helped Sassy roll over. "Looks like you two are political prisoners. Or something."

"Wow, listen to Miky," Zooker said. "Taking charge."

"This is war, motherfucker," Spud said. He squatted and pressed the gun's muzzle into Benjamin Nighthorse's forehead. "And you can be K-I-A in a heartbeat."

"Listen to Spud," Miky said with a you-can't-be-serious look at Spud. "Going to blow people away."

"He's not," Benjamin Nighthorse said.

"Don't bet on it," Spud said.

Benjamin chuckled. He tried in vain to pull away but Spud pinned him to the ground with the muzzle to his forehead. "I'm half drunk," Benjamin said, "and I can tell you're no killer, although you do appear to be intent on skewering me with that thing."

"Why don't you think Spud will kill you?" Zooker said.

"He has a sort of feminine quality about him," Benjamin said. "I think he's in touch with that side of himself. And part of him is empathetic with my situation here. Definitely not a killer."

Spud frowned. Zooker smiled. There was something he liked about this Indian guy. "Spud, lighten up, buddy. Him fighting back was just what you would've done. No harm done."

"I said 'political prisoners;' you're more like prisoners of war, I guess," Miky said. She looked down at Sassy, who was now on her back, hands still behind her. She looked uncomfortable. Miky offered her a hand. Sassy made a face and twisted away.

"Thought you guys didn't liked being called Indian," Zooker said.

Sassy Bones groaned and rolled her eyes. "Don't go there."

"Actually, if you were to ask, you'd find most of my people prefer it," Benjamin Nighthorse said. "After several hundred years the name has become a part of our identity. The term 'Native American' is an attempt, if you will, to complete the eradication of the people who called North America home when the first European conquerors arrived centuries ago."

"Wow. Listen to you. You some kind of professor?" Zooker said. "Or a lawyer or what?"

"I am neither. I am merely an advocate for fairness," Benjamin said.

"He's been talking like that since Windsor," Sassy said, still refusing to look at any of them.

"You're from Windsor?" Miky said.

"Yes, I'm from Windsor. You got a problem?"

Miky thought for a moment. "No," she said and looked at Zooker, "but we might."

"Un-fucking-tie me," Sassy Bones said and shot Miky a stare.

"You sure you're not from Detroit?" Miky said. "That would help a little. Or Milwaukee; that'd be even better."

"Windsor born and raised. It's where I live."

"Shit," Zooker said. "Canada."

"That's what I'm getting at," Miky said.

Zooker looked at Benjamin and nodded toward the Hummer. "That sweet ride of yours has Wisconsin plates."

"I am a native of this state, yes, and a pretty well-regarded one," Benjamin said.

Spud glared at Zooker. "You let him keep going on and on like that. Like he's your buddy all the sudden."

"We're OK with this one, Mik," Zooker said. To Spud he said, "Sorry but I kind of like this guy. I like his attitude."

"What about her?" Miky said.

"Jury's still out. But he reminds me of a guy we captured on the wrong side of the wire one night near Kuwait City. Ended up shooting the shit with him half the night. A terrorist like the rest of them, but a good talker."

"No. What about her? She is not from Michigan or Wisconsin or even America," Miky said.

Zooker frowned. "She just happened to be in the car. I'm thinking it's like what they call collateral damage or whatever, right?"

Miky shook her head and closed her eyes.

"Sounds to me like you've made some miscalculations," Benjamin said.

"Sounds to me like I'm going to have to bust a bomb up your ass," Spud said.

"What did you just say?" Zooker said.

Spud stuck out his jaw. "You heard me."

Zooker laughed. "Bust a bomb. Up his ass?"

Miky said, "I think he means 'bust a cap' or something."

"I have no idea what he means by 'bomb' or how he intends to drop it," Benjamin said.

"That's what you call physically impossible, Spud," Zooker said.

"Or at the very least it's a maneuver requiring medical supervision, and some pretty small munitions," Benjamin said.

"Spud here does not know how to talk," Miky said to Sassy. "Or how to communicate with the civilized world, for that matter." She took another look at Sassy, then at Benjamin. The situation seemed calm enough. She had no plan, no idea of what to do to get them out of this mess; keeping things calm appeared to be the best strategy for now. "Spud, let's just have you take a deep breath here."

Spud, jaw clenched, gun planted firmly on Benjamin Nighthorse's forehead, stared into Benjamin's eyes and said, "I am telling you, ordering you as my prisoner, to shut your Native American feather ass up."

Benjamin closed his eyes and said, "I have been given permission to speak by the spirit of the people who sanctified the ground you're corrupting. The same people whom your government double-crossed. The people your forefathers so artfully swindled."

Spud's eyes were slits. His arms trembled. He shifted his weight from one foot to the other.

"We're no big fans of the federal government ourselves," Zooker said.

"This thing with you is political, then?" Benjamin said.

"I should blow this dickstick away anyway," Spud said. He cocked the gun.

"Oh my gawd," Sassy Bones said.

"Spud," Zooker said.

"Dickstick?" Miky said.

"Don't worry, folks, he's harmless," Benjamin Nighthorse said, his eyes now locked on Spud's.

"Spud. Come on. Holster that sidearm," Miky said. "And stop talking like..."

"Clint Eastwood?" Zooker said. "Rambo?"

"No, no," Miky said, frowning. "I was thinking, like, Chuck Norris. In seventh grade." She couldn't help herself. She laughed.

"Mission was 'engage the enemy,'" Spud said.

"Actually, it was 'hostiles.' Engage 'hostiles,' I believe," Miky said. "There is nobody here who looks hostile. Except maybe you, Spud."

Now Zooker had his arm around Spud, his mouth near Spud's ear. "Look at that car," Zooker said. "Look at him. Listen to him. He's got value; you just know he does."

"Don't worry, he hasn't any intention to do a thing," Benjamin said. "It's just not in him to hurt me."

Zooker shot a look at Benjamin. "You're not helping me here," Zooker said.

"Let him be, Spud," Miky said. "C'mon."

Spud thought about it for several seconds. Finally, he slowly straightened and stepped back.

Benjamin Nighthorse closed his eye and sighed. "As I expected."

Zooker patted Spud on the back. "Look, man." He gestured at the ugly red welt on Benjamin's forehead. "He's a dot Indian now."

# Chapter Twenty-Three

Back when Zooker was in high school, he'd spent a lot of time at his girlfriend's, Sheila's, house mostly because he liked Sheila's mom, liked her a lot, way more than he liked his own mom and a little more than he liked Sheila, a fact that became an issue and led to Sheila dumping him in a wild, screaming fit one afternoon when they were in Sheila's basement rec-room and he was hoping to maybe get to second base with Sheila and had ended up instead spending all of his energy denying that he liked her mom "that way."

It was Sheila's mom who'd told him you get more flies with honey than you get with vinegar. He didn't know exactly what sort of flies he needed to get from Benjamin Nighthorse and Sassy Bones, but his gut told him they'd eventually buzz into view. So as they rolled down the highway, Miky driving the Hummer, Zooker riding shotgun, Sassy Bones and Benjamin Nighthorse in the rear seat, handcuffed hands in their laps, Spud trailing, driving his pickup, Zooker figured he'd chat them up, draw the prisoners in, get them comfortable. He'd seen guys do it before with POWs. Mostly in Gulf I. Besides, he kind of liked talking to the Indian.

It took about ten miles to explain the whole deal to the two of them (Zooker, of course, glossed over the secret parts and just covered the high points of the prairie dogs, monkeypox, and Denton McAllister), after which Benjamin Nighthorse said, "Now that is one serious crock of spectacular shit."

"Which part?" Zooker said.

"The whole thing."

"There are some details about it I'm not going to be telling you but it's definitely the real deal," Zooker said, trying to convey the seriousness of the situation. "This is a major, major conspiracy some of your state people are up to."

"Major Major?" Benjamin said. "Like, Joseph Heller?"

"Great book," Miky said softly.

"One of you can read," Benjamin Nighthorse said. "That's a relief."

"So you kidnapped us," Sassy Bones said.

"Captured," Miky said. "I think."

"But we're just two people riding down some stupid road in the middle of no-f-ing-where," Sassy said.

"It's a war," Zooker said. "Got to start it somewhere."

"Do we?" Miky let the question slip before she had a chance to gulp it back. "I mean, did we?" She kept her eyes locked on the highway.

Zooker frowned. "Watch yourself, Mik."

"Do I detect dissension in the ranks?" Benjamin said.

Miky let out a long sign.

"You can't just wake up one morning and start attacking people on some stupid highway and say, hey, sorry—war," Sassy Bones said.

"Governments been doing shit like this since beginning of time," Zooker said.

"You're not the government," Sassy said. "You're just some yay-hoos from Michigan, dressed like little toy soldiers or something."

"Before you shoot her for saying that, realize that she does have a point," Benjamin said. "Then again, I'm afraid both of you have points. The legitimacy of your right to protect yourself is unquestioned. However, I don't think that right extends to what is now an adversarial role in some kind of preemptive action against people of another state. While I would support almost any act against a government, you're in hazy legal territory here, my friends. And the story, the background, on this sounds as contrived as anything ever put forth by Hollywood." He laughed. "Who set all this in motion, may I ask?"

Zooker sighed, took a deep breath, and then, for Benjamin, he talked through the convoluted debate he and Spud had conducted earlier. When he was finished, Benjamin said, "I say it again, someone's playing you here, dude. You know that, right?"

"You don't have to tell me that," Miky said.

Zooker shot Miky a look, and then twisted to eye Benjamin. "You watch yourself," Zooker said. "I like you, man. But don't be questioning what we're doing here."

They rode in silence for several seconds. Finally, Benjamin said, "Now I get the deal with her being Canadian. That could be a problem for you, couldn't it?"

"Like I say, collateral damage," Zooker said.

"But that's not what they mean by collateral damage," Miky said. "Collateral damage is, like, when you drop a bomb and it kills more than just—"

"Why not just let me go?" Sassy said. "I mean, what are you going to do with me anyway?"

"He's not sure," Miky said. She stole a glance at Zooker. Zooker grinned.

"She's got a pretty hefty point," Benjamin said. "You guys are flying out here in the wind—responding to what? Some kind of imagined attack? Pretty thin ice."

"It's a first-strike deal like Bush, case you were wondering. How he went into Iraq. Premature, like that," Zooker said.

"You mean pre-emptive," Miky said.

"What I said."

"An historic failure by an imperialist government is what I call it," Benjamin said. "You guys up to that legacy?"

"Do you ever shut up?" Sassy Bones said, falling back into her seat, her voice a hiss.

"Like I told you, you get no arguments from us on Bush and Cheney and Rumsfield—all them," Zooker said.

"Feld," Miky said. "Rums-feld."

"Way we see it," Zooker said, "9/11 gave them an excuse to cut civil liberties, piss on the Bill of Rights, and keep rabble-trousers like us in check, which was all just a starting point for them to launch their big plan to knock off Saddam. Some of us even suspect Bush and all them let the attack happen."

"Paranoid much?" Sassy said.

"What I'm saying is," Zooker said, "once they had their opposition here at home in check, well they were free to waltz into Baghdad and get all that oil for their buddies. That was their plan from the get-go and we all know it. We're no backers of theirs. Not at all. They're part of the Ivy-League-Wall-Street-K-Street-Halliburton-deal that runs this country. They all wanted revenge on account of what Saddam did to Bush's daddy, and it was a way for Halliburton and so on to get their hooks into all that black gold over there. Just like the first Gulf war, which wasn't about revenge, obviously, but was a way for Bush-the-senior to pay back his friends, the Saudis, for them digging up dirty stuff on Dukakis so he, Bush, could win the election in '88; see, Bush-the-senior went in and kept that Kuwait oil out of Saddam's dirty hands, with the help of yours truly, and that kept the old House of Saud happy and also, of course…"

Zooker droned on for several minutes.

"I really could use something to eat right now. I'm starved," Miky said, finally breaking the rant.

Zooker frowned for a moment. "So you actually hungry or just trying to shut me up?"

"Both."

Zooker glanced back at the prisoners. Sassy managed a tight smile. "I got to tinkle," she said.

"Sorry, folks," Zooker said, with a snort. "Always did have a gift of gab, my mom said. Could talk the ears off an acre of corn. Sometimes I get going on this stuff and I could just talk forever, seems like."

"I understand. You have passion. That's not a bad thing," Benjamin Nighthorse said. Benjamin took a deep breath, and then let it out slowly. "Believe it or not, I don't think our views on things are all that different."

Zooker took a second to mull this. Then he said, "Meaning what exactly."

"Meaning, listen to you talk, maybe we should have a meeting of the minds here." Benjamin's words were coming out before he could completely process what he was saying—a fact he knew had something to do with the alcohol still in his system and the knot of fear in his belly. He swallowed. "What I'm saying is, let's stop and get something to eat, sure, and let Ms. Bones relieve her godforsaken bladder. And maybe just talk things over."

Zooker looked at the floor of the truck and thought about it. He'd always trusted his gut, whenever things got weird. Things were weird. And there was something about this guy, something he liked. He looked at Benjamin. Zooker smiled. "OK, then. Let's go get us some Arby's."

Benjamin smiled then. Zooker couldn't help himself. He smiled too.

# Chapter Twenty-Four

History often turns on the most unlikely of details. In this case, there were no Arby's restaurants at the next three exits. So just before the fourth, with Sassy warning of impending disaster, they settled on a Cracker Barrel. Zooker stuck a hand out the window, jabbed a finger at the restaurant chain's billboard, and signaled to Spud to take the exit.

His father had spanked then eight-year-old Spud in a Cracker Barrel bathroom while on a family vacation in Columbus, Ohio. Spud had always hated the smell, the look, the food—everything about the chain. Now, as the familiar, ugly, orangey logo came into view, a cloud of irritation enveloped him. It melded quickly with the still-simmering humiliation of his encounter with the Indian dude, Benjamin Nighthorse, and with Spud's growing impatience with their mission. Zooker smoked a lot of dope. It took the edge off. This was no time for taking the edge off. This was time to get your edge fucking up.

On the exit ramp, Spud honked his horn, flashed his lights, and pulled off onto the shoulder. Miky swore and hit the brakes, wrestled the Hummer to a stop, then hit reverse and backed up to Spud's pickup. Spud was at Zooker's window, pounding like a cop with a warrant on a drug dealer's door, before Miky had the big vehicle in park. Zooker buzzed down the window.

"I know you're all chill and 'let's take this one step at a time,' but I just… hear me out."

Zooker shot Miky a frown then turned back to Spud. "What's on your mind, man?" He grinned. "Although I think I know what you're about to say."

"Zook. Let's do this thing. Let's attack these sons of bitches. Here. Now. The Cracker Barrel, I mean. Them," Spud said, jerking his head in the direction of the restaurant, eyes shining, his voice a razor. "Let's take the place down, Zook. Make a statement." Spittle flecked his days-old stubble. He jabbed a finger into Zooker's armor-protected chest.

Zooker let the thought hang there, the smile on his face lingering. "Well, we are all dressed up."

"I know, right?" Spud grinned. He punched Zooker in the shoulder. "Let's do this." Punch. "Let's." Punch. "Do. This." Punch, punch.

"Whoa there, Tonto," Benjamin Nighthorse said. The leather seats protested as he leaned forward. "I thought we were going to have a conversation after some lunch."

Miky's stomach felt like a fist. Later, she would question why she stayed silent. The only answer she ever had for herself was that she wanted to let the air out of the balloon. The problem was, Spud and Zooker were going to attack someone sooner or later, weren't they?

The Cracker Barrel stood just off a busy street lined with the usual assortment of chain retailers and gas stations. The restaurant was in an asphalt ocean, the other shoreline of which was a Menards home improvement warehouse. Long, landscaped islands defined the restaurant's share of the parking bounty.

At Menards, a few customers were coming and going amid a smattering of vehicles. On the street, traffic was heavy. Spud's truck peeled off from the scrum, roared into the parking lot and stopped abruptly, straddling the yellow-lined parking places, fifty feet or so from the door of the Cracker Barrel. It was a reckless, pointless move, Miky thought, Spud's way of announcing their arrival. Zooker insisted she do the same. "This is nuts," she said as she hastily completed a similar maneuver, shoved the Hummer into park and shut off the ignition.

Before Miky had the keys out of the ignition, Zooker was out of the vehicle and opening the rear door. "Let's move, people." He pulled Sassy Bones from the back seat and kicked her door shut. Pushing her ahead of him, he came around the back of the Hummer and opened the rear door on the driver's side. "Come on," he said to Benjamin.

"Let me go. I'm telling you," Sassy said.

"Let it be, babe. Let it be," Benjamin said. He stepped out. Zooker, still holding Sassy, grabbed Benjamin by an arm.

"We don't have to make a scene, you know," Miky said. She risked a glance toward the street. A couple of cars had slowed, creating gaps in the traffic approaching a traffic light, the drivers looking their way, the vehicles behind them suddenly forced to brake. A bearded guy wearing a baseball cap and sunglasses and driving an old Volvo station wagon had rolled down his window, as though that would help him see better. Miky could read his lips as he leaned his head out the window to gawk: "What the fu…?"

She realized how ridiculous they looked in their military gear next to the green Hummer. She wanted to crawl into a hole and disappear.

Spud jogged up. He already had pulled his weapon; it was pointed down at the pavement. The knot tightened in Miky's gut. She swung her gaze across the nearly empty parking lot, felt a gasp of relief, but then looked toward Menards. A fat woman in a pink sweatshirt, black yoga pants, and sunglasses was looking toward them, mouth open. The woman called to a skinny, blue-jeaned man who was sauntering ahead of her. The man stopped and followed her gaze as the woman turned and pointed toward Miky.

Miky looked at Spud and Zooker. "This is stupid," she said. "We stand out like…"

"…Like a red ruby up a white goat's ass," Spud said with a wicked laugh. "That's sort of the point, baby girl." He was bouncing on the toes of his boots, a crazy light in his eyes. From the street, a horn honked. The door of the Cracker Barrel swung open, and a teenaged girl in a Cracker Barrel uniform came out. She stared their way, a hand cupped over her eyes to shield against the sun. Spud turned, looked toward the street. Traffic was slowing to a gaper's crawl. He turned back to Miky and grinned. "This is it, Miky. This is absolutely it." Spud grabbed Benjamin by the arm. "Let's go, Zook."

Spud and Zooker, each towing a struggling prisoner, jogged toward the Cracker Barrel, guns drawn. Miky, following at a half-jog, opened her mouth to yell something, anything, to stop them. *Hold up*, she was thinking. *This is stupid*. To the right of the restaurant's doors, a pretty blonde woman Miky hadn't noticed was sitting on a bench with a little girl. The girl matched the woman all the way down to her skinny jeans. The woman's mouth was unhinging, her forehead wrinkling, the little girl's doing the same—mirror images of "Huh?" as their brains skipped between fight and flight. Miky, suddenly unable to connect with her voice box, felt something click in her chest, something like a small bone snapping. They'd crossed a line. There was no way to back up. Spud, Zooker, Sassy Bones, and Benjamin were in her periphery, all about twenty feet from the restaurant's porch;

208

the double doors of the restaurant were swinging open and two big men in police uniforms, both talking—one potbellied, a toothpick in his mouth, the other younger, slimmer, and good-looking—were walking out. To her right, Spud was coming to a stop, letting go of Benjamin's hand, his weapon swinging up, going level; he was planting his feet, his left hand coming up to meet the right, squeezing the pistol grip in the textbook two-hand grasp. The Cracker Barrel girl was turning to the cops, mouth open, trying to form a word. One of the cops made eye contact with Spud. Miky watched as the police officer's face went quickly from shock to the recognition of a threat. Miky saw her own free hand coming up and waving uselessly—as though a hand could stop bullets—and heard what she thought was her voice, far off, weak and useless, yelling, "Noooo." The potbellied cop was unclipping the holster on his belt. In a heartbeat, he swiveled and leveled his gun at Spud, pausing to yell in a husky rumble of a cop voice, "Drop your weapon," the toothpick floating out of his mouth, tumbling down down down. Spud laughed, pulled back the hammer on the Mag and squinted. The big cop squeezed off a round, the Cracker Barrel girl screamed, and Spud's head exploded. Benjamin, freed from Spud's grip, trundled toward the Cracker Barrel, hands up, screaming, "I'm a prisoner. I'm a prisoner."

The cop had shot Spud in the face. Miky turned away and fought back the urge to vomit. Blood was pooling quickly under his head on the black pavement. He was dead. Miky slowly swung back toward Zooker. He had pushed Sassy Bones out of the line of fire and was swinging his weapon up, assuming the two-handed grip with his boots a shoulder-width apart. Before he could shoot, the cop fired again.

Zooker's head snapped. Blood, hair, gray matter, and bone spouted in a grisly mist. He was down.

Miky knew at a glance that he was dead too.

# Chapter Twenty-Five

Governor Bill picked up his office phone and called Kelli's extension. The phone buzzed in his ear. There was an echoing whir from her office. Buzz. Whir. Buzz. He hung up, went to the door and opened it. "Kell?"

The office was empty. But the phone was still whirring. Governor Bill looked back at the phone on his desk, then to Kelli's phone. It whirred again. He walked to her desk, paused. On the phone's screen, several lines were flashing. Whir. Whir. Whir. Blink. Blink. Blink. His cell phone vibrated. He answered the cell. "Hello?"

"Governor? Tuttle," Tuttle said.

Governor Bill looked at the frantic phone on Kelli's desk. "Yes?" He looked toward the elevators.

"Sir, I need to inform you we have engaged the enemy. And there have been casualties."

"You don't know where my secretary is, do you?" Governor Bill said. He walked back into his office and shut the door, muffling the whirs.

"Sir, I…"

"Kelli. My office manager. She's gone," Governor Bill said. He sat in his chair. He looked at his computer screen.

The document, the speech, was open, the cursor blinking expectantly in the white space after the last word: *naked*. "So is Deanna. Gone."

"Who, sir?"

"She's media relations. She was helping me with my speech."

"Sir, if I may, what speech?"

Governor Bill frowned. "You said something about casualties?"

"Yes, governor. Our lead unit captured two prisoners on Wisconsin soil, then established a target, engaged that target, and now two of our resources are KIA."

"KIA."

"Killed in action. Yes, governor," Tuttle said. "Tragic, sir, but not, as we discussed, not unexpected."

Governor Bill fumbled through the mess on his desk for a pen, found one, then a Post-it note, clicked the pen, and wrote *KIA!* on the Post-it. "We've captured prisoners?"

"Yes, sir. Two. A male and female, and they were cooperating," Tuttle said, "but now their status is undetermined."

"So they're no longer prisoners."

"I'm not sure, sir. Not at this time."

"But you do know we've KIA'd two." Governor Bill circled *KIA!* His eyes drifted from the Post-it to the computer screen. He started re-reading the speech.

"No, governor. No. The enemy fired, sir. And we've confirmed that two of our, well, of the militia members—are deceased."

"It's for next week," Governor Bill said.

"Sir?"

"The speech. For the Mt. Clemens Rotary Club. They invited me six months ago and I just realized it's on the docket. I know people—some people—don't want me making speeches at a time like this so I'm telling you I'm not, like, creating a speech about Ham or anything."

"Governor, if I may, let me explain the magnitude of the situation we're in."

"This is the speech I was going to give next week but I'm going to run it by the folks here today. I mean, we have the podium out on the lawn. My people set that up after Ham, after Ham's situation, for Deanna to hold a press event. And I realize what you said but I'm going to just give this little speech. Run it up the flagpole. See who salutes. I'm saying general stuff like about the state of our state and the importance of protecting ourselves in a, like, a dangerous world," Governor Bill said. "Me and Deanna are, like, adapting it a bit to talk in a very subtle way about, about our current situation. I say 'me and Deanna,' but to tell the truth, I may have to wrap up this puppy myself." Governor Bill eyed the persistently blinking cursor and the *naked*. "Kelli and Deanna are both gone now and the phones are ringing off the hook."

"Sir, I'm not in a position to advise you politically," Tuttle said. "But from a security perspective, in my universe, this is not an optimal time for any sort of outward-facing communication."

Governor Bill leaned forward and stared at the Post-it. "I know you doubt me, Tuttle. A lot of folks out there do. But I am very capable of this speech, of anything, really. It was my mom who always said that. My dad always called me a wingnut; said I couldn't concentrate on shi… stuff or be serious or find my way out of my ass, but not Mom." Governor Bill sighed. "Course I was in sixth grade, you know, when she… Did I ever tell you? She tried to kill her… suicide. Tried to commit suicide. Once."

"Yes, sir. I am aware of that. Very unfortunate," Tuttle said. "Now…"

"I was at school. Cafeteria. Never forget it. My dad was away on business. They sent one of my teachers to get me," Governor Bill said with a laugh. "I was blowing milk out of my nose through a straw. Albert Carter had dared me, he and these guys, and I was doing it—for, like, thirty-seven cents, all the money they had on them, to blow the milk, you know—when Mr. Gropp came and got me. Never figured why they sent Mr. Gropp; guess he drew the short straw." Governor Bill paused. "Short straw." He giggled. "Comedy genius, I am, Tut-ster." Governor Bill looked at the Post-it note on his desk. "She took pills, I guess. That's what they told me, anyway. Too many pills. Or not enough, in a way."

From Tuttle's side of the conversation, a muffled, tinny voice said, "Could I help you?"

"Tell whoever that is I said 'no.' No need to help me, Tut. I'm good. Nothing you can do. Spilled milk, as they say." He smiled and shook his head. "Get that one, Tut?" Governor Bill said. "The spilled milk reference?"

"Hold on. Hold on," Tuttle said. "Sorry, governor, we had to make a drive-thru run. Who else wants a pie? They're two for a buck." Tuttle's voice faded. "Governor, let me call you back in a minute." The line went dead.

"Sir, thanks for your patience," Tuttle said, their phone call resumed. He cleared his throat, hoping to get down to business. "I am outbound with Senator Griffendorf and Representative Vanderway and my mobile secure team op force. We successfully traversed a drive-thru and are now back on our forward vector. Our ETA at target is" —Tuttle paused—"ohhh, approximately 13:30."

"Nice military talk, Tut. You kill me with that. 'ETA.' Estimated time of… of…".

"Arrival, sir."

"Yes, that's right. Say, that pie deal sounded awfully good, Tuttle. Maybe you could bring me back a couple," Governor Bill said. "I like a good pie, you know. My mom used to make a boysenberry. Sprinkled this crumble on the top. Always made it for my dad when he was in a mood; you know, to soften him up. Dad always said he would've killed a guy for a piece of that pie," Governor Bill said. He laughed.

"I understand, sir," Tuttle said.

"The perfect pie. That woman made it," Governor Bill said. He took a deep breath, scanned the Post-its, and found the relevant one. "OK." He sighed. "Guess we should get back to this 'KIA.' What's up with that?"

"There were local law enforcement officers present, governor."

"Local... like cops?"

"Yes, sir. They chose to engage."

Governor Bill wrote *engage* on the now-crowded Post-it; the g's on "engage" were cut off at the bottom edge of the Post-it. He'd finished the g's on the desktop. Governor Bill licked a finger on his free hand and tried to rub the ink away. It smeared. He frowned. "I take it there was some kind of confrontation?"

"Yes."

Governor Bill kneaded his forehead with the fingers of his free hand, and sighed again. "Where was this, this engagement, Tuttle?"

"Wisconsin."

"Where in Wisconsin?"

"A restaurant. A Cracker Barrel, governor."

"Good Lord," Governor Bill said. "What town?"

"Governor, I can't tell you that. Sorry."

Governor Bill wasn't paranoid; at least he didn't think he was. He just felt that sometimes the people around him, Ham included, hid things from him or maybe, sometimes, lied. He wasn't about to let that happen, not now. Not today. "You can't tell me. Why? I mean, if there are secrets, aren't I supposed to know them?" Governor Bill said.

"Governor, I just forgot to ask what city the Cracker Barrel was in. I imagine it was somewhere along I-94. I can find out, sir. My apologies," Tuttle said.

"So you don't know."

"No, sir."

"Then how do you know for sure what happened?" For Governor Bill, a headache threatened, a cloud of gray pain in his forehead. He had gotten what his mom called "special headaches," as a child, especially when he was tense. His mom had treated his special headaches with aspirin and a warm washcloth to the forehead. He breathed deeply and inhaled a memory of his mother, felt the cool touch of her hand. He wondered why he kept thinking about his mom. He forced himself to focus on the job at hand. "I still want to know everything, Tuttle. I am in charge here."

Tuttle sighed. "Governor, look, from the moment we launched this operation, our cyber security folks have been monitoring social media, police communications, and certain Wisconsin-specific chat rooms. Based on our understanding of the vector our militia friends were taking and a sudden burst of chatter vis-a-vis a violent incident at a Cracker Barrel that was along that route, we guessed those might be our people. This was confirmed moments ago by one of your militia folks there on the ground, via text."

"So you have a direct line to them—the militia?" Governor Bill heard a door slamming in the building and imagined it was his father slamming the front door, storming out of the house because of something he, just-a-goofy-kid-a-long-long-way-from-Governor-Bill, had done to disappoint him again. He felt his mom's hand pressing the cloth against his head. The gray cloud drifted through his skull, unthwarted.

"Governor, yes. One of our people on the ground, a female, was able to send a text or two. We had an initial penetration from our militia folks, and then some resistance. As I said, regional tactical assets, police officers, were present. They engaged. Two of our resources countered and were, unfortunately, eliminated."

"English, Tuttle."

"The cops fucking shot two of our people."

"The language, Tuttle. Jesus."

"My point is," Tuttle said, trying to swallow his impatience, "we're in a real shitstorm now, governor."

"Well, I sure pictured this differently, let me tell you. Dead people are one tough sell, Tuttle. People are really not going to be good with that."

"Look. Governor," Tuttle said. He paused, took a breath, and composed his thoughts. "Senator DenBraber, sir, and the others who've been exposed to this horrible virus; they were defenseless. A preemptory strike to avoid future attacks was absolutely warranted. It was your choice to make that strike. And it was your choice to use the militia option."

"Tell me something I don't know, Tuttle," Governor Bill said, suddenly irritated.

"Well, just keep in mind as we forward-lean from here, we are going to incur damage as a result of the tough choice you had to make. In this case the enemy has fired first. But that is the typical return on any war or war-like investment. Human capital will be negatively impacted. As you lead us through the battle ahead, remember, sir, to keep your eyes on the objective."

Governor Bill frowned. "So, it's back to the whatchacallit? The get? That it?'"

"Yes," Tuttle said with another sigh.

Governor Bill looked at the spot on the rug where Ham had fallen. His train of thought meandered down a memory lane crowded with misty images: Ham working through classwork with him late at night; Ham and Marci nudging him to call the wealthy, pretty Ellen Young—she of the wealthy, politically connected Saginaw Youngs—out for the first date that would lead to many dates and, eventually, a wedding with Ham as best man; Ham writing a speech for him at not-yet-Governor-Bill's kitchen table during his first run for the Michigan House of Representatives while Ellen stirred a great steaming pot of pasta on the stove; Ham teaching him how to eat raw oysters, at a biker bar in Manistee where they'd gone to campaign for governor and where Ham ended up holding his, not-yet-Governor-Bill's, head over a sink in the kitchen as he puked after Ham had kept warning him all night bad oysters are common in restaurants far from oceans. Ham had been his right hand, heck, his both hands, since that first encounter at U of M. Other than his dad, well, there was nobody else he could really talk to now.

"This sucks, Tuttle," Governor Bill said. He thought again of calling his father. The problem was that he and his father had always had what Ellen called a "frictional" relationship. All Governor Bill knew was his dad, like Ham, was a great source of thinking when he couldn't think, which was a lot of the time.

Governor Bill strained to hear the music coming from the radio in Tuttle's SUV. Sounded like "Kung Fu Fighting," a song he'd heard on the car radio when he was a kid. "You got some 70s going there, Tuttle?"

"Definitely, sir."

"You like your oldies."

"Soothes the beast, governor."

"You think I could get hold of my dad now and maybe talk this through with him?" As the words left his mouth, Governor Bill was surprised he'd said them. He wanted to take them back.

Tuttle thought for a moment. With his Bluetooth headset on for the call, he could grip the wheel with his left hand as he licked the sticky, gelatinous filling of the cherry pie off the fingers of his right hand. Out of habit, he glanced in the rearview mirror. The vehicle, built for transporting prisoners, was equipped with a soundproof, bulletproof partition that separated the front seat from the rear. He couldn't see out the rearview, so he corrected himself and looked at the driver's side mirror to check traffic behind him. He appreciated the partition. His passengers couldn't hear the conversation.

Uninvited, a fantasy—Babsy riding a white horse in the rain, drinking from a Mason jar, dye from her hair running in purple streaks down her naked back—cantered through Tuttle's mind. He shook his head, sending Babsy into the subconscious mist, although the fact that she was there pleased him. He'd grown more attached to the woman than he'd thought. Something in his gut wanted to—what? Please her? Yes. And there was little doubt of it. This feeling was foreign to him; it was making Tuttle uncertain of himself. He was distracted. By lust and fury. He couldn't trust her. She couldn't trust him. What they'd had was beautiful.

"Tuttle? You there?"

Tuttle sat up. He cleared his throat. *Focus on your objective here*, he told himself. He and Will had planned for Will's idiot son to take responsibility for every decision. Now Tuttle needed to wiggle out of his own role in the scheme, implicate the governor and his crazy-ass father. And deal with Babsy, well, however he wanted to deal with Babsy.

"Governor," Tuttle said, choosing his words like a sniper selecting his target in a crowded Vietnamese market, "I want you to make sure you're giving your strategy time to work. You chose the militia as your combat force. If it works, you need to get credit."

Governor Bill opened the drawer in his desk and pulled out the Sig Sauer. He slid the drawer shut with the barrel. It felt good—the heft of the gun. "I hear you, Tuttle, about me getting credit. I'm just, you know, wondering about running some stuff by the old man." Again, he was surprised to hear the words coming out of his mouth.

"I most definitely hear you," Tuttle said. "That might not be a bad idea. The two of you could, you know, collaborate or whatever—that what you're thinking?"

"I'm just saying this whole notion of militia people defending Michigan and then getting in a gun battle at a Cracker Barrel, well, it's not how I pictured this whole thing going." Cracker Barrel made a nice apple crisp. The thought of apple crisp made Governor Bill hungry. He tapped the gun barrel on the edge of his desk and wondered what Ellen had planned for supper and then wondered if he should make a show of not eating cheese, given the Wisconsin situation. He felt a surge of pride that he'd thought of that. That would be your smart optics, right there. He wrote *CHEESE* on the top Post-it on the pad, but didn't remove the Post-it from the pad. Silently he cursed, knowing the word "cheese" would now be engraved on several Post-its.

Tuttle guided the SUV off the interstate and onto the two-lane road that led to Silver Eagle's headquarters. "This is all your call, governor. Just remember, as long as you've got the right goal, the good get, then history's on your side; the death factor in this will just be a minor part of the story. Your poll numbers, well, they could actually go way up. Especially if you stand up and take credit for being proactive on behalf of your state." Tuttle smiled. That had come out perfectly. "Of course, you can also move to talking with your father, if you so wish. The two of you in this together—not a bad thought by any means."

Governor Bill imagined some of the black-booted personnel from Silver Eagle dropping down in Madison, on the lawn of the capitol, their parachutes with a big silver eagle on them. "I'm sorely tempted to do that, Tuttle. Sorely. I mean, would professionals have done it this way?" Governor Bill looked down at his Post-its. "Would they have engaged these guys in a restaurant?"

"Probably not, sir. But as you know, it was your choice to not use the security people in the first place," Tuttle said.

Governor Bill thought about this. "I'll be honest, Tuttle," he said. "Deep down, it was probably dumb, involving the militia.

But if I pulled them out right now, if I called in, say, Silver Eagle instead, well, how do I explain that?"

"Governor, if I may be frank?"

"Be frank, Tuttle. Be franker than frank."

"For now, stay the course. Let's see how this nets out. For the sake of you and your… your legacy. But when the time feels right, if things don't turn out one hundred and ten percent in our favor, well then you might reach out to your father. I do believe your father, Silver Eagle, would agree on an arrangement that would be value-positive, and perhaps his organization could ramp up quickly and handle the military portion of this as well as the public relations—including the explanation for the militia involvement. Silver Eagle is a one-stop resource for this type of thing. I dare say their people could transform this incident—this initial battle, if you will—into a net positive, a real game changer for you."

Governor Bill picked up his gun and racked the slide. He loved the sound of it. He considered Tuttle's sales pitch and smiled. Handing this thing off to his father, if it came to that, would be tough but at the same time easy.

"Governor, if you choose to call in Silver Eagle, your father would most definitely see the leadership. And so would your constituents." Tuttle allowed himself a smile as he added, "It wasn't George W. who fought the war, sir. He made the choices. He was the decider."

Governor Bill closed his eyes and saw George W. Bush in the oval office, speaking like a leader, talking about the surge in Iraq. Deciding. Delegating. Kicking ass. Without planning to, he said, "Tuttle, I'm not going to wait long. If this thing keeps going in this direction, I'm inclined to call off the militia boys and bring in Silver Eagle."

"Excellent, sir. Very… excellent."

Governor Bill pictured Silver Eagle Security human military resources (HMR)—that's what the marketing materials called them—marching in procession in front of the Wisconsin capitol building.

The door to Kelli's office was open. From her desk, he could hear the whir of another incoming call or, perhaps, many calls. For the moment, the chaos was a good thing. He was a man above it all. He was the man. In charge.

Governor Bill sniffed, stood, and walked to the window—an emperor surveying his domain. "It's already a zoo here. Because of the Ham thing. I have at least five of those satellite trucks. They've set up chairs on the lawn." Directly beneath his window, five members of the MSU pep band, a pretty cheerleader whose name, he recalled from previous photo sessions, was Vicky, and two muscular guys in matching sleeveless T-shirts and sunglasses were chatting. Sparty walked away from the group toward the entrance to the capitol building, stepped over a wind-wobbled ribbon of yellow police tape stretched between two plastic chairs, ducked his huge Sparty head, and went inside. The cheerleader, Vicky, turned a cartwheel on the lawn, narrowly missing a reporter who was holding a microphone and speaking to a camera. Her legs were pretty; so was Vicky. Governor Bill turned from the window, walked to his desk and sat down. He studied the Post-it notes. "We've got the media covering this deal with Ham and probably soon they'll be on that—our incident at the Cracker Barrel—there. But the two of them—the two mediums—they're not on, like, the same wavelength. So no worries there, for now."

"You've got it, sir."

The elevator in the hallway outside Kelli's office dinged. The doors slid open. Sparty walked into Kelli's office, big head tilted to the side, scraping the ceiling, and crossed to the governor's open door. Head cocked, Sparty looked through the door at the governor. Governor Bill frowned. Sparty held his hands up—a gesture of surrender. Governor Bill realized he was pointing the gun at Sparty and lowered it. He gestured at Sparty to come in. Sparty obeyed. Governor Bill held up an index finger. He mouthed the words "Hold on" to Sparty and wondered if Sparty could tell what he mouthed. Where were the eyeholes in that big head? To Tuttle, he said, "So, Tuttle, go ahead. Do nothing. For now. But be ready."

"I'll be waiting for your call, sir." There was a smile in Tuttle's voice that rang like a tiny bell deep in Governor Bill's brain. "This is all up to you now. And your father."

Governor Bill thought about it. The eyeholes just had to be there and he couldn't see them. This, he vaguely realized, was ironic.

"Sir?" Tuttle said.

"Yes, Tuttle. OK." Governor Bill tried to twirl the gun the way cowboys did in movies but, as always, his index finger slipped out of the trigger guard; the 9mm somersaulted to the floor. Governor Bill grimaced, crabwalked his office chair across the carpet, picked up the pistol, and slid the chair back to the desk. "Tuttle, yes. OK. Keep me posted and I will, ummm, do the same." Governor Bill punched the button to end the call.

For the first time since Ham had collapsed, for the first time maybe ever, Governor Bill felt in almost, somewhat total command of something important, something that would have an impact in a way that even his dad would appreciate. Gun in hand, Governor Bill took a long, deep breath, and slowly swung his feet from the desktop, sending the Sparky Anderson bobblehead over the edge. He lurched down to swipe at the bobblehead and hit his head on the edge of the desk. "Damn it," Governor Bill said. He grabbed the bobblehead and put it back in its place. Sparky, grinning, bobbled wildly. "Damn. That hurt. Good Lord." Governor Bill carefully touched his head. He winced and glanced at the fingertips. No blood. "Sorry for the language. Just hit my big fat head," he said to whoever was in the Sparty costume. For a moment, despite the pain, he worried

that Sparty would be offended by the "big fat head" comment—
Sparty was bent over awkwardly and Governor Bill wondered
why the person inside didn't just take off the darn head. Governor
Bill almost asked but Ham had taught him to be careful about
what he said spontaneously in public. So instead, he looked at
the mascot and said again, "Sorry. For the language."

"No problem." The response was muffled. As before, he was
surprised it was a girl's voice.

The girl-voiced Sparty took a step toward the governor.
"Governor, I was just going to ask, if I could take just a minute
of your time…"

Governor Bill sat up straight, wincing. He felt dizzy, a little
disoriented.

"Are you OK?" Sparty said.

"I… I'm fine, just a little woozy." He forced himself to smile
at Sparty, and gestured at her with the gun.

The gun fired. Sparty stumbled backward, and then crumpled
to the floor.

It took the rest of FBI special agent Babsy Witt's lifetime, about
four minutes, for the governor of Michigan to realize he'd killed
her. Babsy spent those four minutes on her back in roughly
the same place on the carpet of the governor's office on which
Ham DenBraber had fallen earlier, bleeding from a wound in
her chest, an ugly hole in the green plastic breastplate of the
Sparty mascot costume she was wearing showing the path of
the bullet. The governor sat, staring, wondering what to do or
say as Babsy, from inside the costume, let out a last heavy sigh.

Governor Bill couldn't move. Couldn't. Think. The smell of
the gun, the sound of it—which seemed trapped in the office,
unable to escape—pressed in on him. He couldn't breathe.

A girl.

Was dead?

# Chapter Twenty-Six

The Dobermans had come loping from their cages, which were concealed in the tree line on the far side of the Silver Eagle Security compound. Within seconds they would be upon the trainee. Will smiled and slid his SUV into reverse, backed out of the parking place, dropped the big vehicle into drive, punched the gas, and turned hard to the right. He looped through the empty parking lot, and turned onto one of the three tree-lined streets that crisscrossed the compound. From a pocket in his Silver Eagle windbreaker, a cell phone whirred. Will retrieved the phone and glanced at the screen. The cell phone whirred again. Will pressed the answer button, brought the device to his ear. "You have news for me?" Will heard and felt a thump. He reflexively gripped the wheel harder and glanced in his rearview mirror. A dog, broken and bloody, was tumbling into the weeds along the shoulder of the road. Had he hit the thing? Will made a mental note to have the car washed.

"The silver eagle flies," Tuttle said.

"Say again," Will said.

"I believe we're locked on target."

"Speak English, you chicken-brained bastard."

"Sorry, Will. I think he's ready to call you in."

"This business at the Burger King soured him on the militia boys, that it?"

"Burger King?" Tuttle said.

"Big Boy."

"Big?"

"Applebee's. Chili's. Whatever it was. The restaurant."

"Oh. Oh. Oh, the Cracker Barrel..."

"That's what I said. The Cracker Barrel."

"Well, yes, yes. The engagement there certainly has him a bit off kilter," Tuttle said.

"Can't say it didn't surprise me a bit. Didn't think they'd make trouble that quickly."

"Ditto, here, sir. Like all of us, I believe he did not anticipate blood being spilled in the manner in which it was, didn't expect cops to be present."

"Never could handle blood."

"Really."

"Yes, from childhood, basically, always was wobbly kneed when it came to blood."

"Would never have guessed that about you."

"I meant my idiot son, asshole, and you know it."

"Of course you did."

Will slowed the SUV and eased into the main parking lot. He guided the vehicle past the rows of parked cars toward the Silver Eagle world headquarters building, a three-story, windowless concrete structure he'd designed on a napkin over lunch with an architect who didn't understand his vision and who'd been fired before dessert. It was a hulking gray box with no signage that somehow managed to be sinister rather than simply nondescript. The firm's management team had nicknamed the building, with his proud blessing, The Fort, and he always felt proud when he saw it. Now as he approached, his mood soured.

"Shit. Hold on, Tuttle," Will said. "Some asshole is in my parking space." He braked, considered getting out and raising holy hell but thought better of it. He wheeled his vehicle past the offending black SUV, arced into the space just beyond it, and stopped. "Give me the skinny, Tuttle," Will said. The other SUV's engine was running and through the heavily tinted glass William Hoeksma, Sr. could see there were people inside of it; they looked like shadows behind the tinting. "When you're done I'll kick these idiots who took my space back to wherever they came from."

"Sure thing," Tuttle said. "Well…"

"You can start by explaining my son's little tirade on the phone to me awhile ago."

"You talked to him?"

"Yes. Called that receptionist of his and she's half hysterical and she put me through. Why a woman has to react that way is beyond me. Given all I've paid her, given the fact that we, I, let her have the job, you'd think she'd hold it together when things finally hit the fan."

"He told me he couldn't find her."

"Couldn't find who?"

"The receptionist. Sounded like she wasn't there."

"Well, she was there when I called him, Tuttle," Will said. "Good Lord." He closed his eyes and leaned back against the leather headrest. "Woman seemed like a basket case. Should have seen this coming." Will allowed himself a chuckle.

"Sorry, Will, I… Hold on," Tuttle said. He groaned. Will could hear Tuttle's car door open and slam. "You were saying? The receptionist?"

Eyes still closed, Will sighed. "The receptionist."

"Yes, what's-her-name. Your little keeper-of-the-governor."

"Oh, oh, yes." Will opened his eyes. "That little nutcase. She went off on me about DenBraber and something about being pregnant and me taking care of her new little family if anything bad happened. Seemed to think that by being my little mole she could hit me up for some kind of protection." Will laughed. "Like I was part of the decision for her and her hubby to have sex."

Tuttle laughed.

"Like I had anything directly to do with DenBraber getting sick. Good God."

Tuttle's laugh drained away. "Yeah, right," he said. "Right."

Will sat up. A guy from the SUV next to his had gotten out of the vehicle and was talking on his phone. The guy had his back to Will, and was now kicking at the turf at the edge of the sidewalk. He was tall, thin, in green overalls and a baseball cap. "Tuttle," Will said.

"Yes," Tuttle said. The guy in front of Will turned and stared off across the parking lot.

"You're parked in my damn parking spot, you idiot."

# Chapter Twenty-Seven

Later, when she recounted the events of that day, Miky would often say the first shot, the one that killed Spud, stopped the world from spinning. The second shot, the one that ended Zooker's combat-booted earthly sojourn, set the world spinning out of control. Benjamin Nighthorse barreled into the potbellied policeman and tackled him, the momentum taking both of them into the other cop. All three sprawled to the pavement. Sassy, screaming, fighting a full bladder and high heels, tripped and sprawled on top of the three men. The Cracker Barrel girl fled across the parking lot, yelling, "Stop, stop, stop." The shooter-cop shouted, "Get off of me, getthehelloffofme." The front doors of the Cracker Barrel swung open and despite the obvious danger, panicked customers and staff gushed out, a human flood, most rushing toward the Menards.

Miky stood between the dead Zooker and the dead Spud and tried to process it all. Despite the years of target practice and training, she'd never seen a violent death, let alone two violent deaths so close at hand. She heard screaming and realized it was coming from deep inside her, a river of sound and hurt and fear that burned her throat and seemed to leak from her eyes. Her father's voice, or a version of it, growled in her head to *get a grip, get a grip*. *GET A GRIP*. This became *SPUD IS DEAD*, which segued to *ZOOKER IS DEAD, ZOOKER IS DEAD, ZOOKER IS DEAD*, which led Miky to glance at the horrifying remains of her comrades, which led her to look away to the entangled pile of Benjamin, Sassy, and the two cops.

Was this real?

The crazy pile of people was sorting itself, the cop who'd fired the shots getting to his knees.

Miky's heart was beating in her throat, saying *flee-flee, flee-flee* and, for a shameful, trembling handful of seconds, the urge to bolt nearly won. The flow of people through the front door had stopped but she could see others cautiously escaping from the rear—parents holding babies, an aproned cook holding a spatula, two suit-coated businesspeople, one looking at the screen of his smartphone, talking as they jogged away. From his knees on the porch, the shooter-cop reached for the arm of a rocking chair. Miky crouched behind a car, drew her sidearm, peeked around the car, aimed, and squeezed the trigger, hoping to scare him. The chair splintered, the cop recoiled with a shout; he landed on his butt, his hat once again falling off. Sassy and Benjamin instinctively, simultaneously, curled into fetal positions, Sassy screaming. The gunshot, like the two that had preceded it, seemed foreign and out of context—a sonic fart in a quiet church. For a moment, Miky felt an apology rising in her throat, an "Oh, sorry, folks, didn't mean to scare you, sorry." But her training and instincts kicked in. She felt vulnerable, exposed. The objective, the Cracker Barrel, was right in front of her. Gun in her hand at her side, she jogged cautiously toward the restaurant, not sure what she'd do there, vaguely aware of more people running away, distant sirens crying, and a few terrified yet stupefyingly curious customers still in the restaurant's gift store leering out at her from between jars of marmalade and racks of country apparel. Those customers' eyes widened when Miky reached the front door, swung it open, and ran inside.

The people who remained in the Cracker Barrel scattered like roaches under a spotlight. An elderly couple from Kenosha, Joe and Kathy Monahan, brushed past Miky and out the front door, Joe still holding the box of chocolate peanut clusters he'd hoped to buy and later would return, fully intact, via Federal Express, with a note of apology. Most of the rest stumbled, shuffled, and wheeled (Ruth Kragt of Oshkosh, visiting her recently widowed sister Sonja, was in a wheelchair due to an ill-timed flare-up of gout) toward the rear of the building and whatever exit they could find. From the edge of a clearance sale (50% Off Items!) shelf near the door, a Santa snow globe teetered, fell to the floor, bounced once, twice, and skittered to a stop, oozing liquid from its plastic skin, Santa still inside and smiling gamely with a red-mittened hand raised in greeting. The now-broken globe rested against the pink-sneakered left foot of a chubby four-year-old named Emma. Emma had put the snow globe back on the clearance display hastily when the shooting started and was now hiding behind her mother, Clare, who was angry with Emma for picking the thing up and putting it back on the shelf inappropriately. Her displeasure showed as, tightlipped, she took Emma by the hand and left through the front door.

Inside the restaurant, the aroma of food—a distinctively Cracker Barrel mix of coffee, cooked apples, fried potatoes, and ham—blended with a silence as striking and unnatural as the gunshots in the parking lot. Miky didn't think. She couldn't think. The shooting of Zooker and Spud was an evil vine looping and looping and looping in her head. She felt disconnected and terribly afraid yet disturbingly calm. She was, unexpectedly, in charge and she was fine with that. She wanted to yell, "Nobody move!" but there was nobody to move. She half-jogged a quick recon of the building, weaving between tables, arms slightly extended with her gun held in a two-fisted grip. She found no one in the dining areas. There was no one in the kitchen; a lone egg, sunny side up, burned in a black iron skillet. Miky turned off the burner under the skillet. She allowed herself a sigh of relief. She ended up at the checkout counter in the gift shop. Miky didn't know what to do and, for a moment, there was a buzzing in her head. She felt like she did in mile twenty-two of a marathon. She fought the urge to quit but that damn voice inside her said this was what she'd trained for. The voice, which sounded alternately like Rub and like her college cross-country coach, told her to smooth her breathing, to evaluate the situation and, above all, to stay calm and be ready to handle trouble.

Through the windows, Miky could see the Indian guy had somehow wormed free of the cops and was running—plodding—across the parking lot toward Zooker's body. One of the cops—the non-shooter—was helping Sassy Bones stand; in her tight skirt and heels, it was a challenge. The shooter cop stood, raised his weapon, and took wobbly aim at the Indian guy—Benjamin; the name popped into her head, sounding again like a funny name for an Indian. Benjamin picked up Zooker's gun from next to what was left of Zooker's head. He turned, bellowed what sounded like a war whoop—in fact, it was; he'd learned it from his grandfather—and Benjamin the Indian ran toward the Cracker Barrel. The shooter cop, mouth agape, didn't shoot.

Despite trembling hands, Miky sent another text to the number she'd been given—the same number she'd messaged about the shootings of Zooker and Spud. She kept this one simple: *2 pris. alive. One armed.*

The text was forwarded through a series of cell phones owned by militia sympathizers until it reached a burner phone carried by Tuttle.

Tuttle informed Will of the situation. With a Wisconsin pris. now armed, clearly the situation had become dangerous.

# Chapter Twenty-Eight

Seven minutes, give or take. That was how long it took officers Smith and Dunkel to get Hank Vanderway and Frances Griffendorf processed and settled into Silver Eagle's Secure Nest (SEC NEST) deep in a subbasement of the headquarters building. The SEC NEST was a self-sufficient living space with a fully stocked kitchenette, a bathroom, two bedrooms, and a living room, all of it two levels below ground and protected by a series of locked steel doors and elevators. Tuttle and Will took an additional five minutes to traverse the series of security checks, including retinal and fingerprint scans at each floor and a strip search at the final stop, necessary to reach Silver Eagle's Strategic Critical Analysis Room (SCAR), which was three floors below the SEC NEST.

Now Tuttle sat across the SCAR's conference table from Will. Next to Will was the copywriter, Lindquist, who was very close to throwing up. Lindquist was trying to fathom how he'd gotten into this situation. He'd been ordered to meet with Will Hoeksma at Will Hoeksma's request, but neither Lindquist nor his superiors at his ad agency—Joe Johnson, John Johnson, and Don Dean—had a clue why. The request from Hoeksma had been, "I want to meet with the writer who's been writing my stuff and no one else." William Hoeksma, Sr.'s business represented 33 percent of the Johnson, Dean, and Johnson annual billings and everyone on the Silver Eagle Security account team at Johnson, Dean, and Johnson was scared to death of the man. The account exec who received the request had talked to the head of account services, Don Dean, who'd talked to the creative director, Joe Johnson, who'd talked to the agency president, John Johnson, who'd said, "Well, hell, who's been writing most of their stuff?" After a series of emails and phone calls between members of the account services team and three emergency meetings between Joe Johnson and other stakeholders on the Silver Eagle account, the answer had come back "Lindquist." So, despite the agency's long-standing policy against ever letting the creative staff members call, email, text, visit or contact in any way a client without a member of account services present, and despite the fact that Will Hoeksma was, by anyone at the ad agency's estimation, the single most difficult client with whom to meet, they'd sent the inexperienced, talented, and somewhat flaky Lindquist with the warning that he should just listen to William Hoeksma and above all not fuck up their relationship with Silver Eagle Security, which was, they reminded him, 33 percent of Johnson, Dean, and Johnson's total annual billings, not to mention that William Hoeksma was one of the more powerful men in the state, if not the whole country, and the father of the governor.

Lindquist sat, stomach churning and notepad open on his lap. Head down, eyes on the floor. He was only twenty-five, wasn't even a senior level staff member. Good at his job; heck yes, he was good. He'd been the lead writer on three award-winning campaigns the year before and had been the writer on a billboard campaign for the Michigan Peach Institute that had been featured in *Adweek* magazine. But he didn't want to talk to clients. He hated to talk to clients. He dreaded being anywhere near clients. He'd had to buy a sports coat just to have something other than jeans and a T-shirt to wear to this stupid meeting with this client. Before leaving the office, Lindquist had told his creative partner and work buddy, art director Freda Peters, that he was so far out of his comfort zone he might break away from earth's gravitational pull. He and Freda had had a good laugh about that. But this, this moment deep in the bunker that was Silver Eagle Security's global headquarters, was no laughing f-ing matter. Lindquist had given up his phone at the first security checkpoint but now wished he had it; if he did he would text Freda, *This is no laughing f-ing matter*, because he knew Freda would laugh at such a text and making Freda laugh made Lindquist think maybe he still had a shot at Freda. This despite the fact that Freda had confided in him that she was currently considering an intimate opportunity with her roommate, which made Lindquist want his own opportunity with Freda even more. Just the possibility of texting Freda made Lindquist smile, but then he looked up and realized Commander Tuttle and William Hoeksma were staring at him, and they were not smiling. Lindquist tried to look confident. He edged his chair out from the conference room table. He crossed one leg over the other and gripped a black Sharpie in his sweaty right hand. He tap tap tapped the top of the pen against the wire-spiral binding of the notebook and jiggled his foot. Both Hoeksma and Tuttle weren't talking. They just sat there, looking at him, nursing cups of coffee drawn from the pump pot in the SCAR's kitchenette. Lindquist was thankful he'd turned down the offer of coffee; his hands were shaking too much to hold a cup, and the deal with Hoeksma was— according to the creative director—"never show him your fear." Now Lindquist was trying not to react as Hoeksma told Tuttle that the pump pot in the kitchenette, which had been developed for the Pentagon, contained a sensor that turned liquids bright pink if it detected any of 328 poisons. It had cost $750,000. Will had fired the Silver Eagle purchasing associate who'd bought it from a backdoor source at the Pentagon. When the associate's supervisor told him the pot was non-returnable, he had also fired the supervisor.

The thought of poison got Lindquist to doodling a skull and crossbones on the open page of the notebook. His hand was so unsteady the skull turned out misshapen, pear-like, like it had water on the brain. He'd had a cousin, Ricky, who'd had water on the brain. Ricky had died when they were little kids. Lindquist tried to convert the doodle into a drawing of Ricky. But the more he clawed at the memory and, subsequently, the drawing, the more Lindquist realized he could no longer picture Ricky. That's when it dawned on him that Will Hoeksma was staring at him. Rather than look up and face whatever wrath might come, Lindquist kept his head down and dramatically scribbled over the doodle. He wrote *Meeting, Silver Eagle w/W. Hoeksma* under the scribble, and waited.

Tuttle had always annoyed Will Hoeksma and on countless occasions, such as this one, Tuttle also had been very useful to him. Hoeksma shifted his gaze from Lindquist and for several seconds stared stonily at Tuttle, who sat across from him at the massive conference room table. Two recessed lights over the table, the only lights on in the room, gave Tuttle's skin a deathly, pale glow. Beyond Tuttle, the cavernous room's details disappeared in shadow. The effect was somewhat sinister, just as Will had planned. He knew the copywriter was nervous. He hoped Tuttle was nervous too.

Will jumped to his feet. Lindquist shoved his chair back, dropped his pen, and nearly tumbled over backwards. Lindquist steadied himself by grabbing the edge of the table with one trembling hand. Will Hoeksma paused, looked at him, snorted, and shook his head, then walked to the light switch and snapped the room into darkness.

The three of them sat in blackened silence. Lindquist swallowed a giggle.

Finally, Tuttle said, "Well."

William Hoeksma, from the direction of his chair, said, "Yes, Tuttle. Well, indeed."

"Well," Tuttle said, "about the secretary then…"

"What about her?"

"She suspect anything?"

"Suspect what?" Will said. "What would that little slut suspect?"

Lindquist cleared his throat. "Am I supposed to be taking notes?" he said, his voice cracking. The room was incredibly dark. He couldn't believe how dark. And he had no idea where his pen was. Or why he was there.

"Shut up, Rimquest," Hoeksma said, his voice a cannon and just inches from his ear. Lindquist snapped back and almost tipped over again. He could smell William Hoeksma's breath. It smelled like pickles. "That's right, Rimquest, I'm watching you," the pickled breath said.

"Lindquist, sir. It's Lindquist," he said and wished immediately that he hadn't said it.

"Your name is whatever he says it is," Tuttle said, his voice suddenly a whisper in Lindquist's other ear. Lindquist recoiled. Something brushed his cheek. A bat? A hand? Nothing. It was nothing. For a moment, he thought he'd wet himself. He tried to slow his breathing. This had taken a very not-funny turn. He wanted to die and was afraid he would.

"Relax, brand-man," Hoeksma said, his voice now from a comfortable distance and cloaked in a warm laugh. "Just listen for now. The notes come later." He cleared his throat. "You were saying, Tuttle? About that little whore in my son's office?"

"Well, I don't know," Tuttle said, his voice now up near the ceiling. "She knew DenBraber very well, from what I understand and…"

"He's standing on the table?" Lindquist said.

"What's that, Numbcrest?" Hoeksma said.

"It's just so dark, I can't…"

"Pipe down, Palmquick," Tuttle said, now near his original position—his chair. "Pipe down before you're piped down."

"Are you intentionally distracting us?" Hoeksma said.

"No, no, I would never… sir, it's just so dark…" Lindquist said, his voice a tinny warble.

"I'm not talking to you, copyboy. I'm talking to our commander, Mr. Tuttle." Hoeksma's voice was a whisper in Lindquist's right ear; he could feel Hoeksma's breath on his cheek. Lindquist snapped back so fast his chair tumbled over, his head bouncing off the carpeted floor. Tuttle and Hoeksma laughed, Tuttle pounding the table and hooting.

Still in blackness, Lindquist scrambled to his feet, fumbled for the chair, righted it, felt for the seat and sat down. His breathing was ragged. He wondered if he was going to have a heart attack, and if he did would he know what it was. He hated Hoeksma. He hated Tuttle. He hated his choice of career. He wanted desperately to impress both of these men and, by extension, everyone back at the agency, especially Freda Peters. "Sorry, I lost my balance there," he managed to say to the blackness.

Both men were silent. Lindquist waited. There was no sound, except his own breathing.

"Sir? Sirs?" Lindquist said.

Nothing.

Lindquist waited. Minutes passed.

"C'mon, OK. I get it. You're, like, testing me or something."

More time passed. Lindquist began to lose his bearings. The darkness was beginning to play with his sense of direction. There was not so much as a sliver of light under a door. He started playing a mental game to describe the darkness. It was black as a bowling ball at the bottom of an abandoned coalmine. It was as black as the rectum of a black panther at midnight. It was black as…

"You were saying, Will?" Tuttle's voice was from Lindquist's left. The lights came on. Tuttle stood next to the light switch. Lindquist blinked, closed his eyes, opened them and noticed for the first time that Tuttle had a bit of blood and a gooey residue on his upper lip. He'd seen Tuttle on TV and online. But Lindquist was shocked at his appearance—wild-eyed and in some kind of work uniform with a bloody upper lip. Lindquist, out of habit, reached for where his phone should be; he wanted to take a pic he could post. But they'd taken his phone, damn them.

William Hoeksma had taken a seat at the head of the table. Tuttle circled to return to his original seat across from Lindquist. Tuttle opened his mouth to speak. William Hoeksma cut him off. "Tuttle, where would you say my son is right now?"

"Lansing?"

"No, I mean emotionally, in relation to his father? Specifically. Where?" Will Hoeksma shot Lindquist a smile and a wink.

"Well," Tuttle said. With the tip of his tongue he licked at the clotted blood on his upper lip. "Well, I would say he's worried and wants to talk with you."

"Would you say he's seen the light?" He looked at Lindquist again. Another wink. "Like our little creative writer friend here is about to see it. You're ready to see the light, right, Lindquat?"

Lindquist managed a nod.

Will Hoeksma turned back to Tuttle. "I mean, in the time since my son ranted to me about bloodletting and so on; you're assuring me, you're guaranteeing me, that he may be ready to help take my little company here to the next level?"

"Yes, sir," Tuttle said. "He's what I'd call target-ready."

"Good. He totally gummed up our original plan. But it seems the other shoe is dropping now with his militia friends mucking everything up. He's aware this is to be his call? Need him to own this."

"Exactly, sir. He is well aware of that. This is his call. And… and yours."

"And he's ready."

"State-wise, yes," Tuttle said. An image of Babsy, drowning, floated through his mind. "There is the little matter of the federal people, however. About how we, uh, keep them in check."

William Hoeksma laughed and shook his head. "Tuttle, you underestimate my capabilities here," he said.

"Maybe so, Will, but…"

"You let me worry about the boys and girls in Washington." Will turned at last to Lindquist, who was staring at his notepad. "OK, Tongue-twist. You're on."

"I am?"

"Yes. You am. First, let me remind you that as a member of my team at your little ad agency there, you have signed a non-disclosure agreement. All of the background stuff we're about to tell you is extremely confidential. Everything you've heard up to now is extremely confidential."

"All of it. Every word," Tuttle said, nodding in agreement.

Lindquist coughed and looked down at his trembling right hand, gripping his pen. He nodded yes.

"You know what guerrilla marketing is, Lundquist? Of course, you do. If you didn't, I'd be forced to kill you." Will Hoeksma shot the kid a wicked grin. Lindquist tried to return the grin but his face didn't feel up to it. "Just kidding, there, young man. I wouldn't kill you. Not yet, anyway."

Tuttle snorted a laugh.

"I know what it is, guerilla marketing I mean. I know all about it."

Will Hoeksma smiled at Tuttle. "Listen to Mr. Assertive, here. Told you this kid had gonads."

Lindquist forced a tense smile. "It's, like, all about tactics," he said. "It's basically a way to promote your business or whatever out in the real world—instead of, like, an ad. Could be almost anything—graffiti on a sidewalk or some kind of flash mob deal. It can actually be kind of cool." Lindquist looked down. He wondered if he'd said too much. He had a habit of saying too much when he was nervous.

"Well done, Limenuts. You apparently paid attention in college."

The name thing was getting old. Todd swallowed his irritation and managed a crooked nod.

Will Hoeksma and Tuttle locked eyes for a moment, a nerve in Will's jaw twitching. When he spoke, his voice was cooler. "You heard this deal about prairie dogs and monkeypox in Wisconsin? It's been on talk shows and all over the Internet."

Todd Lindquist frowned. "Ah, yeah. Yes. I mean, I heard about it. A lot of people have." He paused, and then proceeded with caution. "I'm not sure I believe it, though."

"You're not a right winger, not a big fan of the conservative talkers or bloggers, that it?"

"Well, uh…"

"Let's cut to the chase, kid. All of that nonsense was us. It was made up. Just like a lot of the ads and such you write. All fiction. Guerilla marketing. And a little public relations thrown in." Will smacked the table, laughed, and looked at Tuttle. "Well, except the part that affected our dear friend, Senator DenBraber. Unfortunately, that got a little real—had to. It was our launching point of phase two."

Lindquist's heart lurched. "Senator DenBraber? I heard... Was that—part of this?"

"You're a bright kid, Lamwad. It's why I like you."

"But. The senator is really sick. That's what I heard. He, like, collapsed, right?"

Will glanced at Tuttle then swung his gaze back to Lindquist. "The senator's illness might suggest a certain capacity for viral warfare, if taken in the right light, correct?"

Lindquist felt a snake twisting in his gut.

"I believe the expression is 'see what we did there?'" Tuttle said.

Lindquist was afraid to breathe. He thought for a moment that if he did, this man, these crazy old men, would do something unthinkable to him. Will Hoeksma had a weird look in his eyes.

"The point is not what we've done. It's what we're going to do in response to what's supposedly been done to our dear state," Will said with a wry grin. "Tuttle can maybe make it clearer for you. Isn't that right, Tuttle?"

Tuttle didn't answer. He'd let his mind wander off to Babsy and her betrayal. He felt stupid for not seeing through her— for believing she was attracted to him merely for his looks and lovemaking skills. She'd used him. Now as he looked across the desk at his boss, Tuttle thought about how Will Hoeksma was using him too. He'd known this for a long time but the fact of it popped into his head like a pimple. He saw red, blinked.

Will, impatient with Tuttle, turned back to Lindquist. "Pretty soon everyone, *everyone*, will be talking about the brave men and women of Silver Eagle Security. That is, if my security expert here can hold his shit together. And if my dumbnuts kid doesn't botch it with any more of his idiot ideas."

Lindquist avoided eye contact, stared at the desktop, shuffling through thoughts like cards in a deck. Finally, head still down, he said, "So you, like, did something to the senator..."

"Someone did something to the senator," Will Hoeksma said. "And for all practical purposes, 'someone' appears to be Wisconsin."

"So that's what the governor thinks?" Lindquist said, his eyes locked on the table. "I mean, the prairie dog thing? Why would anyone even believe that?" He was horrified that he'd asked the question. He sneaked a peak at Will Hoeksma and was relieved to see a smile on the man's face.

Will Hoeksma chuckled. "Ohhh, young man. You have so much to learn about today's world. Or about what you do for a living."

"People believe what they want to believe," Tuttle said quietly.

"Damn straight, Tuttle. And you know what else, Lardquest?" Will Hoeksma leaned toward him, wagging an index finger. "Today, people want to believe what other people *don't* believe. They want to be the ones who" —Will paused and drew air quotes with his fingers—"'get it.'" Will paused for a moment to let that sink in. "My son the governor is no different. You play to your audience's ego, kid, and that's when you've got them. By the balls. Right, Tuttle?"

Tuttle nodded, his lips pressed tightly.

Lindquist wasn't good at thinking before he spoke—his superiors at the agency had made that critical point during his performance reviews each year. True to form, his next thought shotgunned out of his mouth: "So what the hell does this have to do with me?"

Both men stared at him. Lindquist froze. He lowered his gaze and stared at his open notebook. His wildly active brain leaped through a series of images involving him bleeding, him being dumped in a shallow grave, and Freda Peters crying over her loss. A small element of this fantasy appealed to Lindquist.

Will Hoeksma finally said, slowly and deliberately, "Well, once Silver Eagle has deployed assets and mopped up our little conflict in Wisconsin, which we're preparing to do even as we speak, you're going to help us tell our story. Which, in turn, will help us reach the objective of this whole thing."

"Which is?"

"Market share, young man. Market. Share." Will pounded his gloved fist on the table, underscoring each word. He smiled at Lindquist. "You are going to write the scripts and the Twitters and what-have-yous and whatever else we ask you to do—to communicate the capabilities and skillset employed by Silver Eagle in defending the State of Michigan. I'll explain all of the details and what is expected of you in a written brief as soon as we get you settled."

"Settled?"

"As of right now, at this moment, you are onsite, with us. I work directly with you. You will communicate with needed resources at the agency, from here. But you will be onsite for the duration."

"Onsite. Like, how 'onsite?' I mean, I can leave for, like, lunch or whatever, right?"

Will shook his head. "There's much to do, Lundersmith. We've prepared a place for you in the building. Tuttle's people are transporting your belongings from your apartment. To here. You're my number one choice on this. And I want you to be comfortable…"

"You broke into my place?"

"Careful," Tuttle said sharply, suddenly alert and defensive. "It was not a break-in."

Lindquist looked at Tuttle, then back at Will, then back at Tuttle. Lindquist was angry and not a little scared. More like a lot. A lot scared. "But you can't do that." He started to stand. Tuttle shot him a look that said, clearly, *Sit.*

Lindquist stood.

Tuttle, now fully alert, slowly rose. He put a hand in a bulging pocket of his coveralls. "Hold on there, Livernuts." His voice had an edge to it.

Lindquist cursed his lack of impulse control. He wanted to sit but was afraid the movement would provoke Tuttle.

Tuttle pulled a banana out of the pocket. He placed the banana on the table. "This look familiar?"

Lindquist, momentarily relieved, frowned. "It's a banana."

"It's your banana."

Lindquist thought for a moment. "My... from my kitchen?"

"We grabbed your clean underwear too. Although there wasn't much of it that was clean."

Lindquist's face was red. He looked from Tuttle to Will Hoeksma. "You can't. This is crazy."

"We had official clearance. Governor's office OK'd it."

Lindquist studied the doodles he'd made in his notebook, trying to imagine strangers clawing through his closet; he was clenching and unclenching his fists. He hoped they hadn't found his weed.

"We found your weed, by the way," Tuttle said. "Good shit."

Lindquist froze.

"Mr. Lindquist," Will Hoeksma said softly. "Sit. Sit."

The use of his real name had the desired effect. Lindquist slowly sat. Tuttle sat too.

Will stared at the skinny, twitchy kid in his sports coat and skinny jeans. Now that Lindquist knew the deal, he had his head down and was staring at his notepad. His burst of independence had sputtered. Good. Head down, nose clean. Perfect.

"I guarantee, once the event is over today—and it should be over today; we are very good at what we do—we will have a week to ten days of you helping us get our follow-up messaging campaign out there. In the meantime, I can't have you sharing anything you've learned with anyone. And I really can't have you running all over yakking about what you're working on."

Tuttle was eating the banana without peeling it. "If you reveal any of the classified information about the background—the secret stuff we shared…"

"…which is all of the stuff we shared," Will said.

"Yes, all of it," Tuttle said. He swallowed, made a face, and then took another bite.

"If you fail us in any way," Will said, "I will pull my account from your agency. I am sure you know what that will mean to your superiors. And that's only the business end of it. Don't ask what we'll do to you personally." Will looked at Tuttle.

"Yes, don't even ask," Tuttle said, talking around a bulge of banana. He swallowed, with difficulty, and then took a swig of now-lukewarm coffee, which washed down the remaining banana. He held the bottom third of the banana in his fingertips, gestured to Lindquist with a *Want this?* look. Lindquist frowned. Tuttle cocked a hip in the air and slipped the partially eaten fruit back into his pocket. He settled into his chair and sat, staring at Lindquist, sucking on his bloody, gluey upper lip. Lindquist looked away.

Lindquist's breathing was returning to normal but his head was spinning. He imagined himself getting up and walking out. He could do it, he figured, if he moved quickly. Tuttle and Hoeksma were both looking at him. Had they actually just admitted to breaking into his apartment? Were they threatening him? Was this all some kind of joke? The journalism jones he'd suppressed while in late adolescence was now again in full flower—there was a big news story happening here—but Lindquist was worried that he should ignore it and just run. He mentally retraced the gauntlet of security procedures they had taken to reach the room. He glanced up at Will Hoeksma. Their eyes met.

"You're in this, Lindquist, like it or not. We're just waiting for the governor's call, since this will all be, literally, his call," Tuttle said. Lindquist looked down at his notepad. For some stupid reason, he was kind of excited.

Will's phone chirped and he looked at the screen. He smiled and turned his gaze to Tuttle. "Speak of the devil."

# Chapter Twenty-Nine

Tuttle pointed to his ears and then made a swirling motion with both of his index fingers. Will frowned. Tuttle whispered loudly, "We're recording." Will smiled and nodded. The room was equipped with a digital recording system and Tuttle had activated it. Will pulled his phone away from his ear, tapped "speaker" on its screen and quietly placed the device on the conference room table.

"Hello, governor," Will Hoeksma said. "I hear you have a situation developing." Will smiled at Tuttle and shot Lindquist a sideways wink. He was feeling especially winky. This was going to be a good day after all.

Across the table, Lindquist sat, preparing to take notes. An alarm in the back of his brain was telling him he was in danger of knowing too much; things always ended badly for guys who knew too much, didn't they? This notion sent fear crawling through his gut like the remnants of a bad burrito—that's how he would describe it, years later, in a book about the events of that day; the book would become a feature film that would make Lindquist a wealthy man respected by some for his talent and courage but resented by others for being an opportunist.

A sharp rap on the table startled Lindquist. Will Hoeksma was pointing at his right ear. "Listen up." To the phone, he said,

"Tuttle's kept me informed, my boy. Looks like you started this thing with Wisconsin, using your militia friends, but that hasn't exactly worked out?"

There was no response.

"Governor?" Will said. "Bill?"

Governor Bill didn't know what to say. He was staring at the dead Sparty and the gun was still in his hand. He placed the gun carefully on the desk. He thought he heard the elevator rising, coming his way, and wondered if someone had heard the shot. Of course. Of course, someone had. He kept staring and wondered if it was possible for Sparty to be not dead. He closed his eyes and prayed she would get up and maybe laugh—haw haw—like this was all a prank. When he opened his eyes she hadn't moved. If it was a prank, she was an awfully good prankster.

"Are you there, governor?" Tuttle said.

"Yeah, yeah. I'm here," Governor Bill said, half to the phone and half to the costumed and clearly dead body in his office.

"Governor, listen," Tuttle said. "Let's make this simple right now. I could not recommend and did not in good conscience recommend this brazen action by members of the Michigan militia. But if I may say so, this situation you find yourself in is right in Silver Eagle's sweet spot. From a resources standpoint, as we discussed previously, you won't find a company with greater bandwidth. Between Silver Eagles' capabilities and equipment in the key verticals and their best practices, well, governor, let's just say our opponent will regret this day, if you choose to have Silver Eagle move into an aggressive, offensive, action-positive, fully weaponized response. And make no mistake, that's where the next step would be, were you—as governor and... and... the decider—to decide to take a next step."

"I... ummm... I... yes. I know. I hear you. I'm just... something..." Bill tried to focus on the issue at hand. But that was awfully hard to do. "I was thinking..."

"Oh for gosh sakes, spit it out," Will said. "Spit. It. Out." Billy was his mother's son. Nothing from the deep end of the gene pool had survived the sperm-egg collision when they'd conceived this kid. Nothing. He looked at Tuttle, who was shaking his head. Tuttle had both palms facing down, pushing downward—*bring it down a notch*. Will clenched his teeth, swallowed, then said, "What are your thoughts right now on this, uh, situation, governor?"

Governor Bill swallowed and struggled to think. The elevator had stopped climbing, at the floor below. Governor Bill was looking away from the dead mascot, his eyes resting on the wobbly Sparky Anderson bobblehead. Sparky seemed judgmental now, his head bobbling disapproval. Governor Bill's heart punched against his ribs. He had an urge to look out the window, to see if the media and people below had heard the gunshot. How could they have not heard it? He imagined them, openmouthed, staring at the window. He couldn't look. *Focus*, he told himself. *Focus on the first get.* "I'm not even sure I can legally, you know, do this," he said. "Tuttle and Ham told me Wisconsin needed to be stopped but now it turns out maybe I shouldn't have done the militia deal because it looks like they're in over their heads or maybe this is just going to blow up into something big or whatever." Governor Bill knew he was rambling and that his dad hated it when people rambled. "So, what I'm saying is, at least I can bring in the best people, the best company available, you know, to handle this thing. We can figure the rest of this out later, right?" He said the last part to the dead female Sparty, who still hadn't moved; the duration of the not moving sent a chill through Governor Bill. He fought the urge to run. Or scream. Or scream while running. He willed himself to finish his thought. "So, what I'm saying is, could you, like, handle this situation we have here with Wisconsin? We'll just, like, call off the militia guys and have you jump in or something, somehow."

Will Hoeksma smiled, looked at Tuttle, and nodded. "Well, yes, yes, certainly. You're asking me to put our boots on the ground, correct? To use all means necessary? To defend our state?"

Governor Bill felt an unexpected rush of relief. He ran a hand through his hair and wondered if he should get a haircut today. He quickly decided he wouldn't have time. He made a mental note to write a note to not get a haircut. He realized his father was waiting for his answer; he could picture him, standing with his phone in his hand and massaging his forehead while the muscles in his neck bulged and that nerve in his jaw twitched.

"Yes, whatever it takes," Governor Bill said. "Boots. Boats. Planes. Whatever. And…" He thought for a moment; there was something else, something important. At last, it popped into his frantically spinning head. "You can do, like, public relations—right? I mean, with Ham down right now, I'm pretty short-handed as far as, like, advisors and people who can deal with the public and so on. You can handle all of that, right? I mean you have, like, a staff that handles PR and stuff. We want good optics here, right?"

"Yes. Yes. Of course."

Governor Bill sighed. "OK. Yes. Go ahead. All of it. Do."

William Hoeksma smiled. "It's official then. I accept your request, governor." Another wink, this one aimed at no one in particular. "And believe me, we'll manage the optics."

"Well, OK. Ummmm. Thanks. Thanks, ummm, Dad, sir. And the costs?"

William Hoeksma was ready for the question. "Governor, listen. Given the rapidly developing situation, a situation we did not see coming but feel it is our duty to confront, now that you've made it clear that you want us to do so, Silver Eagle will sacrifice our standard rate card in order to work within your budget constraints. This is our home state. We have been attacked. You have asked us to counter that attack. It is in times such as these that we must all come together. We are, ultimately, all Michiganians and patriots."

"Don't you mean Michiganders?"

"What?"

"Never mind." Governor Bill sighed; it felt good to be shifting the responsibility to Silver Eagle. His eyes drifted back to the dead girl. He sighed again—this time the sigh was wrapped in a sob. He'd momentarily forgotten he'd shot Sparty. He tried to ignore the growing certainty that this Sparty thing was going to become even harder to handle than the deal with Wisconsin. He felt the weight of it growing, spreading through him. His organs—especially his heart and his stomach—seemed to be getting heavier and heavier. He heard what he thought was the elevator resuming its journey, creeping upward toward him. He remembered all the talk about focusing on the get and he decided the get was, right now, the Wisconsin thing but after that, it was probably going to be the dead girl thing. So many gets. How was he to handle them all? "OK then. What… what now? I mean, what do we do from here?" Governor Bill said, trying not to look at Sparty.

In the Silver Eagle conference room, Will Hoeksma's smile returned. He winked at Lindquist. Lindquist's face seemed gray. "Well, governor, if our math is accurate, you now have one remaining militia resource onsite who is still viable. It is a female. She is a Michigan resident and it's our duty to do whatever we can to protect her. In addition, there are two remaining POWs—as I understand it, the prisoners were taken by your militia team in Wisconsin in some sort of random engagement but our latest report indicates one of them is now armed and we can only assume he is a threat to us. So…"

Governor Bill's heart lurched. "One of… Wait, what?" His voice came out strangled. "Who? One of the who has a gun?"

Will rolled his eyes. Before he could respond, Tuttle held up a palm and leaned toward the cell phone. "Governor, listen, we must move forward with all urgency. The situation is deteriorating. But this is something your father's operation can be on top of rather quickly. Just to be clear, we just need to double-confirm here, if I may" —Tuttle looked at Will—"that you are giving Silver Eagle the go ahead to manage all of this. The two of you are on the same page here, right?"

For Governor Bill, Tuttle's voice, his manner, was a balm. He imagined a Silver Eagle SUV driving up to the Cracker Barrel in somewhere, Wisconsin, Silver Eagle guys in full combat gear getting out, quickly shooting the prisoner who had armed himself and then telling everyone, "Hey, we'll just take what's ours and get on our way." His mental picture of the scene—the Silver Eagle guys pointing their guns at the Wisconsin people while telling the militia member from Michigan who was still alive to get into the vehicle. In his mind's eye, Governor Bill could see the Silver Eagle guys carefully picking up the dead guys and sliding them into the back of the SUV. One of the Silver Eagle guys would close the doors not with a slam but with a soft, reverent push-shut and click followed perhaps by a respect-filled pat on the back window. The SUV would then roll out of the parking lot as slowly as a hearse, the Wisconsin people suddenly keenly aware of the costs of war. He wondered if maybe he could be home in time for dinner with the family. He saw himself sitting down at the table, leading the family in a heartfelt prayer of thanksgiving, the details of the prayer—"… please remember Ham DenBraber's family and the brave people from Michigan who died serving our state…"—mixing with the media coverage they'd no doubt seen and heard to give the family just a taste of how tough his day had been. He imagined that he, with a sigh, would open his eyes and tell them about the tough day as his wife patted his arm. He imagined wrapping up the day by calling Tuttle and asking for his help with the dead girl, perhaps Tuttle stopping by the house to chat about it, Tuttle patting him on the back. "I've got this," Tuttle would say as they stood in the dewy coolness of Governor Bill's back yard.

"Governor, do we have your official confirmation?" Tuttle was saying.

"Yes. Yes," Governor Bill said. "Go ahead. With whatever. All of it."

Will rubbed his palms together, leaned back in his chair. He mouthed, "Thank you, Jesus" to the steel-reinforced ceiling.

Tuttle leaned forward, reached under the conference table and fumbled for the button that activated the recording system. He switched it off and signaled to Will that he had.

Will nodded to Tuttle and said, "Under the governor's request, let's authorize immediate deployment of a UAV for reconnaissance and a possible strike at the current point of conflict."

"Already done, sir," Tuttle said.

"Really." Will looked surprised.

Tuttle shrugged.

"UA-what?" Governor Bill said.

"UAV, governor. A drone."

"We—you, Silver Eagle—have, has, drones?"

"Affirm that, governor," Tuttle said. He glanced at Will. "Silver Eagle pre-located its drone fleet to an airfield that is, by the grace of God and advance planning, near the big lake. Assuming a positive outcome of this conversation, I requested a drone launch just prior to this call." This time, Tuttle winked at Will. Will smiled. Sometimes Tuttle surprised him. "The drone is approaching the Wisconsin shoreline even as we speak, on what appears to be a training run. But it is armed and ready to make a statement if you choose to have it do so."

"You have drones in, like, Wisconsin?" Governor Bill said.

"They are here in Michigan, sir. We launch them from here."

"They're in Wisconsin now?"

"One is. Almost. Yes. Again, being proactive."

"Wow. That's amazing."

"Silver Eagle was prepared, governor," Tuttle said. "It's a strategic advantage they've leveraged before." He smiled at Will. Will nodded. "Good," he mouthed. "Good. Good."

"But where—how? Drones?"

"Yes. Drones." Tuttle said. "And we're not talking about the little ones you buy online, sir. These are military-grade, airplane-size, fully equipped drones that have seen combat. They were procured from the Pentagon through back channels, governor. An excellent strategic purchase. Hired a team of retired military personnel to pilot them from right here" —Tuttle tapped the conference room table twice—"in this building. We'll show you the operation when this is over, governor." Again, it was Tuttle who winked. "Damn impressive. Very handy in a time like this."

"You said something about 'a possible strike.' Are you sure we need to just, like, start dropping bombs?"

"They'd be missiles, actually, governor," Will Hoeksma said. "We'll first perform a high-altitude recon and get some initial visual data, of course, to ascertain where our people are and evaluate the conditions on the ground. No firing without clear objectives and provable targets. And absolutely nothing without your OK, Billy. This whole thing is your call."

Governor Bill Hoeksma frowned. "Thanks, ahh, Dad… sir."

"So, if I may, governor," Tuttle said, "I'd suggest you prepare yourself to make a decision based on the video we get from that bird currently aloft."

Governor Bill tried to think through all that had led them here. For the first time all day, he fully recalled the briefings with Ham and Tuttle and the discussions he'd heard on Graham Parker's radio show about the Wisconsin threat. He closed his eyes and saw the blurry photos of the "chemical plants" and the mobile labs, then his internal gaze shifted; he saw Ham on the floor of his office and imagined Governor Oleson of Wisconsin going to lunch instead of making funeral arrangements for his wife. He pictured Denton McAllister in the movie *The Deer Hunter*, and then realized that it was Christopher Walken in *The Deer Hunter*, not Denton McAllister. He recalled Christopher Walken and Will Ferrell on *Saturday Night Live* playing that Blue Öyster Cult song and arguing over a cowbell. This was funny and had nothing to do with any of the rest of it and Bill knew why: His therapist said he "diverted" his thoughts when he wanted to duck decisions. Governor Bill knew he needed to focus and appear strong. Being strong meant not looking like a stupid puppet. Governor Bill was sick of being a puppet. He had an image in his head of the drones sending video back to screens somewhere in his father's building, and he thought, *Hey, I should be the one looking at those video screens.* "I need to be on top of this," Governor Bill said, trying to sound strong, assertive—governor-ish. "Dad, yes, you're, like, gonna handle this—Silver Eagle is. But nothing happens without my, um, say so or call or approval or whatever. I want a video feed or something, so I can be in charge of the actual, decisions, you know."

Will looked at Tuttle and gave him a thumps up and a questioning look. This was working better than he'd figured it would. The Silver Eagle strategic plan was to show Silver Eagle's breadth of capabilities to the marketplace—not get ass-deep in some kind of contrived freaking war.

Tuttle thought for a moment. Then shrugged and said, "Not a problem. I'll get a secure portal. You can see all the pictures you want, sir. Might as well pipe it into the SEC NEST so Vanderway and Griffendorf can have a ringside seat, too."

# Chapter Thirty

As agreed upon, the school bus pulled up to the rear entrance of the Cracker Barrel. The air brakes hissed, the engine groaned and fell silent, and the door swung open with a tired squeak. Nathan Sleeper, today feeling every minute of his twenty-seven years, stepped down the three steps and out of the vehicle, then turned to face it. Nathan had spent the night before grading papers and creating nametags for twenty-two third-graders. He'd had much less sleep and more wine than he should have had. Oblivious to what was happening inside and in front of the building, he watched with arms crossed as the first of his students, Trevor, whom he'd semi-privately nicknamed "Chucky," bounced down the steps, swinging the backpack he'd been told to leave on the bus. Before Nathan could stop him, Trevor tripped himself with the backpack and pitched forward onto the asphalt, his chin taking the brunt of the landing. He began wailing and bleeding. Nathan closed his bloodshot eyes. It was Trevor's mom, the Cracker Barrel regional manager, who'd arranged/forced upon him the field trip. She saw it as a way to show children how a restaurant worked. Also, she thought the "community outreach idea" would put her in good stead with her boss, who was big on "community outreach." Nathan Sleeper just saw the whole thing as a pain in the ass.

In the restaurant gift shop, Miky stood staring at Benjamin Nighthorse. Benjamin raised his hand that wasn't holding a gun, palm out. In a growl-whisper, he said, "I come in peace." He attempted a smile. It looked more like a grimace.

Miky frowned. A sigh of relief betrayed her. She needed all the help she could get.

"I don't know what the capital F is going on," Benjamin said, "but I'm about all you've got. I've always detested our government. Now I detest it even more."

Miky nodded. Her heart was beating in her ears. Her voice was surprisingly calm, steady. "Ok," she said. "OK." She knew what she had to do. All her years of committing to the cause, of being the person her father and Bo wanted her to be seemed, well, lame. She'd been acting, hadn't she? In a way, yeah, she had been. Even in her marriage, well, she'd been kidding herself. Bo was married to the cause and she was merely dating it. But was that so bad? She didn't know. She'd sort out her relationship issues later.

Miky glanced out the window. One of the cops had Sassy by an elbow and was guiding her, at a stumbling jog, away from the restaurant. The other cop was facing the Cracker Barrel, gun in a two-handed grip, half raised, but he was also backing away. Miky figured the cops, uncertain about the situation inside the restaurant, would set up a perimeter and wait for reinforcements. She needed to move quickly.

She studied Benjamin. "You need to lose the gun," she said. It was an order.

Benjamin frowned. He opened his mouth.

"Hand it to me," she said. Benjamin obeyed.

Miky looked for a wastebasket, found one, and dropped the gun in it. She glanced out the window—nothing new; the cops were clearly waiting for backup. Miky unbuttoned her camo top, took it off, sat on the floor and wiggled out of the pants. She

258

rolled up the army gear in a ball and stood, removed her helmet, and shoved it all into the trashcan. She took off the shoulder holster and, with the heavy gun still in it, dropped it into the trashcan, too. She was suddenly a young woman ready for a run.

There was a creak—a door opening?—in the rear of the restaurant. Voices? Yes, children's voices bounced against the walls and tumbled through the building. From the rear, also an adult's voice, a man's, demanded quiet and got it, the children's voices going to whispers, covered now by their footsteps and shhhhhh's.

The door from the kitchen banged against the wall. A young man, rumpled and harried, stepped cautiously into the room. "Hello?"

"Whoa there. Who are you?" Miky said. She looked at Benjamin. Both moved toward the hopelessly confused Nathan Sleeper. "You have to get out of here," she said. "Now. You have to hurry."

Tuttle hung up the landline. "We're closing in on our target," he said with a grim smile. Will Hoeksma slapped the table triumphantly, making the already jumpy Lindquist jump. Will picked up a remote control and pressed a button. From the ceiling at one end of the room, a large video screen hummed its way down the wall and clicked softly to a stop. Will pressed another button on the remote. The screen flickered, and then suddenly the three of them—Lindquist, Will, and Tuttle— were seeing the world from the nose of a Predator drone as it skimmed through Wisconsin airspace. To the plane's port side, the wide-angle lens picked up a flicker of blue-gray on the horizon—Lake Michigan. The drone had crossed the lake and was tracking south.

Lindquist swallowed hard. He hated flying. On airplanes, he always picked the aisle seat because it was farthest from the window and closest to the exit. He always listened to the entire safety message at the beginning of each flight; he knew every detail by heart. In just a few seconds, the video feed was making him nauseous. He turned away briefly, hoping to force the feeling to pass. The other men's upturned faces seemed to glow in the light from the video. Will seemed—what was the word? Euphoric. Yes. Yes. Euphoric. Lindquist turned back to the screen. Far beneath the Predator, Wisconsin's boasted bounty of lakes and streams sliced and splashed a checkerboard of farmland and forest.

"Ten minutes out," Tuttle said.

"From… from where?" Lindquist asked, a bit too weakly. He hated that his voice warbled when he was around tough, powerful older guys like Tuttle and Will Hoeksma. To make things worse, something was seriously, frighteningly bad about all of this. Something was very very bad. A small part of Lindquist wanted to stop it. Another part wanted to make sure that, whatever was about to happen, he got his part in it right. Lindquist did not want to piss these men off. He hoped no one got hurt, especially that he didn't get hurt. He cleared his throat. "I mean, what's happening exactly?"

"Just a minute, Limburger," Will said. He glanced at Tuttle. "You send numbnuts the link to this?" Will said.

"Who, sir?"

"The governor." Will half-snorted the title. "My boy."

Tuttle pulled out his cell phone. After considerable swiping and tapping, he looked up. "I sent it."

"And we're ten minutes to target?"

Tuttle's phone vibrated. He looked at the screen. "The governor has opened the link. He's watching."

"Time to destination?" Will said impatiently.

Tuttle thought for a moment and then glanced at his watch. "I'd say eight minutes now. Ish."

"Well, let's just conference the governor back in. On speakerphone. Might as well get this party started. This is his baby; we want him to own it."

"Roger that." Tuttle punched a button on the landline. From the conference call speaker, a dial tone hummed. Lindquist turned to the screen. The drone was flying over a small town, or maybe a big town; it was tough to tell. He could feel his heart rate picking up. The governor's dad had called the governor "numbnuts." Lindquist tried to get his head around that. Seemed funny and also not good.

Governor Bill glanced at the huge costumed body on the floor. Sparty seemed deflated and the costume, with the hole in the chest and the dead person inside was, well, not like the proud mascot it had been. Had he done that? Governor Bill swallowed the fear and sadness bubbling in his throat and turned back to the video feed on his laptop. The idea that they were moving toward certain armed conflict excited and frightened him. All of the meetings and briefings with Ham and Tuttle, all of the conversations and emails about the Wisconsin threat—details he'd only half heard when he'd been briefed—were now dancing in his head with George W. Bush and that bullhorn. Now, he was the man on the rubble. Was he ready? Damn straight, he was. Yes. Maybe.

The fourth ring jarred him. Eyes locked on the Predator video feed, he picked up his cell from his desk, glanced down just long enough to see the number, which he didn't recognize. He swiped the screen to answer: "Governor Hoeksma." The quilt of land and lake beneath the drone made him a bit sad. Wisconsin was a beautiful state, after all. But, Governor Bill thought, this was about the get. He whispered it. "The get." In his mouth, at the moment, the word had heft. He liked it. This was what leadership was about. It was about men who knew the get and got it. He allowed his eyes to wander back to the body on the floor. This was a very weird day, he thought.

The voice from the phone was repeating itself. "Governor? Sir? Governor?"

Governor Bill frowned and sat up. "Yes, Tuttle." His eyes were now on the Ronald Reagan photo; the dead president seemed to be sitting a bit taller in the saddle. The deal with Wisconsin, well, Reagan would've gotten it. He would've gotten the get. Yes, he would have. The thought made Governor Bill feel as though he owed it to Reagan to get it too.

"Sir," Tuttle was saying, "you're back on a conference call from Silver Eagle. Your video feed is up, correct?"

"Yes, yes. Yes it is," Governor Bill said. He closed his eyes and tried again to focus. He saw the images of the World Trade Center towers burning, of Ronald Reagan smiling at him, of the mobile bioweapons labs parked in a Wisconsin loading dock, of the bullhorn president with the guts to keep his eyes on the get after that dark September day. Of Sparty falling to the floor like a crumpled foam-and-plastic warrior.

There was a ding from the outer hall but Governor Bill didn't notice. A sliding sound, too—the elevator door opening. "Tuttle, I am watching," Governor Bill said, the words coming more quickly, more loudly than he expected. Without thinking about it, he slowly stood, his gaze again wandering to the cartoonish figure on the floor.

"Governor, I should advise you. We have a representative from our ad agency here," Tuttle said.

"Oh," Governor Bill said. He walked slowly around his desk and knelt by Sparty's head. "Why? Why someone... From the agency, really?"

"He'll be leading the charge on the creative ideas and videos and such as we roll out the marketing side of this. Just don't you worry your little governor's head about that. That's business, son." His father's voice was booming with authority and Governor Bill felt a familiar tightening low in his digestive tract. "You focus on our enemy here, son, sir. Governor."

"Videos?" Governor Bill frowned. "What kind of videos?" He switched his phone to speaker mode and put it on the floor next to his knee. With trembling hands, one on each side of Sparty's massive head, he took a moment to study the face of the costume and was momentarily delighted to find eyeholes. Then gently, ever so gently, he pulled off the head. He gasped.

"Oh, the videos are for the YouTube and so on. Promotional stuff. Not your concern, sir," Tuttle said. "Marketing materials for our security provider here."

"Kid's name is Limerick," Will said loudly. He winked at Lindquist. Lindquist didn't see the wink. He was focused on a point in the shadows to the right of the video screen, trying to withdraw from the situation or at least disengage. "He's a regular creative genius. He's going to take the footage you're seeing right here—we're recording it—and write a voiceover, mix in some music and create magic for the Internet. Probably come up with some print ads and a few things for our sales force and such. All outward facing, business to business stuff. You wouldn't understand, Billy boy." There was a bounce in his father's voice, one Governor Bill hadn't heard in a long time. "We'll get ourselves one heckofa permission space here once the marketplace gets wind of what we can do."

Sparty was a dead woman, not a girl. She had a pretty face and a purple streak in her graying longish hair. Governor Bill could barely breathe but still managed to respond to his father. "So, so, we're—you're making this into, like, an ad campaign?"

"Marketing, my boy. Something you never really understood. One of many things," his father said.

Governor Bill's gut took a twist for the worse. Eyes still on the woman's face, he reached for his phone and picked it up. He forced himself to find the camera app, tapped to open it, aimed it at the woman, and took her picture.

"We're two minutes from target, governor," Tuttle said.

"Really?"

"Yes, governor."

Phone in hand, Governor Bill stood on wobbly legs. He would send the photo to Tuttle. Tuttle, not his father, would know how to handle this. Definitely not his father. Tuttle. Yes. He walked to his desk, looked at his laptop screen. The drone's-eye-view showed more clutter, buildings and such. They were approaching another town. Governor Bill felt trouble in his gut surging to his throat. He swallowed and wondered if he had any antacids in his desk. He looked away from the laptop to his phone. He tapped the text message app and selected the photo, his heart aching as he considered the woman's face—pretty, despite her eye patch—on his screen. He attached the photo to the text. Took a deep breath, glanced at the real woman's dead face. Glanced back to the laptop—from the drone, more buildings and parking lots—then back to the phone. With trembling thumbs he typed, *I need your help*. He tapped send.

Governor Bill heard a noise and looked up. Ham DenBraber was standing in the doorway in a rumpled, faded, green hospital gown, the kind of gown that tied at the back of the neck and was completely open in the back. Ham had one hand behind him holding the gown closed, his sad eyes fixed on the dead woman in the Sparty costume. Ham sneezed and wiped his nose with the back of a meaty hand. He brushed a lock of hair out of his eyes. Ham looked at Governor Bill and said, "What the fuck, Bill?"

# Chapter Thirty-One

Lindquist was losing it. These men were up to something he didn't quite comprehend, something that could alter the course of history or be illegal or deadly or all of that. The story behind it was some kind of paranoid political crazy man's wet dream involving prairie dogs and biological weapons and Denton Freaking McAllister. It had been swirling around, bits and pieces of it, on the Internet and right wing radio for, like, a year. No one—*no one*—he knew had taken it seriously. But now here he was in a room with the governor's father, who was calling the governor "numbnuts," and they were about to do God knew what to some people in Wisconsin. This was like some kind of elaborate joke or bad movie or a novel that didn't quite work. But it was real. It was happening. He was in the middle of it. And now he had the added stress of having to somehow come up with a video and ad campaign out of it. Lindquist had won a slew of awards for great work but he felt this was going to be an elaborate clusterfuck of a project. It would have been better if an account exec had handled this. Meeting directly with clients was not his strong suit. Not at all. He tried to will his imagination into a nice warm shower with Freda Peters, calling upon his talent for full-color, detailed fantasy to transport himself away from yet another difficult moment with a client, but he couldn't conjure the necessary imagery.

"We are approaching the target, governor." Tuttle's voice halted Lindquist's internal debate. "In fact, we are beginning to circle and switching to Tactical Visual Perspective."

Tuttle's phone vibrated. He reached into a pocket. Lindquist forced himself to look at the video from the drone. The UAV seemed to be circling, the camera zooming in, in, in on a building and a parking lot. The feed was startlingly clear. He could see a few cars parked in front of the building, and two other cars moving, leaving. People were running away. And what was this? It looked like someone or somethings—two, yes—in the parking lot, not moving.

"Behind the building. Is that a school bus?" Governor Bill said.

"Yes, yes. That's what it looks like," Tuttle said. His eyes were on the screen but he was fumbling for his phone, annoyed, as it vibrated again.

In the living room of the SEC NEST, Hank and Frances were side by side in plush recliners, separated by a small coffee table, like an old couple watching TV on a Saturday night. The only light came from a lamp on the table and from the flat screen that hung on the wall ten feet in front of them. Both were hunched forward, forearms on thighs, staring at the video feed from the drone. Hank was having trouble concentrating. He'd chugged nearly half a bottle of the Nyquil he'd found in the SEC NEST's bathroom medicine cabinet.

It was Frances who saw the bus first. Before she could react, Hank slowly stood, stumbled to within inches of the TV, and squinted hard at the image. When Hank turned around to face her, Frances already knew what he was going to say. Hank's face was pale, his eyes wide. In a voice lathered in cough and cold medicine, he said, "A g-damn mobile lab. Right in the g-damn parking lot where we hit them first. What are the odds?" He looked at the screen again, a smile on his face. "This is gonna be good."

Frances contemplated the image for several minutes, a cold knot in her gut. Hank stumbled back to his chair and fell into it. Eyes back on the screen, he said, "Looks like we've got those bastards right where we want them."

Frances took a deep breath, closed her eyes, and whispered a prayer for courage. "I need to take a leak," she said. She stood. "You let me know what happens."

There were children, a lot of them, in the kitchen, in a single file that snaked from the entrance, to the dining area, to the back door. These kids were restless. Two women—30-something; Miky's teacher radar told her they were moms—were moving down the line, trying to maintain order. It was clear none of them—the adults or the children—knew what had happened at the front of the building. The young man held up a hand, palm out, facing the kids. The moms took his cue and immediately raised their hands. The chattering mob began shushing each other.

Nathan turned to Miky. "We're here for a field trip. It was arranged months ago, but it doesn't seem well-organized." He sounded annoyed because he was. He looked Miky up and down. In her running gear, she looked like the coach and athlete that she was. "Oh, hold on. Sorry. I assumed... I mean, do you even work here?"

Miky looked at him, then glanced at the moms; both were petite and cute—yoga-pants-and-brightly-colored-running-shoes cute. She turned back to the young teacher, took a deep breath, and said, "You need to be out of here. Five minutes ago."

\*\*\*

"Dad? Let me call you back," Governor Bill said. He reached a trembling finger to his office phone, fumbled for the conference call button, and ended the call to Silver Eagle.

Ham DenBraber stood in the doorway to the governor's office for a moment, staring at the body on the floor. Finally, he walked in and slowly circled the large mascot costume with the dead woman inside, one hand still holding the rear of the hospital gown closed, his sad eyes taking in the pretty, eye-patched face of the woman.

"It just... the gun went off. An accident," Governor Bill said.

Ham's eyes seemed to grow weary as they shifted to Governor Bill and then quickly back to the body. Ham paused for a moment to contemplate the purple streak in her hair; a frown stuttered across his brow as if he were asking, "Why would anyone her age want a purple streak?" Then his wide, bare feet plod, plod, plodded slowly around her, his big Ham head bent forward. A lock of hair fell over his eyes; he kept brushing it back with his free hand. He stopped in front of the governor's desk, and took another long look at the body before turning again to Governor Bill. Ham had always been calm in times of trouble. Now he looked calmed. But he also looked like shit.

"She's a federal agent. FBI." Ham coughed. Sniffed. "Name's Babsy Witt. She has a thing for costumes, undercover surveillance, and a certain state police commander."

Governor Bill's throat was dry. He tried to avoid looking at the body. "You know... How do you... Seriously, the gun... It was an accident..." Governor Bill frowned. "How did you even get out of the hospital?"

"You shot her?" Ham said.

"Yeah, no, like I... it went off. The gun."

Ham turned back to Babsy and sighed. He stared at her, lost in thought. "I called an Uber."

"You couldn't get, like, dressed first?"

"Snuck out when the nurse shift changed. No time."

"I thought you'd been poisoned or something."

"Look. Listen," Ham said, looking at his old friend. "I'm sick, yeah. But it wasn't Wisconsin, those guys, the prairie dogs. That was all… It was your father. And Tuttle. They made that up. They exposed me to some kind of virus—just a really bad cold."

Governor Bill couldn't think. Couldn't breathe. He couldn't look at Ham. He stared at the gun on his desk, his eyes wide. "Are you, like, contagious?"

Ham coughed. "Probably past that stage. I got dehydrated is all—why I fainted. I figure Tuttle and one of his creepy friends found a way to isolate the virus and expose some of us. He's got a million of them out there—guys who can do this kind of thing."

"You're saying they made this up?" Governor Bill's gaze had fallen to his gun. "I can't buy that."

"I know. It's crazy." Ham sighed. He ran his hand through his hair. "I didn't exactly, like, lie. I mean, I'm on your side in this." Ham began to pace. He looked at the body, as though he was seeing it for the first time. "Holy… what are we even talking about right now? This woman is dead. Damn it, Bill—I mean, how?"

Governor Bill stared at the body and felt again the brittle echo of the fatal gunshot. Somewhere between his eyes and his nervous system, a faucet was opening and the reality of taking someone's life was spilling out. This particular reality was an awfully cold one. He shivered and wrapped his arms around himself. Tears rose. Governor Bill's eyes looked to Ham's pale and sagging face for reassurance. "The safety was on. I'm sure."

Ham looked again at the body and shook his head. "Do not under any circumstances tell Tuttle about this. Not yet anyway."

Governor Bill studied the Post-it notes on his desk. He felt heat now, in his chest, and his stomach churned. He wondered again if he could be coming down with something. Nervous for something to do with his hands, and anxious to divert attention from the dead Babsy, he picked up the gun, jabbed it toward the body. "How do you know her?"

"I don't know her. I know about her. Long story. Not sure you want to hear it at this point." Ham turned and looked at him. "And I'm not sure you want to be messing with that right now."

Governor Bill looked at the gun in his hand. He imagined cops in his office again, this time coming for him. He closed his eyes and tried to swallow a growing panic attack, counting to ten, then twenty, stumbling through the breathing exercise a long-ago therapy session had taught him, coaxing the air toward his quivering diaphragm. The respite helped and a thought, as clear and cold a thought as he ever got, popped into his head. He sat straight, opened his eyes, shoved the laptop out of the way, spied the decorative Kleenex dispenser, and took two tissues out of it. Frantic, he rubbed one side of the gun the way he'd seen criminals do in movies and on TV. When he figured he'd done a thorough job, he did it again, and then gripped it with the Kleenex, flipped it over, and repeated the cleaning on the other side. He wrapped another tissue around it, picked up the gun with his fingertips and held it out—a 9mm dead fish—toward Ham. "Here, get rid of this." When Ham didn't respond, Governor Bill looked at him with pleading eyes. "Please, man. I'm begging you. You get rid of it and we can, I don't know, come up with a story or whatever…"

Ham hesitated, then let go of the rear of his hospital gown, strode to the desk, and took the gun. The weapon out of his hands, Governor Bill's pulse slowed, his breathing smoothed.

He became keenly aware of Ham's proximity. Eyes on his friend, Governor Bill backed his chair slowly away from his desk.

"I'm seriously not contagious at this point," Ham said, disgust in his voice.

"Not taking any chances."

Ham swallowed a response. His eyes wandered to the laptop screen. He froze, and pointed the gun at the computer. "What's going on there?" Ham used the gun to nudge the laptop around so both of them could see it clearly. On the screen, the aerial view offered a dizzying, circling perspective of a suburban retail plaza. The camera zoomed in on a building—Ham's heart sank as he recognized a Cracker Barrel restaurant; it looked innocent, vulnerable. The high-def picture clearly showed cars in the parking lot and what looked like a school bus behind the restaurant. "Is this…?" Ham took a deep breath, sneezed, sniffed, coughed, closed his eyes, opened his eyes, and said, "Your father and Tuttle… is this them? They doing this?"

Governor Bill looked at Ham but didn't answer.

"Good Lord," Ham said. With his free hand, Ham picked up the receiver of the governor's desk phone. He handed it to Bill. "Call them. Now. Tell them to pull back. Tell them you know what's going on."

"But I don't."

"You don't what?"

"Know."

Ham hung up the phone, took a deep breath, and then told Bill the whole lousy story. For the sake of time, Ham skipped the minor details, but he filled him in on the conspiracy—how the whole thing had been one elaborate lie to get him, the governor, to authorize Silver Eagle Security to attack citizens of Wisconsin.

"It's all his idea of a stupid, demonic marketing stunt," Ham said.

Governor Bill couldn't get his head around it all. "You came here this morning to suck me in to all this, to get me in deep, didn't you?" he said. "You were part of this. I know you were."

"Tough to believe me, I know, Bill. But seriously, I was sitting in that hospital and I had a come-to-Jesus moment," Ham said. He sighed. "Honest, man. I'm lying there, thinking, *Wait a minute*. So I called a guy I know at the FBI to tell him about this whole stupid mess. Found out the feds were already investigating Will and Silver Eagle. The guy I know told me about this undercover deal, about your friend Babsy Witt with the purple hair. They knew your dad was up to something. She was here to help get to the bottom of it."

Governor Bill tried to comprehend Ham's near-betrayal and his father's and Tuttle's trickery. He couldn't. So he again contemplated the dead federal agent in his office. Solving that issue seemed, to his beleaguered mind, to be the more pressing get. "What about her?"

Ham leaned toward the screen and squinted. The drone's camera was zooming in on the rear of the Cracker Barrel, on the bus parked there. "Let me figure that out. Looks like we might have a bigger problem."

Will frowned at the conference room phone, irritated. But before he could curse his son for ending their call, he noticed the bus.

"Damn," Will said. "We can't engage when there's a bunch of snot-nosed brats inside the restaurant; that's just bad business."

Tuttle studied the video and for a moment tried to convince himself the vehicle at the rear of the restaurant wasn't a school bus. The bus triggered a memory. He looked at the ceiling and chuckled. "Hold on, Will. Hold on." He shook his head. "This is perfect."

"No, it's a damn school bus is what it is."

"No, no, stop. I mean, yes. Sure. It is." Tuttle slapped the table. "This is... Don't you see? Our scenario. Remember? Mobile labs on buses? That's what we called those buses in our pictures—mobile weapons labs."

In the glow of the video monitor, Will Hoeksma's face was stern. "Kids wreck everything. I'm talking from the communications standpoint. We hurt a bunch of children, automatically we're in a negative space, even with the Third World market. Cardinal rule of the security business: no naked napalmed babies running down the road."

"Oh I hear you, Will. But this is our proof—the proof we need to rationalize engagement."

"Don't know that we need it. Proof, I mean. We've got a damn verbal contract with the State of Michigan. Just don't want kids in the way."

"You and I both know that 'verbal contract' only goes so far. But the bus—it really optimizes us from a public relations standpoint. We can tie A to B—the pictures to this video. It's a we-had-no-choice situation. Mobile weapons lab. Perfect. Get it?"

Will Hoeksma thought about it. A smile slithered across his face. "Not like we want to drop a bomb on kids or anything."

"But we don't know there are kids in there," Tuttle said. The drone's view widened slightly, revealing the scene in front of the Cracker Barrel: the now unmistakable bodies lying in the parking lot, a scattering of parked cars. Tuttle's phone buzzed. He had a text. From Governor Bill. Still smiling, he slid his thumb onto its home button to activate the fingerprint security access. His eyes were locked on the video feed. "For all we know, it's one of those labs. Our goal is getting rid of the threat—to us," Tuttle said. "To our client..."

Now Will was chuckling. "Yes, to our client who authorized this. That's cold, even for you Tuttle. But it works."

The conference room phone trilled. Lindquist, who was staring at the video feed with his mouth open, jumped. Will stretched from his chair without standing and jabbed the conference button on the phone. "Yes?" he shouted.

"Sir, it's Donahue."

"Donahue?"

"Our pilot, Will. He's in the control room here, driving the Predator." Tuttle spoke without looking up. He was reading the governor's text, his face suddenly a mask. He squinted at his phone's screen, trying to digest the message. He sucked at his upper lip, tasted blood, frowned, and studied the image Governor Bill had sent. He read the governor's message for a second time. Tuttle used his fingertips to zoom in on the face of the apparently dead woman in the Sparty costume. The purple streak in her hair was clear, her pretty-ish face so familiar. For a moment, Tuttle could barely breathe. He thought about the last time he and Babsy had been together. He thought about her threat to him and her amazing body and tried to understand how it was possible she'd shown up in the governor's office dressed as Sparty and was now dead, apparently at the hands of the governor. He considered then dismissed the idea that this all was some kind of counterplot or a trick. He studied the photo on his phone again. Then he thought a little more about Babsy's body. Then he thought about how he'd needed to get out of the mess with her. Then he felt something sharp stabbing his heart. Tuttle stood. "I've gotta go," he said. And before Bill could say "What the fu…", Tuttle was gone.

With Benjamin's help, Miky turned the children around and channeled them toward the restaurant's rear exit. As the bubbling mob meandered through the kitchen, she gave the teacher, whose name was Nathan, a carefully worded and not accurate summary of what was happening at the Cracker Barrel:

"Some men came to the restaurant, probably planning a mass shooting, and the police shot two of them. There appears to be a standoff with the remaining ones." This, as Miky hoped, lit a fire. Within minutes, Nathan, the chaperone-moms, and the wiggling, protesting children were out the door of the restaurant and getting back on the bus.

Miky and Benjamin helped the teacher hustle the last of the children onboard. Roaring engines and screeching brakes announced the arrival of more police to the front of the restaurant. From their perspective at the rear of the building, Miky could see a SWAT vehicle. On foot, armored officers, AR15s cocked skyward, were cautiously approaching the front porch, some angling to see what was happening in the rear with the bus. Her militia training told Miky the cops were making a huge tactical error; they weren't sending vehicles and manpower around to the rear of the building. Not yet anyway. They obviously were uncertain about the layout or were scared. Or both.

"Now what?" Benjamin said; he was out of breath, his face red and shining with sweat.

"Now, I'm hoping the cops are planning a standoff," Miky said. "At least for a little while."

The school bus driver, a heavyset woman with wild red hair and a badge on a lanyard around her neck that said *Pearl*, fired up the engine, slammed the folding door, shoved the bus into gear, and eased up the clutch.

Miky slapped the side of the vehicle. "Hold up," she said.

Pearl braked. The door protested but opened. Pearl was visibly annoyed. Miky gave her a tight smile, held up an index finger. "One second." She turned to Benjamin, grabbed him by a shoulder, and said, "I'm sorry for what happened to you. You need to go. Get yourself and these kids out of here. Now."

Something flickered between them, something that for Miky was exciting and worrisome but for Benjamin was just exciting.

"I want to help you," Benjamin said firmly. She held his gaze a second longer. He saw doubt, anger, and what he hoped was lust.

"No. This isn't your deal. You guys never should've been involved," she said, shouting to be heard above the truck's engine. "Some bad shit going on here."

"Duh. I'm all about the bad shit."

A faint grin threatened Miky's composed face. She liked this guy. She really did. But this was no time for getting soft. Time to go hardcore, as Bo and Rub would say. "Get on the bus. Seriously. Now."

"But what are you going to do?" There was concern in his eyes. Seemed genuine.

"I'm going to end this." Miky looked down. One of her running shoes was untied. Irritated, she knelt to tie it. "Someone has to." She glanced over her shoulder, then turned back to Benjamin.

People were shouting. From the front of the building, a large vehicle bellowed; air brakes hissed. Benjamin said, "You're not going to end anything. Not without a whole lot of help you're not."

Miky gritted her teeth. She opened her mouth to speak just as a red dot bloomed on Benjamin's forehead and quivered there. Miky swung around. A cop in SWAT gear. He'd made his way to a post at the corner of the Cracker Barrel's front porch. He trained his laser-sighted rifle on Benjamin. How had he gotten there without her realizing it? She mentally kicked herself.

"Hold your fire!" she screamed, her hands in the air. "He's not part of this!" Miky stepped in front of Benjamin. "We're not involved! Neither one of us!" The sunglassed sniper hesitated. "I'm serious! There are kids here!" Miky said, still yelling to be heard but less anxious, trying to slow the moment, calming her breathing—all things she'd learned from her father. The cop seemed to buy it. His body language relaxed; he dropped his left hand and pointed the weapon skyward with his right, his elbow to his hip.

Miky turned to Benjamin, her mind suddenly clear. There were two types of soldiers, she'd been told. The first was all shoot now, ask questions later. The other knew there were times to fight and times to flee, Rub had always said. The trick to living was recognizing which was which.

"Change of plans. Let's both get on the bus," Miky said. And as they did, without turning, she held her hand in the air. "We're with them!" she said loudly enough for the cop to hear. To Benjamin, she added, "You were a dot Indian there for a second. I think I just kept it from being permanent."

# Chapter Thirty-Two

"Donahue," Will said toward the phone. "Let's lock on target. The mobile weapons lab."

"Sir?"

"The school bus. It's not a bus."

"Say again?"

"Lock on the mobile weapons lab that looks like a school bus. In the rear of the building. The school bus."

"Roger that." The probe's camera began zooming toward the bus behind the Cracker Barrel. "It's moving, sir."

The bus was slowly pulling away. Two figures were standing in the parking lot near it. One of them struck the side of the vehicle. The vehicle stopped.

"It stopped, sir."

"Ready full payload, Donahue."

"Full…?"

"Don't question me."

"Roger that. Stand by for confirmation."

On the screen, the two people next to the bus seemed to be talking.

"Go macro, Donahue."

"Again, sir?"

"Widen out."

The video feed blinked to a wider view. A half dozen or more police cars, including a military-style vehicle, a stream of figures spilling out of it, formed a semicircle in the parking lot about fifty yards from the entrance to the Cracker Barrel. The rest of the parking lot was empty now, except for the two bodies, alone and unattended midway between the police and the restaurant.

As they watched, a helmeted cop, rifle at the ready, crept out from under the building's porch roof. The cop stopped at the corner of the building, back to the wall, peeked around it, then crouched and raced to the rear corner, flattened there, peeked, then stood straight, braced himself against the building, brought the rifle into firing position, and aimed the weapon toward the two figures near the bus.

One of the figures, hands in the air, stepped in front of the other. There was a moment of uncertainty, and then the cop seemed to back down. The two figures turned and got on the bus; the vehicle accelerated quickly away from the Cracker Barrel.

"The bus is moving again, sir."

"I see that, Donahue."

"Are you, uh, shouldn't you… Where did, umm… Mr. Tuttle go?" Lindquist said with a croak.

Will barely heard him; his eyes were locked on the screen. He was working through the task at hand the way he always did—methodically, logically. He had no idea what was going on with that loopy Tuttle; the guy had always been a wingnut—that he'd bailed on him at this moment was predictable. There was no time to worry over that. The shooting of two Michigan citizens was a gift; it gave him the rationale to counterattack. There was a school bus present—good Lord, what a miracle—and he had "evidence" of school buses used in the production of deadly weapons. He had no idea if there were kids on that bus.

In his mind, as head of Silver Eagle Security, it didn't matter. His objective, his mission, were clear. School buses were part of the plot against his client. Sure, there'd be public outcry. But the risk was the governor's. Governments and companies everywhere would be lining up for Silver Eagle's services, once the smoke cleared. This was an unsafe world. To the defenders go the spoils.

Will, eyes on the moving bus, allowed himself a slight smile. "Hold on to your panties, Linglang," he said. "This is about to get interesting."

Lindquist blanched. "But…"

"Go big or go home, that's what I always say," Will said, even though he'd never said it. "Right, Donahue?"

"Ahhh, sure, sir," Donahue said from the speaker. "Sir, confirming, target locked and payload ready. We are go… One second… hold…?"

The video screen went blank.

When he'd admitted them to the Silver Eagle building, Tuttle had given Hank and Frances a single, shared high-security visitor badge. Hank had let Frances keep the badge. And for that, Frances was now grateful. The badge's magnetic strip gave access to the elevators and, therefore, to each floor of the Silver Eagle building. Frances used the tiny map of the Silver Eagle headquarters layout on the back of the badge to find the Drone Operations Command (DOC) center—a tiny office on the third floor.

Air Force protocol dictated a two-person operation for drones, but Silver Eagle's founder demanded a lean operation. Clay Donahue, the company's soft-spoken, crew-cutted DOC Commander (DOCC) had double duty. He was both the drones' operator—handling the cameras, lasers, and other information-gathering equipment as well as guiding the Hellfire missiles—and the pilot in charge of deciding when to pull the trigger that launched the Hellfires. It was a stressful job. There had been an uptick in demand for Silver Eagle's UAV technology. The pilotless birds had been carted to a slew of third-world hotspots—when launched they'd always been controlled by Donahue from his Silver Eagle cubbyhole. A former US Air Force airman who'd piloted Predators over Afghanistan, where he was credited with seven confirmed kills, Donahue was up to multitasking. But each mission inevitably ended in someone's death. When you added the job-juggling with the killing, the gig tended to wear on him. Donahue had picked up a habit of eating crappy food while he worked—an emotional crutch that was softening his formerly rock-hard abdomen but, as he told his worried wife, it "sure beats blowing your brains out."

Under Silver Eagle's Guide for Employee Appearance and Decorum (GEAD), Donahue was required to carry and be "well versed in the operation of" a sidearm. Junk food addiction aside, Donahue was a smart and sober Texan with a Southern Baptist sensibility for rules and order. However, he typically slipped his shoulder-holstered Ruger .45 into a desk drawer—a violation of the letter of the rule if not the intent. This decision, based on comfort and a streak of Texas independence, was to prove unfortunate.

Before Clay could process that the heavyset elderly woman opening the door to his cramped office meant harm and that he needed his gun to defend against it, the lady had pulled from a wall-mounted surge protector the power cord to the computer system that controlled the Predator. For good measure, she also yanked out the cord to Donahue's coffeemaker and the one for the hot pot Donahue used to warm jalapeño-cheese sauce for nachos. On the video screen, *Error* flashed white in a sea of electronic black. On his cluttered desk, the hot pot choked on a gurgle and the coffeemaker hissed in defeat.

Donahue, trained to manage crises under stress, spoke calmly into his wireless headset. "Sir, we have a problem here. I think it's one of those congressmen. The woman congressman, sir." He pushed his chair back, opened a drawer, and reached for the Ruger. Frances lunged across the desk to stop him, sending an open bag of tortilla chips to the floor and knocking over the hot pot. Hot jalapeño-cheese sauce splashed across the keyboard and onto Donahue. The usually unshakable Texan let out a yelp and wiped frantically at the hot orangey-yellow mess. Frances grabbed the Ruger.

"Stop. Right now. Just stop," Frances said. She fumbled with the holster, managed to get the gun free and point it at Donahue. "Just. Stop. Stop this."

Donahue swung his chair around to face Frances; the chair's casters rolled over tortilla chips, the chips crunching at the offense. He slowly raised both hands, palms out, cheese smeared from face to ear. "Easy. Easy. Nobody needs to get shot here."

"Just. Don't. Just stop the drone. Stop all of this. This is crazy. Stop it now." Frances leveled the gun at Donahue's head, with obvious reluctance.

"What the hell is going on there, Donahue?" Will Hoeksma's voice was fire in his ear. "You let that… that bitch shut us down? She has a gun?"

"Roger that. It's a complete disconnect with the bird."

"That fat old dyke waltzed in and what—overpowered you? Is that what I'm hearing? Good God, man. What in the name of sweet baby Jesus am I paying you for?"

"Yes, yes, yes, I know, sir. I can explain." Donahue looked at his assailant. Senator Griffendorf was now holding the weapon as though she knew how to use it and was considering that possibility. Donahue glanced at the insistent error message on the video screen.

"You have no gun and apparently no backup system," Will Hoeksma said.

"No, sir."

"Who in hell would build an operation like that one without a backup?"

"Well, sir, as I understand it…" Donahue paused.

"Who, Donahue?"

"You said no to the expenditure for a backup system or even a generator."

Frances Griffendorf pulled the Bluetooth headset from Donahue's head. She struggled to put it on her own head while still pointing the gun at the drone pilot, fumbled the headset and dropped it. She and Donahue lunged for it. Frances somehow—"I think it was unintentional," she would later say—struck Donahue; a hard, glancing blow to the head; with the gun. Donahue's cheese-slathered head hit the floor. After that, Donahue didn't move.

# Chapter Thirty-Three

Tuttle had acquired a great many skills in his lifetime. In his elderly years, he would tell a biographer he was most pleased to have learned (during an extended leave in Brisbane during the Vietnam War) to safely neuter puppies with minimal blood loss (for the puppies) and to fly, also safely, helicopters. He hustled the Silver Eagle Hughes MH-6 Little Bird to Lansing in about a half an hour—no flight plan, no radio contact—and landed it on the Sparrow Hospital helipad. A nervous ER crew and potbellied security guard met him at the rooftop door. Tuttle, state police badge aloft, pushed through them, shouting, "State police commander, state emergency business." He continued to repeat this loudly— "STATE POLICE COMMANDER, STATE EMERGENCY BUSINESS, STATE POLICE COMMANDER, STATE EMERGENCY BUSINESS"— as he made his way through the hospital—down corridors to elevators, down more corridors to other elevators—to the street. About a block from Sparrow, he lowered the badge and stopped identifying himself—he was attracting attention he didn't need.

Tuttle entered the state capitol through a side door for which he had an access card, avoiding the impatient gaggle of reporters and onlookers still milling near the front entrance. He took the steps three at a time.

The tableau inside the governor's office would have made one hell of a 70s album cover, Tuttle thought. Shockingly, Ham DenBraber, pale and bleary-eyed, gun in hand, rumpled hospital gown with half of his frighteningly hairy butt exposed, was standing there, seemingly transfixed by the scene before him. On the floor, sans helmeted Sparty head, the now-dead Babsy Witt's head was dwarfed by her ridiculously large costume. Governor Bill was behind that big, ornate desk of his with a dumbshit look on his face, staring at the screen of his open laptop. Neither DenBraber nor the governor spoke. Both turned to gawk at Tuttle as he walked in and knelt to the floor next to his former lover. He looked into her eye, which was open, locked on the ceiling and, like the rest of Babsy, unresponsive. There was a gunshot hole in the chest of the Sparty costume. Tuttle was relieved she was gone and shocked to also feel anger and grief. They'd had something between them. And it had been a good thing/bad thing kind of thing. But she'd blown it all sky high. The hit song with those lyrics— the artist and year (Jigsaw, 1975) flashing in his head like a neon beer sign—began to play, an earworm squirming across his memory, wrapping around his heart and squeezing. Babsy and he had made love to that song and others like it, hadn't they? Tuttle missed her for perhaps the hundredth time and wished her dead for the hundred and tenth. He'd gotten his wish. But she hadn't deserved it, had she? Well, yes, she had. The inner debate ping-ponged as it had for much of the day. He finally decided he was relieved she was gone and angry, very angry, to see her this way. She'd been his lover and betrayer, after all. Now she was shot, dead. Didn't betrayed lovers get first dibs on this type of thing?

"Tuttle, thank God you're here. Things are very messed up right now," Governor Bill said. "I... well, there's this... this horrible horrible thing with her." He pointed at Babsy. "And you, my dad? What did you think you were... You made all this up? You tricked me? You have some explaining to do. And now this video... the drone..."

Tuttle heard the governor but didn't acknowledge him. He stood slowly and looked at Ham. "Why are you here?"

"I decided to tell him..."

"Tell him..."

"Everything."

"So you came here and did this," Tuttle said, cutting Ham off. A statement.

Ham stared back, opened his mouth. A croak came out. Ham looked like hell. Tuttle made a mental note to email the guy in Columbia who'd helped him virally infect Ham and Hank Vanderway. Job well done, amigo.

Governor Bill was frantic, overwhelmed with issues. "What's up with this drone? I can't seem to... the video? I can't tell what's going on. Are they, like, launching a bomb? Tuttle, there's a school bus."

Tuttle held a hand up, palm out, toward the governor. To Ham he said, "You know she's FBI, right? That give you a reason to kill her? You got something to cover up, senator?"

"I..." A coughing fit seized Ham, his face going scarlet. When he at last had it under control, he turned his sad, glazed eyes to Tuttle. "I walked in and..." The coughing resumed. Ham buried his mouth in the crook of his right elbow, the gun swinging crazily in his right hand. His body shuddered dramatically. His hospital gown flapped open, momentarily revealing more of himself than anyone wanted to see.

"Ham, good Lord," Governor Bill said, glancing up at his friend and then back at his computer. "The drone. A bomb or missile or whatever. They could be firing and I have no clue what's going on."

Tuttle stood. He shifted his gaze slowly back to Ham. The senator looked disgusting. This irritated Tuttle. And suddenly, everything—Governor Bill and Will and the whole sorry cheese conspiracy—irritated him. The deal with Babsy—whatever was going on in his head and heart about her—just the fact that it was a deal, well, that irritated him too. At the same time, in the back of his mind, he knew this was a moment. His goal had been to somehow wiggle free of all this and now here it was. Bam. Opportunity.

Ham met Tuttle's gaze with glassy eyes. Ham sniffed and wiped his nose with the back of his gun hand. Tuttle reached into a coverall pocket and fumbled for something.

"The feed is dead. Should I restart an app or something?" Governor Bill was jabbing a single key on the laptop's keyboard. "I hate technology."

Tuttle found his weapon, pulled it, and pointed it at Ham DenBraber. "Drop the gun, senator. I'm arresting you for the murder of FBI special agent Babsy Witt."

From his perch at Kenosha Regional Airport, air traffic controller Chip Kincaid had been monitoring the progress of Silver Eagle's Predator drone for an hour or more. Silver Eagle's UAVs were well known to the Kenosha tower. In recent months, the Michigan-based private security firm had chosen the shorelines on either side of the big lake for test flights. Chip had trained to pilot Predators during the Gulf War, but his military career was cut short by a staph infection that had run amuck. He'd come home to Kenosha for several subsequent surgeries and to learn how to be an air traffic controller. Chip was bored with his new gig. Now, as the Silver Eagle Predator began to deviate from its flight path, his pulse quickened. Chip informed aircraft in the vicinity to stay clear. His supervisor in the relatively sleepy Kenosha tower relayed concerns about the suddenly errant unmanned aircraft to other controllers in the region. When Chip couldn't raise Silver Eagle's pilot and the Predator began losing altitude, prevailing west winds pushed the drone-turned-glider back toward the shoreline. Chip prayed mightily, if a little guiltily, that the runaway bird would stay off course; if it did, he'd have to scramble fighter jets from Naval Station Great Lakes to knock it out of the sky.

Before anyone or anything could scramble, however, the Predator ditched itself into the big lake about twenty miles offshore, thus ending Chip Kincaid's dreams of heroism and Will Hoeksma's plan for war, in one fell swoop.

# Chapter Thirty-Four

The bus roared into the school parking lot with a Wisconsin State Police escort: two cars, one leading the other following. Parents, reporters, and other gawkers, alerted by news of the shootings at the Cracker Barrel, were waiting. In the crush of humanity—moms and dads finding their children, reporters begging to talk with someone, anyone, about the standoff, the Wisconsin cops trying to sort it all out—Miky slipped away. Within eight minutes or so, she was a mile from the school, just another runner out for an afternoon workout.

Miky knew she could escape the Cracker Barrel and the school kids, but she knew she couldn't get away with her part in the day's events. She didn't want to get away with it. She just wanted to approach the police on her terms; she needed space to think through what she would tell them. As she ran, she did what runners do: she processed what she'd just been through and imagined what would happen next.

She was done with the militia; she knew that much. There was no way she could go back. The trickier issue, the one gnawing at the edge of her heart, was her marriage. Truth be told, things hadn't been great between her and Bo for a while. He was a true believer. What would he say about her decision to abandon Red Sky? She loved him. She didn't know if she liked him.

A vehicle slowed on the road behind her. She glanced over her shoulder and saw the expected flash of green and chrome. The Hummer pulled over, crunching gravel. Miky slowed to a shuffle, then a walk. She pulled up the front of her shirt and wiped her face. The breeze felt good on her abs. Chest heaving but feeling loose and calm, Miky circled back and approached the driver's window. The window lowered.

"Was beginning to think you were going to make me run twenty miles."

Benjamin looked down at her through mirrored sunglasses and smiled. "Took forever to get done with the cops and get them to take me back to the Cracker Barrel. Get in the back." He nodded toward the rear seat. "I already got someone riding shotgun."

Miky climbed in, slammed the door. Sassy Bones turned around in the front passenger's seat and said, quietly, "Hi."

Before Miky could speak, Benjamin said, "Don't worry. I explained some stuff to her, based on our conversation in the bus and, you know, what you did back there at the restaurant. Sassy's cool. She gets it."

The two women managed tight smiles and nods.

Benjamin shifted into drive, checked his mirrors, and guided the Hummer back on the road. In minutes, they were heading toward Michigan.

"If you look behind you there, you'll see all your shit."

Miky twisted around, spotted her gear. She sighed. "Cool. Thanks."

"Cops don't know I got it. I was quick."

"And the phone?"

"Taken care of," Benjamin said.

"You do what we talked about?"

"Yes, ma'am."

"Annnd?"

Benjamin Nighthorse smiled again; let her wait for it.

"C'mon."

"It's that Tuttle creep you told me about. The police folks were pretty stunned. I'm guessing the story is all the way up to the governor now—Oleson, I mean."

"No shit?" Miky sat back in her seat and let it sink in. The number she'd used to send the last text had been the one weak link in the chain of secrecy. And by suggesting the cops call that number, well, she realized it would also mark the end of her time in the militia, regardless of how she felt. Militia members didn't like Tuttle but that didn't matter. She would be a snitch now. They hated snitches more than they hated anybody. Fine. So be it.

"Sounds like they got the FBI after him, over there in Lansing, he being state police and all. Can't trust his state people to take him in."

"Yeah, and if it's Tuttle that did this, then it's probably everybody. Governor Hoeksma, his old man—the rumors were true, I guess."

"Correct."

Miky laughed. "I'm guessing the part about Denton McAllister was Tuttle's doing. Heard Tuttle's one weird dude."

"Denton McAllister? Like, the actor?"

Miky sighed. "Someday, I'll tell you all the shit that was supposedly part of their big 'conspiracy.'" She air-quoted the last word. "I'm guessing this thing had something to do with Silver Eagle, Papa Hoeksma's little mercenary army." She thought for a moment. "Whatever." Another sigh. "It's over."

Benjamin eyed her in the rearview. "They'll be waiting for you in Paw Paw. FBI there, too. Just like you wanted. I drop you off. You turn yourself in. You good with that?"

"I'm good with that." Miky thought for a minute about Zooker and Spud. "Sorry about all this with you two. Really, I am." She sighed. "I wouldn't have done this to you. Honest."

"Awww, those guys were assholes, right, Sass?" Benjamin glanced at Sassy Bones. She nodded and stared out the window. He shot Miky a look in the mirror. "We'll let you make it up to us someday." He laughed.

Miky thought about it. "Yeah, Zook and Spud were morons. Right? But. Feel awful that it had to go the way—those two guys getting…" She pictured the shootings and felt a surge of emotion—the day had been way too difficult in so many ways.

They rode in silence, lost in thought, for several minutes, until Benjamin said, "You guys do Arby's?"

Frances sat in Donahue's chair and tried to calm her pounding heart. She managed to pull the cell phone from her pants pocket. Willing her hands to hold steady, Frances scrolled through her recent calls. She found the number and called it. Donahue stirred, opened his eyes, and twisted into a sitting position on the floor; he sat there, dazed, wiped some cheese from his head and face and then looked for a place to wipe it from his hand; he chose his pants. The gun in her lap, Frances eyed Donahue as she spoke briefly to her contact at the FBI. Frances ended the call, got up from the chair, nudged it out of the way, and extended her hand. She and Donahue groaned as Donahue stood. Frances grabbed the chair and guided the young airman to it. The fog in his head lifting, Donahue sat for a moment with a frown on his face.

"Here," Frances said. She handed Donahue the gun. "You can put this away. And I'm sorry; for the record, I didn't mean to hit you." She reached to the power strip and plugged in the dangling cords. "As you might have judged from my call, the FBI is on its way here, and I'm guessing they'll bring along some ATF agents and what-have-you. I figure you have very little idea of what just happened. And that's good, for your sake. Ignorance is bliss and let's just keep it that way for now. Of primary concern for the authorities will be your boss and our dear friend Colonel Tuttle."

Donahue blinked several times, twisted his neck to the left and then the right. He looked at the gun in his hand, thought, held Frances's gaze, and made a decision. Donahue scrounged for the holster, shoved the pistol in it, and returned both to his drawer.

"I have one request," Frances said. "I'm guessing that drone crashed somewhere. I'm hoping for all of our sakes it was away from people."

Still silent, Donahue pressed the button to reboot his system.

The video screen in the Silver Eagle conference room flickered, uttered a loud electronic burp, and then bloomed to life. Lindquist gushed out a sigh of relief. "It's back up, sir."

"No shit, Sherlock," Will said. In the gray-blue-white of the screen, Lindquist could see the veins bulging in the older man's neck and forehead. Will's breathing was audible; his fists were clenched. "Are you there, Donahue?" He barked the words at the phone speaker and stood, jaw knotted, eyes locked on the screen. The phone responded with muffled voices and other, unidentifiable sounds.

Lindquist followed Will's gaze. Both watched as the Predator's camera sniffed a broad, seemingly endless expanse of water, the perspective tilting to starboard as the UAV's altitude dropped lower, lower, lower and then, again, the screen was black.

Will Hoeksma grunted, gasped; eyes blank but still on the screen, he sank ever so slowly into his chair.

From the phone, an unfamiliar voice—an older woman's voice Lindquist would later learn belonged to Frances

Griffendorf—said, "Is that you, Will Hoeksma? Are you there? If you are, and I'm guessing you are, this mess is over. Do you understand me? It's over."

But Will Hoeksma didn't hear Frances Griffendorf. Nor did he hear Lindquist, who was yelling, yelling, yelling, "Sir, are you OK?" like some kind of idiot. Will simply felt a white knife of pain through his skull, and then nothing at all. Ever again.

# Epilogue

Hank slurped his coffee and speared a chunk of fried potato with his fork. He put the mug down and stared across the restaurant table at Frances. "Put that thing away and go buy a newspaper like a regular human being. You look like a crazy woman."

Frances looked up from her iPad. "Thought we had a deal."

"Who said anything about a deal?"

Eyes back to the tablet, Frances swiped through a story on freep.com. "Deal was, no matter what, you stop calling me things like 'crazy woman' and I won't bring up the other, the thing."

Hank grimaced and motioned to Julie the waitress, who was looking their way from across the crowded diner. He pointed at his coffee and mouthed "Warm up," with a smile. "Trials are over. People in jail. Folks getting on with their lives. The Great American Cheese War That Never Happened is all ancient history. So's our deal."

"Not according to the *Detroit Free Press*," Frances said. She tilted her head back slightly to read the screen through the lower portion of her lenses. "Says here Ham DenBraber's considering running for his old senate seat. What's next, Billy

Hoeksma, Junior coming out from wherever he's hiding to run for congress or something?"

"Don't blame Ham. Good man. Like some of us, he just got caught up in something. Jury cleared him. Public forgave him. That bastard Tuttle tried to make it look like Ham killed what's-her-name—the FBI gal. Everyone knew Tuttle did it, especially once they heard the governor's testimony and all. And the part about them being lovers, Tuttle and that gal. Made sense he killed her." Hank paused. "Still sounds weird to say all that. Been what, a year and a half? Still doesn't seem real." He took a drink of his coffee just as Julie sidled up to the booth, steaming carafe in hand.

"Doesn't seem real you bought into a conspiracy involving cheese and prairie dogs and some such. And Devon El Chop Chop or whatever's his name," Frances said softly, with a smile.

"Now see there," Hank said sharply. "That's what we agreed we'd stop talking about. That's the kind of sh—"

"You brought it up. Again, see my previous comment re: 'crazy woman.'"

"Fact of the matter is, no one has really said at least some of that wasn't true. I'm telling you, I still don't trust that Oleson. Or none of those Hollywood types. And yeah, turned out it wasn't monkeypox. But I was sick as a dog. So was Ham. Sick. As. A. Dog."

"You guys arguing about all that again?" Julie topped off Hank's coffee cup, drew back slightly and held the carafe over Frances's cup. "More joe, Frances?"

Frances put her hand over the cup. "Better not."

Julie straightened, free hand on a hip, pursed her lips, and blew a wisp of her hair from her forehead. Hank sighed. "You still smell good."

"Your crush is showing," Frances said. She turned to Julie. "For the record, you do smell good."

Hank shot her a look.

Julie gently punched Frances's shoulder. "Well, at least I've got that going for me." She gave Hank a smile that stabbed his heart. "Can I get you two anything else—like, oh, say, a new topic to discuss?"

"She brought it up," Hank said, nodding at Frances. "Even though we had a deal."

"Oh, now the deal's back on?" Frances said.

"Like I said, you brought it up."

"I 'brought up' your crush or I 'brought up' the time someone thought Wisconsin was trying to attack Michigan over cheese and things got all crazy with the militia and the Hoeksmas and the head of the state police and an FBI agent ended up dead in the governor's office and the head of the state police ended up in jail?"

Julie giggled. "You forgot about the part where the governor was impeached and his evil billionaire dad died of a stroke. And some militia guys got shot by cops. Oh, and that you were the hero with the whole drone thing while handsome here"— she looked at Hank and stuck out her tongue playfully—"slept through it all."

Hank put down his coffee cup and pounded the table with a fist. The plates and silverware rattled; coffee sloshed from his cup. "Careful there, young man," Julie said. She leaned over Hank, snapped two napkins from the dispenser and blotted up the mess. "Or I'll take away your personal Sparty coffee cup."

"Sometimes you guys push things too far." Hank sniffed, sounding hurt. Julie straightened and looked at him. They held each other's gaze. Finally, Julie said, "Do you want me to hold you, poor baby?" Hank couldn't help himself. He smiled gleefully and nodded.

"You guys make me ill," Frances said.

\*\*\*

Bill Hoeksma, Jr., former governor of Michigan, watched the trainees carefully. The new men, recruited from reams of encrypted resumes, were tough dudes. Three were former Navy Seals, one was an ex-Army Ranger, and four were former Marines whose backgrounds weren't entirely clear. However, this was the most brutal day in Silver Eagle basic training. Each man was buried up to his neck in sand. It was 85 degrees in the South Carolina sun. Ex-governor Bill sat in the air-conditioned trainee observation room (TOR) and silently wished one of the men would crack and demand to be released before the 320-minute time endurance test ended.

Ex-governor Bill was bored.

Just as Will Hoeksma had figured, business for Silver Eagle was booming. But he hadn't needed an ad campaign. Operation Cheesus, as many had come to call it, had generated intense media coverage and, subsequently, attracted clients from all over the globe. The quirky, gun-loving, militia-connected, ex-governor Bill's stock was high among military and paramilitary personnel. Impeachment was his badge of honor.

The copywriter's, Lindquist's, book was about to hit bookstores. Ex-governor Bill had given an interview—Ham had advised Bill to tell the truth (about everything except Babsy), so he figured, *What the heck?* The kid had done it right, as far as he could tell. He'd talked to everyone involved who was still alive, including Governor Oleson and Denton McAllister.

Bill thought about his dad and wondered if he'd ever really miss him. He thought about Ham and how they'd stayed friends. He thought about Babsy Witt. Emotions—anger, worry, doubt, fear—stirred. Ex-governor Bill pushed those feelings away.

Their father's will had been clear: Silver Eagle was to stay in the family. Bill's siblings didn't want to be involved with it. When the impeachment and all of the related trials ended, his brother and sister asked Bill to take on the job, with the stipulation that he and Silver Eagle leave Michigan. Bill had few other options. So his siblings bought an abandoned military base in the Carolina low country. And ex-governor Bill became Commander Bill.

The months he'd spent in South Carolina had been almost as challenging as the preceding year and a half. The ex-governor was forced to keep a low profile. His wife and kids were not happy here. They were living under a false name, Branagan, in a semi-witness-protection program. It was weird.

He looked out at the shimmering heat waves, at the sweating, silent heads lined up in the white sand. He unscrewed a bottled water and took a long drink. Again, he thought of Babsy Witt and how his gun had misfired that day. Outside, one of the men began to moan loudly enough to hear. On the table in front of him, ex-governor Bill's phone buzzed. He looked at the screen. He had missed multiple calls. This one was from Qatar. He took another drink and let it go to voicemail. He didn't know anyone named Qatar.

Miky took the steps to the front porch slowly. The workout—800 meter repeats at 5k pace—was the type she'd relished in her younger, competitive days. It really kicked her butt now, she thought with a wan smile, and the altitude didn't help. She heard a crunch of gravel and turned. A battered Jeep Renegade, towing an equally weary horse trailer, rolled up the driveway and turned toward her weather-worn barn, which squatted about fifty yards behind the house. Her vet, Helen, waved. Miky gave Helen a thumbs up. With a sigh, she picked up the Mason jar filled with water she'd left for herself on the top step.

After a long drink, Miky sat, enjoying the sweat and fog of fatigue that came from a good run. She surveyed the mountains in the distance, took a deep breath of the thin and at-the-moment-insufficiently-oxygenated air, and whispered a prayer of thanks. The move here, to Colorado, had been the right one.

Bo had never accepted what she'd done at the Cracker Barrel and during the subsequent investigations and trial. Her decision to flee the scene, to him, was cowardly. Then, when she'd renounced the militia movement and betrayed the militia in her testimony, well, that had been too much.

After her own trial, she'd discovered local school boards aren't all that friendly to a teacher caught up in a political conspiracy and fake-war crimes, even when the courts agreed the teacher handled herself as well as could be expected. So she lost her job in addition to Bo.

Once she'd served a brief probation for her role in the mess, she'd taken stock. She still loved to teach. Loved to coach. And she always had dreamed of owning her own farm or ranch—something that felt like her childhood. Scouring the job sites had led her to Crested Butte and an open-minded superintendent in desperate need of an English teacher and a cross-country coach. A hipster biology teacher with a serious beard and a battered Honda had shown her this place. She'd used a chunk of her savings for the down payment.

A whinny from the horse and laughter from the vet told her all was well with the first major purchase she'd allowed herself after buying the ranch, a coal-black filly. She groaned and stood. Thought about the possibility that Benjamin might call. She loved talking to Benjamin—loved reminding him she'd named her female horse after him. Nighthorse. It still made them laugh.

Behind her, from the house, she could also here the whine of her other family member, a yellow Lab she'd rescued from a shelter in Denver.

"Coming, Rub," she said loudly and chuckled at the sound of that name.

She thought briefly about how happy she'd become. The past flitted by. She let it go.

# Acknowledgements

Thanks to my daughter Tracey; my brothers, John and Bill; and my long-time writer-critics, Bob Young and Dave Kagan, for opining on early drafts. Thanks to Abbie Headon and the team at Farrago for all of their work in bringing this story to life. And thanks to my wife, Lori, for supporting the dream.

# About the Author

**Paul Flower** was born and raised in Michigan and still resides there. He has been writing professionally for more than 37 years. While much of his career has been spent in advertising and marketing, he worked in broadcasting for a short time. Paul has one previously published novel to his credit, and his writing has appeared in national and regional magazines. He and his wife have four grown children and a rapidly evolving number of incredibly beautiful and intelligent grandchildren.